Praise for Alice Peterson

'This is a **wonderful portrait** of the different dynamics within **an unusual family**' *Daily Mail*

'My **break-away book this summer** so far' *Telegraph* magazine

'A lovely example of **realistic fiction** that many women will be able to relate to' *Sun*

'**Couldn't put it down**! . . . What a beautiful, **uplifting, unconventional** love story' Paige Toon, author of *Thirteen Weddings*

'Moving, sensitive and **thought-provoking**' Alison Mercer, author of *After I Left You*

'A **spellbinding** story' *The Bookbag*

D1324755

Alice Peterson's first book, *A Will to Win* – now republished as *Another Alice* – is her personal story of her tennis days (she was one of the top ten juniors in the country), followed by her fight to beat rheumatoid arthritis. Since then she has written six novels, including *Monday to Friday Man*, the dog-walking romantic comedy that knocked *Fifty Shades of Grey* off the top of the eBook chart. She lives in west London with her Lucas terrier, Mr Darcy.

Also by Alice Peterson

LETTERS
FROM MY
SISTER

ALICE PETERSON

Quercus

First published in Great Britain in 2005 as *Look the World in the Eye*
by Black Swan
Published in ebook in 2012 by Quercus
This paperback version published in 2016 by

Quercus Editions Ltd
Carmelite House
50 Victoria Embankment
London EC4Y 0DZ

An Hachette UK company

Copyright © 2005 Alice Peterson

The moral right of Alice Peterson to be
identified as the author of this work has been
asserted in accordance with the Copyright,
Designs and Patents Act, 1988.

All rights reserved. No part of this publication
may be reproduced or transmitted in any form
or by any means, electronic or mechanical,
including photocopy, recording, or any
information storage and retrieval system,
without permission in writing from the publisher.

A CIP catalogue record for this book is available
from the British Library

PB ISBN 978 1 78648 062 0
EBOOK ISBN 978 1 78206 324 7

This book is a work of fiction. Names, characters,
businesses, organizations, places and events are
either the product of the author's imagination
or used fictitiously. Any resemblance to
actual persons, living or dead, events or
locales is entirely coincidental.

10 9 8 7 6 5 4 3 2 1

Typeset by Jouve (UK), Milton Keynes

Printed and bound in Great Britain by Clays Ltd, St Ives plc

To my sister, Helen.
And to Sophie, for inspiring the story.

1

2004

'Morning, Eddie.'

'The usual, Katie?' He turns to operate the cappuccino machine. 'You've been away, haven't you?'

'Well, I was in Paris for two weeks on business. Catwalk shows . . .'

'Paris and models? Sounds like a holiday to me.'

'And racking through three thousand designers' clothes. After a while it's not much fun, I promise! It was like a cattle market.'

'One cappuccino, organic chocolate on the top.'

'Wonderful.'

'Busy day ahead?'

'Yes, very. Never stops, does it?'

'You've changed your hair again,' he notes.

I nod. 'It's my fashion show tonight.' I rummage in my

purse, trying to find the right change. 'I've got plenty of tickets left, Eddie.'

He laughs. 'Maybe next time. See you tomorrow.'

'Five minutes!' I call out to the models. The dressing room has an overpowering smell of hairspray and styling solutions. I pace the corridor. Where is Sam? I punch in his number on my mobile.

'Katie, I'm on my way, promise,' he says. 'In a cab right now.' He makes car noises. 'Yes, left here, mate.'

'Sam!' I can hear a phone ringing in the background. 'You're still in the office, aren't you?'

'Half an hour, tops,' he tells me.

'Sam, I really need you here.'

'Don't pull my hair so tightly,' I overhear Henrietta, one of the models, screeching. 'Are you *sure* you're a professional?'

'Please get here soon.' I hang up, take a deep breath and walk back into the dressing room. Hen sits in the corner, stroking a strand of her blonde hair protectively. 'Hen, five minutes,' I say, counting them off on my fingers. 'One, two, three, four, five. No more tantrums, OK? Let her do your hair.'

I look at the chaos of high-heeled shoes and the racks of black clothes waiting to be modelled. I own a shop in Turnham Green called FIB, which stands for Female In Black, selling day and evening wear and accessories, and tonight is the summer fashion show. The clothes, of course, are mainly black, except for the odd accessory and the occasional burst of colour for contrast. I have started to organize fashion shows twice a year; it's hard work but it pays off. This one is being held at a house in Chiswick, owned by a client of Sam. The house is so big you could run a marathon in it. It's a perfect location for a show because my local customers won't have to travel far. The owners have gone for the minimal look: stripped floorboards, white walls, spotlights, modern paintings, gilded mirrors. In fact, it's almost a clone of Sam's house, except his is half the size.

I can hear the audience taking their seats; there's that familiar sound of shuffling and scraping chairs. This is the point when my nerves start to kick in. I pick up a half-full glass of champagne, pink lipstick smudged around the rim.

The first thing Sam ever said to me was, 'Is your glass half-full or half-empty?' followed by, 'Allow me to get you a refill,' finished off with a wink.

If he had been less attractive I probably would have politely refused. I had to look around to make sure he was talking to me; that he had picked up *my* glass of vodka and tonic.

Eve, who works for me at FIB, tells me the photographer wants a quick word before we start, and someone from the press has just arrived. 'Good luck, girls,' I say. 'Look the part, feel the part and you ARE the part.' Was one of the models rolling her eyes at me?

Quick look in the mirror. I'm wearing one of the outfits we are showing tonight: a black halter-neck dress that floats below the knee. There's a panel of silver beading around the neckline and bust, and it's cut low at the back and fastened with sparkling silver buttons. My outfit is finished off with slip-on silver heels. My dark brown hair has been dyed black and is half scooped back with a white rose.

The show begins with a model striding out in a satin top and black hipster skirt, offset by a handcrafted black-and-silver beaded belt that shimmers under the lights. In one hand she clutches a black satin bag with a small silver clasp. In the other she holds a cocktail glass. I wanted to kick-start the evening with a heady injection of glamour. She glides up to the fireplace, smoke weaving its way across the wooden floorboards. The audience marvels at it and claps as the model leaves the room. I see Emma, my old school friend, taking a seat at the back. You can never miss her entry into a room. She's nearly six foot tall and always played goalkeeper in school netball classes. She mouths 'Hello' to me and looks at her programme. *Sam, where are you?*

Sophie Ellis-Bextor's 'Murder on the Dancefloor' plays as the next model, Henrietta, walks on, looking miserable but determined, her hair scraped back into a ponytail. Her mother is in the front row, watching adoringly. 'Henrietta and mother' come together in one package, like bubble and squeak. Hen's mother is lame, but loaded, and after you have sat her down in the corner of my shop on the chaise longue, plied her with a few drinks and generally treated her like royalty, she buys her darling daughter Henrietta almost my entire stock. 'Whatever you want, I don't mind,' she says in a steadily increasing haze. Sam often asks me if the 'old soak in the corner' has been in. He knows it's his lucky night if she has.

As the song reaches its climax, Henrietta turns dramatically, looks at her mother, who grunts and stamps her stick on the ground with approval, and sashays out of the room. Going well so far, I think to myself. Everyone is talking, there's a general buzz and people are looking at programmes with interest, writing down notes – always a good sign.

The next girl waltzes out in a zebra-printed evening dress worn with a scarlet wrap. This is one of my favourite outfits. Her hair is dyed jet-black, bobbed, with a sharp fringe, *Chicago*-style. 'Superstition' by Stevie Wonder starts playing. I shift in my seat. This song always reminds me of home. Being at school. I can hear 'Turn that blasted noise off!' from Mum's studio when 'I Just Called to Say I Love You' was played over and over again from my sister's bedroom. Another world now.

But I do think about Bells. I can still see her letter slipped into my leather diary, that neat familiar handwriting. I haven't even opened it. I feel guilty receiving letters from her because I don't write back. I intend to, and then one thing happens after another – trips abroad, work, going out, yoga classes, parties, Sam . . .

'How long does it take to write one letter?' Dad nags me. 'She really would love to hear from you.'

The photographer from *Tatler* takes a final picture of all the models standing together. 'Lastly, and most import-antly, I would like to thank Mr Todhunter for allowing me to use his fabulous home for the event, especially at such short notice,' I announce. Everyone applauds as I shake his hand. 'Please, everyone, do stay on for a drink, and thank you once again for coming tonight.'

I'm shaking hands, kissing cheeks, moving through them all in a blur of praise, hearing '*Loved* the show, Katie,' or 'Stunning,' or 'Darling! You look a million dol-lars,' my glass of champagne constantly being refilled and the adrenalin kicking in wildly. Eve tells me the photog-rapher would like to take a photograph of me for the article. I swing round to greet him and put on my best smile, while trying hard not to show too many teeth. 'Thank you,' he says after taking the shot. 'Great show,' he adds.

'Well, thank you for coming,' I reply, my balance going

for a second. I'm already feeling quite drunk; I hope he airbrushes the telltale patches of red from my cheeks.

I feel a warm arm slide around my waist, and turn around. 'Sam.'

'Congratulations, babe, it was sensational.' He kisses me, his smooth skin brushing against my cheek.

'You missed half of it.' But I smile, my earlier agitation melting at the sight of him.

'I saw the better half.'

'Sorry for snapping earlier, Sam. I was having my usual panic attack before the show.'

'It's cool, don't worry about it.' He loosens his tie and then leans towards me and whispers, 'Is the old soak in the corner here?'

Emma makes her way towards me, dressed in sensible black working trousers and a turquoise cardigan vivid against her olive skin. She's a clinical psychologist and has probably come straight from the hospital. But before we manage to say hello – 'Katie darling, that was the best show yet,' says Antonia, one of my customers who lives around the corner from the shop. 'I need to get rid of my post-baby stomach, though, before I can even think of buying some of those slinky outfits.'

'You've got your figure back so quickly, Antonia,' I reassure her, 'you could get away with wearing any of my clothes.'

'Really?' She blushes, touching her cheek. 'Well, I might

pop by tomorrow and have a trying-on session. I have an engagement party to go to. A very smart affair, dinner and all that jazz.'

'Well, I'm sure FIB can sort you out. How's the new baby?'

'I might take it back to the shop –' she chuckles at her own joke – 'and ask for a refund. Just a few nights' sleep would be nice.'

Sam, Emma and I make understanding noises, although we don't really have a clue. Emma is the nearest of us to having children, as she's engaged to Jonnie. For me, the idea of a baby is terrifying. I'd rather live on a compost heap than go through all the traumas that Mum went through. 'Antonia, this is Emma, an old school and family friend, and Sam, my . . .' Partner? Other half? No. 'My boyfriend,' I finish.

'Well, I strongly advise that you two take precautions.' She nods at Sam and me, laughing again at her own humour. 'It is *exhausting*. If I'm honest, I never wanted to have more than one child, but poor little Billy really wanted a brother or sister. My husband says it's selfish to have only one child. They always say only children are spoilt brats, don't they?'

'I'm an only child,' chips in Sam, running one hand through his hair. I see him wink at Emma.

Antonia reddens again. 'Do you have family, Katie? I'm sure they're so proud of you and what you've achieved. To have your own business and be doing all of this.' She glances around the room. 'Are they here tonight?'

'No, sadly they couldn't make it.' I look at Emma and Sam, hoping they might change the subject. Instead Sam asks me where the loos are and excuses himself.

'That's a shame. Do you have brothers? Sisters?' she asks inquisitively.

I look around. Sam is out of earshot. 'No, it's just me.' Emma gives me a long hard look. It's funny how one small question can have an instantly sobering effect.

'Oh,' Antonia says. 'Well, never mind. It's OK to be an only child, I mean, like I said, I would have stopped at one,' she continues, digging herself an even deeper hole.

'Emma, don't,' I warn her as we finally move away from Antonia.

'It's up to you,' she says in a spiky tone that makes me feel uneasy.

'It's easier, then I don't get awkward questions or those awful sympathetic smiles.'

'It's fine,' Emma says, but her tone is no more forgiving. 'If you think it's best, you carry on.'

I hate it when she gets all self-righteous. The drinks come round again and we each take a glass.

'Right, back to business,' I say, making my way over to Hen's mother with a glass of champagne.

*

Sam turns the key and we walk inside. He and I have been going out for nine months, and I moved in with him after only three. Sam works in the City. He used to be a currency trader. Now he works in 'mergers and acquisitions', or 'M & A' as he calls it. He lives in Notting Hill, a stone's throw from Portobello Market, the famous travel bookshop and the Electric Cinema. It was an impulsive move on my part, but neither of us could see the point of being apart because I was staying with him almost every night. It's easy for me living here, as it's only a bus journey away from my shop. Also, Sam has a widescreen television in every room, and a steam room on the top floor. How could I say no?

Mum was immediately suspicious, firing questions at me. 'Who is this man? Are you sure you're ready, Katie? You jump from one relationship to another like there's no tomorrow.' Her reaction didn't altogether surprise me, but it made me want to move in with him even more.

Sam picks up the mail, mostly junk – pizza delivery companies, cab firms touting for business, a card saying the electricity meter man came but no one was in. 'Nothing that can't wait here,' he says, chucking it on to the small table in the hallway. He wraps his arms around me.

'I'm tired and happy,' I tell him. 'Tonight went really well, didn't it?'

'You are a fashion goddess, my darling.'

I kiss him. 'Thanks so much for helping me organize this evening.' I know Sam went out of his way to ask

Mr Todhunter if we could use his house for the show. 'I couldn't have done it without you, you know.'

Sam's face burns with pride. 'My pleasure. We're a team, you and me.'

'Well, I think we're a top team.'

'The best.'

I look over his shoulder. The red answerphone light is flashing.

'How about a liqueur?' Sam hums as he skips downstairs to the kitchen.

'Love one.' I slip off my high heels. My feet ache. I stare at the machine again, certain the message is for me.

'A steam?' Sam suggests as I'm about to press the button. He's holding two glasses and a bottle of cognac. 'Leave it till tomorrow, it'll only be Maguire. Come on, I've got a surprise for you.'

I turn away and follow him upstairs.

2

After an early-morning run to blow away the hangover, I arrive at the shop with my usual cappuccino and croissant, and a pain au chocolat for Eve, who is addicted to chocolate. I find her studying the books to see how last night went. 'We have many orders, especially for the French lace dresses, and many people for the mailing list,' she says, looking even more delighted when I hand her the pastry.

'That's wonderful! Last night went even better than I expected. Eve, I have to tell you,' I exclaim, 'Sam is taking me skiing this Christmas! It was a surprise, he left the tickets on my pillow.'

'He is a dream,' she sighs. 'Hector and I, we do not get on very well at the moment.' Hector is her boyfriend. 'You two are very serious, *non*?' Eve is French. When I advertised for a new shop assistant six months ago, she was leagues ahead of anyone else. She arrived on time, wearing a black ribbed polo neck with a camel suede skirt, and her long honey-blonde hair scooped into an immaculate ponytail. She answered my questions so earnestly, as if her future depended on it. 'I like you very much, Katie. I hope I get this job,' she said, and touched my desk, 'touching wood.'

'I guess we are serious. I'm a lucky girl,' I say, for a moment feeling guilty that I blurted it out, when I know Eve isn't getting on too well with Hector.

'And he is lucky too. Perhaps he is "the one", Katie?'

'Perhaps.'

It's late in the evening and I'm about to lock up for the night. There's a tap on the shop window and I see Sam outside wearing shades, holding a bottle of wine wrapped in tissue paper and a bunch of lilies.

He hands me the flowers. 'Thought I'd pick you up from work today, I finished early for a change.'

'What are these for?' I grin. 'Skiing and now flowers *and* a chauffeur. If you keep this up, I'll never want to leave you.'

'That's the whole idea, Kitty-kins,' he says, kissing me. It's a hot summer's evening, and the restaurants and bars have opened their doors. Friends are meeting after work, talking and drinking in the last of the sun.

'Remember, we're going out tonight,' Sam reminds me as he unlocks the front door.

'Are we?'

'I wrote it down in our social calendar, Katie. Dinner with Maguire and his new lady.'

'Sorry, it slipped my mind. It's been hectic today, Eve and I didn't have a moment off, not even for lunch. I'm going to have to employ another person.' I walk over to the answerphone and press the play button. 'Can you fix us a drink, Sam? A nice glass of wine?'

He raises an eyebrow. 'As opposed to a horrid one.'

'Katie, it's your father.'

I stand rooted to the spot. This must be the message from last night. I *knew* something was up.

'I need to talk to you. It's . . .' He coughs. '. . . It's really quite urgent.'

I swallow hard. Oh my God, something has happened to Mum. Or Bells. Has someone in the family died? Aunt Agnes? He must wonder why I haven't called him back.

Sam looks at me curiously. 'Your old man never calls here.'

Sam is right. Dad always calls me at the shop. Why didn't he call me there today if it's so urgent? 'I don't know,' I mutter, pressing my lips together.

'It's your mother. She's been working herself into the ground,' Dad continues, 'you know what she's like, and we haven't had a proper holiday for years. We went to the doctor and he strongly recommended a break. I'm taking her away. *So,*' he lingers on the word, 'we need to talk about Bells.'

Bells. Don't say anything more, Dad, please. Hang up.

14

'Who's Bells? Is that your dog?' Sam asks.

'Wine?' I say, praying he'll walk away.

'Katie, you know I hate pets.'

'Your mother and I are going to France for two weeks,' Dad continues, 'but we can't leave Bells on her own.'

Sam is shaking his head now. 'Sitting next to Mum's dog, Doogle, is like sitting next to an old fish. F. Breath Esquire, I call him.'

'Sam! Go! Drink!' I demand now, feeling myself burning under my skin as I put my hand out to press the stop button, but Sam puts his hand firmly over mine.

'What is it, Katie? Jesus, I thought I had a weird relationship with my parents.'

Sam has always been cagey about his family. 'Who's Julian?' I once asked him. 'My father,' he replied, in an unusually stiff, formal voice which invited no further questions.

'I really need to talk to you,' Dad continues. 'I'm out all day tomorrow, so can you call me back tonight?' There is a lengthy pause. I wish Sam would go away. His presence feels like a loaded gun.

Dad inhales deeply, making Sam laugh. 'It's only a bloody dog, isn't it, Katie? Anyone would think he was talking about the future of the euro,' he says, finally disappearing downstairs.

It's two o'clock in the morning and I can't find my cigarettes. The evening was dismal because I couldn't stop thinking about Bells. Sam would never have known I wasn't enjoying myself. I smiled in all the right places and laughed when Maguire relayed his filthy jokes. But Sam can't massage this problem away. Why did it have to happen now, when things are running so smoothly? Oh Sam! Where have you hidden them? I stare at the cupboards. There's nothing in Sam's kitchen. All the surfaces are kept carefully bare; in fact there's nothing much anywhere, except for the art sculpture in the corner of the room, made out of what looks like coloured milk bottles. Sam tells me it reflects the mood of the modern world.

I open one of the cupboards and run my eyes over the shelves. Maybe Sam tucked the cigarettes into the pressure cooker, as we never use it? Nope. I stand on tiptoe and run my hand along the top of the cupboard. I could kill him. If I want a cigarette, why shouldn't I smoke one?

I open each drawer, slamming it shut when no cigarettes are revealed, my conversation with Dad preying on my mind.

'Katie, we know it's a lot to ask, but I need your help,' he had said to me earlier this evening.

'It's all so sudden, though, why didn't you tell me how tired Mum's been?'

'I can't hear you, speak up.'

I had to repeat the question again, keeping half an ear on what Sam was doing. I could hear him upstairs, opening our wardrobe, running bath water.

'Oh, Katie, you know how proud she is. We'd never go away unless I organized it. Look, it's just for two weeks.'

'How is she?' I asked, biting my lip. 'Dad?'

'She'll be fine, as long as she has a break and we take some time off now.'

'Right,' I acknowledged. 'I know you need a holiday, but I'm not sure I can look after Bells. It's such short notice.'

'It's all booked,' Dad said firmly.

It's so unlike him to go ahead without asking me. How does he know I'm free? I might be going on holiday too, or abroad on business. 'Is there anyone else we can ask?'

'Like who?'

'Aunt Agnes. She'd love to . . .'

'Bells wants to stay with you.'

'Why?' My voice was a loud whisper. 'I can't have her here.'

'Can't or won't?'

'What about my shop? I'm sorry, but I can't drop everything. Let's call Aunt Agnes.'

'Now listen here, Katie. Your mother and I have never asked anything of you until now. We need this time together and Bells specifically asked if she could be with you in London. I told her she must write to ask you herself. Didn't you get her letter?'

'It must have got lost in the post,' I lied, picturing it unopened and hidden in my diary.

'Oh, Katie!' He raised his voice in exasperation. 'Why

won't you write to her? She's always asking after you. "How's Katie? Never see Katie." '

I could hear Bells saying that and my heart melted for a split second. Dad must have felt it too because his voice softened. 'It would mean so much to her, and to us.'

Back to reality. 'Dad, two weeks is a long time. It's not even my own home.'

'I understand you'd have to ask Sam. We would help towards costs and . . .'

'No, it's not about money, Dad.' Sam came downstairs in his towel at this point, asking why I was taking so long. The bath was ready. A thought came to me. I could persuade him to go on a golfing weekend with Maguire and the lads. 'I could have her for a weekend?'

'And where will she stay the rest of the time?'

'Can't she stay in Wales?' was my desperate last attempt.

'Well, she could, but that's miserable, quite frankly,' he said, his voice loaded with frustration.

I understood all of this, but . . . 'I'm sorry, Dad. I really can't. If I had my own apartment . . .'

He cut me short. 'That's not the real reason, is it, Katie?'

I was quiet.

'Isn't it high time you shared some responsibility for your sister? Are you going to pretend she doesn't exist for the rest of your life? You can't always leave it up to your mother and me. What would you do if something happened to us? Bells would be your responsibility then. Have you ever . . . ?'

'Hang on, Dad, what did you mean, if something happened to you? Like what?'

'If you won't have Bells to stay, you call her and tell her yourself,' he continued, his voice was trembling with anger now.

'Dad, what did you mean before?' I pressed him. 'Everything's OK, isn't it?'

'All I meant was, your mother and I aren't always going to be here for Bells. I'm not trying to scare you, but let's face it, it's something you need to think about.'

But I don't want to. Emma has said this to me too. She wishes I would spend more time with Bells. 'After your parents, you are her next of kin,' she says.

'Katie?'

'All right, I'll have her to stay.'

There was this great sigh of relief. 'That's wonderful, thank you,' Dad said.

Frustrated in my search for cigarettes, I stick the kettle on instead. Is it unfair to expect Sam to have Bells to stay for two weeks? If it were my home, well, that'd be different, I reason to myself. Oh, God, who am I fooling? Yet I'm furious that my parents have put me in this position. It cuts both ways, Dad. I have a life to lead. I have a career. I can't drop everything for Bells like you and Mum have. That was always the motto in our household.

I massage my forehead, desperately trying to think of an alternative. Should I phone Aunt Agnes? Bells would have a much nicer time staying with her. I used to love my holidays there.

How am I going to do this? How will I introduce Bells to my friends? To Eve? To Sam?

I dig into my handbag to find my diary. In it is Bells' letter. I open it. The address, date and time are neatly underlined in the right-hand corner.

To my sister Katie Fletcher
Mum and Dad to stay in France and it would be very kind you have me to stay in summer holidays. To stay with Aunt Agnes, Suffolk too far, big thumbs down, would be very loveley to stay with Katie in London please. Its very Longtime, since I saw you and Wales close to London.
Love, Bells xoxoxo

I fold the letter and tuck it back into my diary.

How can I say no?

3

1982

I am seven years old. I like staying with Aunt Agnes, who lives in Suffolk, near the sea. She makes the best Black Forest gâteau with flakes of real dark chocolate, and cooks home-made chips with real potatoes in a large deep pan. She is very pretty and wears glasses, attached to small brown beads like a necklace, and a long checked apron when she's cooking. She has these pointed shoes that look like witch's shoes and a trainset that I play with in her large garden.

Her husband is funny too. Uncle Roger. Once he sat back in his chair and the whole thing collapsed. 'This house is like an old lady,' Aunt Agnes said. 'It needs a bit of cosmetic surgery.'

I think their house is spooky. Uncle Roger swears to me that he has seen the ghost of his father at the top of the stairs. The stairs creak, even my bed creaks. The corridors are dark and smell old, and I run as fast as I can up and down those haunted stairs and into my bedroom. 'She's only a little girl, but sometimes I think she's going to crash right through them,' I overheard Uncle Roger say once.

I'm staying with my uncle and aunt while Mum has her baby. Mum finds being pregnant difficult. She has had three miscarriages – Dad explained to me what they were – and during this last pregnancy she has been in bed most of the time. Now it's time for me to go back home. 'Your mother has had a baby girl,' Aunt Agnes tells me. 'You'll need to help your mum a lot. She will be very tired.' She isn't smiling at all and keeps on glancing sideways at Uncle Roger.

Why is she being so quiet all of a sudden? Up until now Aunt Agnes has been showing me baby knitwear patterns and asking whether she should just 'go for it' and make the booties pink or perhaps 'sit tight' in case it's a boy. Every sentence has begun with either, 'Katie, if your mother has a girl . . .' or, 'I'm sure it's a boy. I can feel it in me bones.' Even when we went to Sainsbury's she told the girl at the till that she was expecting a nephew or niece. Aunt Agnes flaps her arms around when she's excited and her eyes flicker like a butterfly. Sometimes she pokes out her tongue when she's in an especially good mood.

The Sainsbury's girl had black all around her eyes and didn't seem at all interested. As the Club biscuits and mini packets of cereals slid past her she said, 'Me, I'm never gonna have children or get married. Men, they're only good when you want something done.'

Aunt Agnes roared with laughter as she packed everything into bags. 'What a lot that girl will miss out on,' she told me in the car on the way back home. 'When you grow up, Katie, promise me you'll have lots of children. Fill the house with them. Don't be lonely like your old Uncle Roger and me.' Aunt Agnes can't have children. Mum and Dad explained that's why they like to pack me off to go and see her in the holidays. Supper that night was spent deciding what names to call him/her. Now Aunt Agnes looks as if she doesn't know what to say about the new arrival.

She hugs me on the platform and tells me to be a brave girl. I cannot understand it. I always travel on my own to Suffolk. A guard helps me on to the train and then there is Dad to pick me up when we arrive. There's nothing to be brave about. The train trundles back to my parents' home, and I go to the buffet car and pick out a marshmallow biscuit with strawberry filling and a packet of cheese and onion crisps. In between mouthfuls I try to imagine what my baby sister will look like. Will she look like me when I was little? Dad used to say I was blonde and big-eyed with dimpled white skin and chubby legs like baguettes. 'You used to wear your knickers on your head too.' He smiled. 'You pretended they were scarves.'

Dad meets me at the station as usual, wearing his dark-rimmed glasses and looking even thinner and longer than he usually does. My dad is over six foot two inches. Today he is wearing his scruffy jeans that he normally only wears around the house and his knitted chunky grey jumper that matches his hair. He always complains that he turned grey too early in life. He helps me with my shiny red case as I show the platform conductor my crumpled ticket. On the way home I want to ask lots of questions about the new baby. Yet I feel as if I have a marble stuck in my throat. Instead, we drive home in silence. Dad doesn't even put the radio on to hear the news. He loves the news. Eventually Dad says, 'Your mother is tired.' He tells me I must be a good girl. He is gripping the steering wheel so hard I can see his knuckles turning white.

'We're back,' Dad calls loudly. We walk upstairs in silence.

Mum is sitting on her bedside chair with her old quilted bed-jacket on. Dad often tries to buy her another bed-jacket, but she won't give it up. 'It's like comfort food,' she says. 'Sticky toffee pudding.' I kiss her on the cheek but she doesn't move, just sits there quietly, like Granny sits in her armchair when she comes to stay. Her eyes look red and puffy, as if she's been crying. What's wrong? Shouldn't Mum be happy if she has had a baby? Instead she looks small and old and her cheeks are cold and dry.

The crib stands in the middle of the room. It looks lonely and no noise comes from it. Mum looks over to Dad, who seems to be making some kind of secret sign at her.

'Before you see your new sister . . .' Dad says slowly. I know then for certain that something is wrong, and I'm scared. I walk over to the crib and look down.

4

'Did you really think you could keep her a secret for ever?' asks Emma, grinding some pepper on to our hummus. Each Tuesday Emma and I go to a yoga class, followed by supper together. Sam plays poker with Maguire and a few of his other workmates.

Emma tilts her head sideways when she asks questions – she does it when she's watching television too, her forehead furrowed in concentration. Emma and I know almost everything about each other. She was once my next-door neighbour. We went to school together, ballet classes together, until Emma was told she was too 'big-boned' to have a future in pirouetting. She's tall and willowy now, but when she was little she was 'partridge-shaped' as my Dad used to say. She stole bags of crisps from the cardboard box in their kitchen and ate them at the bottom of the garden. I was the other way round; the teacher constantly asked me if I was eating properly.

We used to have a dressing-up box at home and we'd put

on my mother's old fur coats and stilettos and strut down to the shops together with Peggy, Mum's dog, held tightly on the lead. Peggy would never walk with me, I had to drag her and she bumped along the pavement. I spent most of my time at Emma's house. When things at home were difficult or if Mum and Dad were at the hospital visiting Bells, I stayed with Emma. Their family house became my second home. Emma is the only person I can talk to about Bells as she grew up with both of us.

Emma still has that psychologist's expression on her face, which makes me feel unsettled. Of course this would be her reaction.

'I knew Sam would meet her some day, if we were serious,' I finally reply.

'*Are* you serious?' She dips her pitta into the hummus.

'Yes, I think so.'

Emma is absent-mindedly coiling her dark brown hair, but her eyes don't leave mine. 'Then in a way this is the perfect opportunity to tell him. It's given you the push you need. Otherwise, when will you?'

'It's never been a conscious decision not to tell him about Bells.' I fight my own corner. 'He knows I have a sister, I haven't told him much about her, that's all. It hasn't come up in conversation.'

'You're embarrassed, aren't you?'

'Of course I'm not embarrassed.' I blush, feeling defenceless around her, as if she is peeling the protective layers away from me one by one.

Emma chooses not to hear. 'You think the longer you don't mention Bells, the harder it will be to drop her casually into conversation, don't you?'

'Sam's not a curious person,' I defend myself, 'we don't talk about family stuff.' Since going out with Sam I have discovered little scraps of information about his parents. His father worked overseas when he was young. 'Mum and I were fine,' he insisted when I asked him if he'd missed his father. 'We had a great time. Mum had a ball, in fact, when Dad left. Didn't have to pick up his dry-cleaning or put his bloody supper on the table by seven on the dot. She could go out with her friends. Used to take me to all the parties,' he recalled with a short laugh. 'Yeah, we had a grand time, Mum and I. Turned out for the best, I'd say.' Sam doesn't like saying anything is wrong or that someone has hurt him. It's a positive thing, in that he doesn't ever feel sorry for himself or harbour resentment. 'Life is for living, not for dwelling on, Katie,' he always says.

It's not really as simple as Sam makes it sound. Yet I've never felt able to tell him about my family; about how much I hated not seeing more of Mum after Bells arrived. Anyway, it doesn't matter because Sam doesn't ask. That's why I love going out with him. I don't need to explain anything. I can be exactly who I want to be.

'Eat some of this,' Emma demands, pushing the plate of hummus and pitta bread in my direction. 'You haven't touched your food.'

I look at the plate dispassionately. 'I'm not hungry.' Instead I pour myself another glass of wine.

'I think you're overreacting to the whole situation,' she says. 'You're not the only one to go through something like this, you know. Dad did exactly the same thing with Mum.'

'Really?' I look up.

'Yes.' Emma nods. 'He didn't introduce her to his brother, you know, Uncle Spencer? Big ears, plays the piano very badly, rides a motorbike and wears dodgy maroon shirts and purple ties?'

'I know Uncle Spencer.' I smile. 'He's the one who can tell you what day of the week you were born from the date of your birthday, can't he? I used to love that game,' I reminisce. 'I was born on a Friday. I always wanted him to be just one day out, but he didn't slip up, not once. I remember his wobbly "Für Elise" too.' I grin. 'Which came out especially at Christmas, along with a few hymns. "Hark the Herald" was particularly painful.'

'Exactly.' Emma laughs. 'He's wonderful, but he lives on another planet. Dad thought Mum might call off the engagement if she met him. So he was wily and arranged that Mum's visits never coincided with Uncle Spencer's. They "courted" for eight months, were engaged, and Mum finally met Uncle Spencer for the first time at the wedding.'

'In one of his dodgy suits?' For a moment I am forgetting my own dilemma and enjoying the world of Uncle Spencer.

'No, even worse, he arrived on his motorbike wearing a black shirt with a gold tiger on it.' She wrinkles her nose. 'Totally inappropriate, but it didn't surprise anyone.'

'Well, there you go!' I top up my glass of wine. 'Your dad would understand then. *You* should too.' I feel like I have earned back a few points.

'I do understand. But I asked Mum if it would have made any difference had she met Uncle Spencer before they married, and she said no. She was adamant. She would have married Dad anyway. He was a silly old fool who worried too much. She adores Uncle Spencer. We all do. He's entertaining. She finds his sister, Esther, boring and straight.'

'Ems, I do see what you're saying, I just feel Sam has to seriously . . . I mean, seriously,' I emphasize, widening my eyes, 'fall in love with me before I introduce him to Bells. It's only been nine months and they have been fantastic. I'm happy. I don't want to risk Bells meeting him and whacking him hard in the balls.'

Emma's face dissolves into a smile. 'She doesn't do that any more though, does she?'

When Emma and I were at school we used to meet boys in our lunch hour and clumsily snog them behind school fences and gates. I remember fancying two boys, Toby and Ben, but not being able to choose which one to go out with.

So I decided to put them both to the 'Bells Test'. In the past, boys had met Bells and, ten times out of ten, left the house vowing never to return. To begin with I had been mortified, but then I started to turn the situation around. There had to be one boy, surely, who could stand up to the test?

I took Toby home first and watched Bells charge at him full tilt and butt him in the balls. You might wonder where the fun was in that, but the best part lay in studying his reaction. When Bells belted Toby I watched him as he clutched his balls in agony. Then he pretended it hadn't happened at all and asked me what was for tea. Bells started to howl with laughter and Toby said he had forgotten his mum wanted him back for tea after all.

Ben was different. He rugby-tackled Bells and she liked that and kept on asking when he was coming round again. And he did come back! Ben at least had risen to the challenge. Was I scared that Sam wouldn't?

'Come off it, that was when we were . . . what? Fourteen? Fifteen?' Emma continues. 'And we are talking Toby, the prick who wore tight leather jackets and thought he was in *Grease*, and Ben who drew phallic diagrams all over your pencil case and files? What a loss!' she laughs. 'Bells did you a favour.'

'I know,' I concede. 'But, Emma, it's two whole weeks. It's not a weekend, a few days, it's a whole fortnight.'

Emma shakes her head. 'Katie, this is ridiculous. Bells is

not your average sister, but so what? She wants you to be a part of her life, is that so scary? Just this evening I had to see a young girl from a broken home, self-harming . . .' Emma stops, knowing the information on her patients is strictly confidential. 'You need to put it in perspective.'

The waiter takes our plates away. 'You're right,' I say, hanging my head with shame. 'I'm sorry, Emma, your job must be difficult sometimes.'

She shrugs. 'Bells gets on with it. You need to as well. When did you last see her? I mean, properly?'

'Last Christmas. I went home for a night.'

'You never know, you might actually enjoy her company. Things always come along to test us,' Emma continues. 'Life never stays on a nice even keel; it doesn't work like that.' As she is saying this, half of me wants to reply, 'What's ever tested you?' Emma's life is perfect. She gets on with her family, her brother is her best friend, she has a close relationship with her parents, Jonnie adores her, they were *made* for each other, and now she has a large diamond on her finger.

'You don't see enough of your mum either, Katie. You might regret it one day.' She waits for my response. 'What's wrong? There's something else, isn't there?' she probes. 'Is it your mother?'

I tell Emma about my conversation with Dad. 'It seems a bit sudden, that's all. I can't help wondering if he's keeping something from me.'

'Your dad wouldn't lie,' Emma says with conviction. 'Look, I think all they want you to do is make more of an effort with Bells.'

'Mum didn't even ring to ask me how my show went,' I tell her.

'OK, but did she know about it? Did you ask her to be there?' Emma's patience is running out.

'No, not really. Oh,' I wave a hand dismissively, 'I know. I'm nearly thirty, not sixteen. It shouldn't get to me like this.' I sink back into my chair and try to relax. 'I wish I'd told Sam straight away about Bells; it would have made life a lot easier.'

'Tell him your sister's coming to stay. Describe her so he won't be too surprised, and I bet you he'll be fine about it.'

'But . . .'

'No buts.'

'Yes, but what if . . .'

'No buts. I know you would be saying the same thing to me if it were the other way around. And I know it's easy, my sitting here giving you advice,' she admits, 'but tell Sam tonight. Don't put it off any longer. He's not a monster, he's your boyfriend. I tell Jonnie everything, he would be hurt if I shut him out. Don't we go out with people to feel supported? Isn't that the whole point?'

'Yes.'

'You tell him,' she says simply. 'What's the worst that can happen?'

5

1982

'Katie,' Dad says sternly, 'don't upset your mother.'

I can't help it. I peer into the cot again. 'But what's wrong with her?' I turn to look at Mum and Dad. 'Why hasn't my sister got a proper nose? And what's that funny hole between her nose and lip?' Mum is crying now, and Dad crouches down beside her, stroking her arm gently.

'Why does she look so funny?' I ask again. I can't look at the baby any more. It's scaring me.

'Katie,' Dad begins, 'this is the way she was born. I'm afraid not all children are lucky enough to be born perfect.'

'Why?'

Dad takes off his glasses and wipes his eyes. 'Just because. We're going to have to help her. Your sister will have to see a doctor who will make her face better. It's going to be all right. We're . . .'

'Stop!' Mum sobs. 'Nothing's all right. How are we going to cope?'

'We'll manage. We'll make sure we do,' Dad reassures her. 'Katie will help us, won't you, darling?' He looks at me as if to say, Don't just stand there, come over and give your mother a hug.

Was this what Aunt Agnes meant by being brave? I walk over to Mum and put my arms around her.

The doctor is here and I am listening behind the kitchen door.

'There's an excellent local team of specialists in facial-oral problems. They're highly experienced in treating children born with a cleft of the lip and palate,' he says. 'One child in approximately seven hundred and fifty births has this problem. We will also consult a plastic surgeon for advice. He'll talk us through the reconstructive surgical procedures. With a series of operations, we can repair your daughter's lip and palate.'

'When can we start?' Dad asks.

'While she's still a baby, but a bit bigger and able to cope with the surgery.'

'I don't understand why this happened. I felt fine during the pregnancy, I had plenty of rest. What did I do wrong?' Mum pleads for an explanation.

'It's not your fault,' Dad tells her.

The doctor agrees. 'There is no known cause. Is there any family history, do you know?'

'Not that I'm aware. I was so sure I had done everything right,' Mum continues, oblivious. 'But I should have had a scan. I should have . . .'

'Stop it.' Dad raises his voice. 'Stop blaming yourself.'

'The specialists will go through everything with you. I know it's hard to take in, but we are very experienced in this field.' The doctor clears his throat. I can feel a terrible silence stretching out before he adds, 'I am afraid there is a further problem. She could be brain-damaged, though to what extent precisely we do not know at the moment.'

'Brain-damaged?' Mum says numbly.

'Yes. We'll carry out more tests, but she . . .'

'Her name is Isabel,' Dad says, on the verge of tears. 'We've always loved that name.'

'Isabel, right. That's a lovely name. You have another girl too, don't you?' the doctor enquires.

'Yes, Katie. Why?'

'Nothing's certain at this stage, but you may need help. Isabel will need constant attention.'

Poor Mum. This is so unfair. I will help. Let me help.

'We'll be fine.' Dad speaks softly to her. 'We'll get through this together.'

I hear the doctor stand up to leave. I rush away from the door and run upstairs.

Mum doesn't say goodnight to me like she usually does. Dad comes instead. It seems dark and cold in my bedroom and I feel very alone when I hear his heavy footsteps walk away from me.

6

I look at the picture of Sam in the silver frame by my bed-side. He's wearing the white cotton shirt that I bought him for his birthday, sunglasses perched on the top of his head. Sam is handsome and he knows it. Virtually every feature is symmetrical except for one of his nostrils, which is not as open as the other – he puts that down to his mother smoking when she was pregnant with him. 'The moment Dad was out of the house, she smoked like a chimney. Fag in one hand, vodka in the other.' The only other thing he is conscious of is his receding hairline, but I tell him it makes him look distinguished. Noble even. He tells me it makes him look like his father, as he takes a handful of his hair and tries to ruffle it up as much as he can.

I still haven't told him about Bells. I've put it off for a week and now her train's arriving in Paddington tomorrow. I don't know why I believe the problem might go away if I don't talk about it. The phone rings; it's Dad. They're leaving the next day. 'Who are you staying with in France?' I ask.

'The Walters.'

I don't recognize the name. 'Who are they?'

'Old friends. He used to work with me at Sotheby's.'

'I don't remember them.'

'They moved to France when you were about two.' Dad changes the subject quickly. 'Now, you've got my mobile . . .'

'Actually, can I have the Wallers's number?'

'Walters.'

'Right. Can I have their number?'

'You won't need it.'

'Well, you never know.'

'We'll call you.'

'I think I ought to have it.'

'Ring us on the mobile.'

'What if there's an emergency?'

'There won't be.'

'Why are you being so funny about their number?'

'Darling,' Dad finally slows the pace of his answers, 'it's simply easier if you ring us on the mobile. That way you can call us any time.'

I agree to this, unwillingly. 'Remember to turn it on then,' I add.

Dad always says he bought the mobile 'for emergency use only', but fails to understand it's useless in an emergency if it's switched off.

'Darling, I have to go now. Will you thank Sam very much?'

I put the phone down feeling uneasy. I have to tell Sam

about Bells tonight. I rang him from the shop earlier, telling him not to work late this evening, that I was cooking him his favourite meal – steak with homemade chips, just like Aunt Agnes's. I've even made him a pudding: orange ice-cream cake with dark chocolate sauce. It's his mother's recipe and so easy, even I can do it.

'Not sure I can get away early, sweetheart. Busy day,' he told me.

'But I haven't seen you all week.'

He seemed to be considering. 'What have I done to deserve this, Katie?' I could hear his chair swivelling around. 'Are you feeling guilty about shagging someone behind my back?' And then he crowed with incredulity, as if the very idea of someone cheating on him was impossible. Sam has enough arrogance to bottle up and sell internationally. Yet this is what I find most attractive about him. I always thought I would end up falling for an academic or maybe a writer. My last boyfriend was a composer who travelled the world creating soundtracks for television shows and films. I barely saw him, which was why it ended. I knew a relationship like that was heading nowhere. Yet I never thought I would go for someone like Sam. Then again, I fancy Simon Cowell, which says it all.

I put the photograph frame back down on the bedside table and open the sliding doors to our wardrobe, clothes neatly folded into different compartments. What shall I wear? I go for the dark red lace top with the velvet trim around the neck. I'll wear my black lacy bra underneath. Bottom half will be jeans with black boots. Sam loves those boots. I peel off my oyster-grey shirt and toss it into the laundry basket, unzip my skirt and look at myself in the long mirror. My hair, now dyed back to its original dark brown, hangs loose around my face. It's getting long. I pin it up with a clip. I have my father's fine hair. In fact, I have inherited most of my features from Dad; the long Fletcher nose, the wide mouth and my dimple.

I open one of the mirrored cupboards in our bathroom to find some cotton-wool pads and cleanser. Sam gets infuriated with me if I leave my toothpaste or cotton-wool pads lying around in the bathroom – everything has to be packed neatly into the mirrored cupboards. I like it that he is tidy. If he wasn't, his place would look like it had been burgled.

I wipe the day's make-up off my face. From Mum I've inherited a splattering of freckles across my nose and cheeks, and my green eyes. Dad always says he fell for her eyes straight away. They were the colour of olives, and Dad loves olives. When I first met Sam he told me I had 'come to bed' eyes. Wait till he sees Bells' eyes, which are far more beautiful. They're a vivid green with no sludgy grey in them at all. I sit on the edge of the bath and run the water, pouring in a capful of neroli oil, and finally I step into the sweet-scented water. It's been a long day. Tonight will be fine. Sam will be cool about Bells and everything will be

OK, I reassure myself for what must be the hundredth time.

Later I finish laying the table, placing the new napkins I made out of muslin by each plate. Mum could turn her napkins into the shape of lilies. I used to try to copy her as a child. Now I simply fold mine in two. I open the fridge and pour myself a second glass of white wine. Sam should be here any minute now. I hear a key turn in the front door and something jolts sharply inside me. I breathe deeply, I think about Emma's advice to come clean.

'Hi, honey,' I call. The room smells of scented candles and chips frying in golden oil. Music plays softly in the background.

Sam enters the kitchen, hands me a bunch of scarlet and orange tulips. I thank him with a kiss and he wraps his arms around my waist, pulling me close to him. 'Kitty-kins.' He rubs his nose against mine. 'I'm a lucky boy. I raced home. Not too late, am I?'

'Perfect timing. Good day?'

'Great day in the markets. Fabulous. Wham, bam, thank you, ma'am.' He winks. 'And now I'm all yours.'

'That's brilliant, Sam.' When he's excited about closing a deal I have tried to ask him in the past about it, but he always says, 'Top-secret, babe, confidential,' and taps his nose. So I rarely bother now, just make encouraging noises.

'Smells fab, I'm starving.'

'Sit down,' I instruct, leading him to a chair. 'You need to relax.'

'Are you softening me up for something?' Sam murmurs with pleasure when I massage his shoulders.

'Can't a girl spoil her boy?' I run a hand over his back. 'Right, what do you want to drink? Beer or wine?'

We have just finished our first course. What's wrong with me? I haven't said a word about Bells. Instead, I'm listening to Sam tell me that Maguire has bought a Mini Cooper and plans to go racing at the weekend, and would I mind if he goes too?

He leans across the table and strokes my cheek. 'Enough of me, how's the old soak in the corner? Has she been in lately?'

'No, annoyingly not.' I tell him about Eve instead as I clear the plates. 'She ought to be the size of an elephant, not a mouse,' he chuckles.

I open the fridge, telling myself that when I put the pudding on the table, that's when I'll say something. It's not so hard to say, is it? *Sam, my sister's coming to stay tomorrow, is that OK? She's not quite what you'd expect, you might be a bit taken aback . . .* I'm going to scare the living daylights out of him, aren't I?

The pudding sits in front of him. Sam rubs his stomach and smiles. 'I could get used to this star treatment.'

'Sam, there's something I need to . . . oh my God! Is that *the* watch?' I stare at his wrist. 'You actually bought it?'

'Yep.' He beams, shaking his wrist at me. Sam has been going on about this watch for months. It's a special 'emergency' model with an electronic device you can press to alert help in moments of crisis. One of his friends works in advertising and his company was involved in its promotion. Sam and I were so excited when we met Pierce Brosnan at the launch.

'You know, I might buy one. Imagine if I were caught in an avalanche,' I overheard Sam saying seriously to Tim, one of his friends at work.

'Yeah, yeah, yeah. Absolutely, mate,' Tim replied.

'Or when your canoe tips up while you're white-water rafting?' I suggested to them both, trying not to laugh. I didn't remind Sam that he wasn't exactly into extreme sports. Falling into a bunker playing a round of golf was about as dangerous as it got for him.

Now he looks at his watch proudly. 'If you pull the emergency cord by mistake you're fined thousands of pounds, Katie, so be careful, *capisce*? Anyway, what did you want to tell me?' He slices the orange pudding, cream seeping out around the edges and making patterns in the chocolate sauce.

'I should have asked you before, but my sister's coming to London.'

'Really?' He eats a spoonful. 'Yum,' he moans appreciatively. '*Delicioso*. Have you been secretly going to cooking lessons?'

'I was hoping she could stay with us? My sister? Isabel?' I remind him.

'Sure. For how long?'

'Two weeks.'

'Right.' Sam mulls this over, looking surprised that it's for so long. 'No, that's OK, see no reason why not. Isabel's younger than you, isn't she? I could set Maguire up, he needs a bird.'

'But he had a new "lady" only days ago.'

'Nah, didn't work out. Maguire likes it short and sweet. So Isabel's coming up for two weeks? Perfect. Done and dusted.'

'Sam! Don't talk in clichés. Maguire will end up a sad lonely old bachelor if he carries on like that,' I add.

'Does she look like you?' he goes on. 'Just a younger, more wrinkle-free version?'

'Sam,' I say with some irritation. 'Is that all you think about? Image?'

'Yep. Well, it helps if she's not a complete moose. Come on, girls are the same. Blokes are more honest, that's all. Would you have fallen for me if I was ugly as sin?'

I pick up my plate and walk over to the sink.

He holds up his hands in a gesture of apology. 'How old is she then?'

'Twenty-two.' I sit back down, stare at the candle I lit so hopefully. Pudding is over and I still haven't told him the whole truth. By the time it burns out he will know every-thing about Bells, I vow.

'What does she do? Is she a lap-dancer?'

'Oh, Sam,' I sigh.

'Don't tell me . . . she works for MI5 or something exciting like that? Seriously, why don't I get Maguire over one night and introduce them?'

Bill Maguire. Tall, blond hair the colour of egg yolk with eyebrows and lashes to match. Always wears a leather jacket, a predator when it comes to women and loves to tell dirty jokes. 'Um, I don't think so. I mean, Bill's great, but . . .'

'She is single, right?'

I nod. 'Sam, there's something I need to tell you about her, though.' I stare at the candle, watching the flame glow in the dark.

Sam comes over to me.

'I'm looking forward to meeting her, babe. Stop worrying. You stress too much.' He kisses my neck before walking in front of me and kneeling down, putting his hands on my knees. I know that look. He's about to break out into Chris de Burgh's 'Lady In Red' because he knows it makes me laugh. We tease Emma for liking Chris de Burgh, that's how it started. In fact we have his CD too, but that's our little secret.

Sam pulls me to my feet. We love dancing in the kitchen. It's our time together, Sam and me. He spins me around, singing softly in my ear. We laugh.

Why does my family have to be different? I curse quietly to myself as Sam holds me. Wouldn't it be wonderful to be able to say, 'My sister's a lawyer'? Or an architect, philosopher, psychologist, artist, writer, charity worker, hairdresser, chef, whatever. Why can't we be normal, like every other family? Why do I care so much? Surely I should be past this stage? Shouldn't I be mature enough to tell Sam? Like Emma says, if we are in a serious relationship . . .

Finally we stop dancing. 'Thanks for a lovely evening, Katie.' He takes my hand, gently kissing each finger in turn.

I don't want to tell him, it doesn't feel right to say anything now. He will meet Bells tomorrow.

7

1984

As I walk across the school playground I can see my mother standing apart from the cluster of parents waiting by the iron gates. Bells is with her in the pushchair. What's she doing here? A mixture of panic and anger jabs at my chest. Mum never picks me up. Normally I go to Mr Stubbington's corner shop to buy some sherbet dips and marshmallows and then walk home with Emma, my next-door neighbour. I go round to her house for tea because it's nicer there. They light the fire and then we toast our marshmallows.

Mum approaches one of the other mothers and a young girl. She's wearing her grubby apron with paint and oil stains down the front, her bright red shoes that look more like clogs, her auburn hair still pulled back in one of her cotton headscarves. All the other mothers wear long navy skirts and blouses with pearls, and their hair is curled and sits like perfect nests on top of their heads. Why does my mum have to look so different? Why did she have to bring Bells?

'Katie, what is it?' Emma asks impatiently. 'I'm hungry. Come on.'

'Mum's here, with Bells.' I pull her back.

'So?' Emma shrugs.

I haven't told anyone in my class about Bells: they wouldn't understand. Emma is the only one who has seen her from the beginning. Bells' face looks so strange. They laugh at anything that looks weird. Mrs Higson, one of the mothers who stands at the gate, is so fat that everyone calls her Mrs Treestump-Legs. Has Mum seen me? I dart behind the boys' outside loo, but can't stay there for long because it smells. I almost choke. My mother's voice is louder than any of the other mums, I think crossly. I'm sure she does it on purpose. 'Go then,' I tell Emma, waving her away with my hand. 'Tell Mum I had to stay behind in class . . . say anything.'

I can hear people walking off, engines being turned on, prams being pushed, dogs barking. I wait with my fingers clipped firmly to my nose.

'Hello,' I overhear Mum saying, trying to be friendly. 'Don't look so worried, she won't bite you. Her name's Isabel. We call her Bells.'

Who's Mum talking to? I poke my head round the wall. It's Imogen, from the year below, with her mother.

'What's wrong with her?' Imogen asks, unable to take

her eyes away from the baby in the pram. 'What's that big hole in her face?'

'Imogen, don't be rude,' the mother says, blushing. 'It's the inside that counts, isn't it?' she says to Mum.

Mum says nothing.

Imogen still stands rooted to the spot like a mannequin in a shop. Piss off, I want to shout. Her mother eventually pulls her away.

I wait until it is quiet and safe to come out. After roughly ten minutes I poke my head round the wall. Mum is bending down talking to Bells. I bolt sideways and then stroll forward as if I have come from the main school building. 'I don't care what anyone says,' I hear, 'you're my beautiful little girl, and your mother loves you, and we are having a lovely time, aren't we?'

'Hi, Mum. I had to tidy up the paints . . . and stuff,' I falter.

Mum eyes me suspiciously. 'Emma said you were showing your needlework to the headmistress.'

We walk back home, my head hung low.

'Are your feet suddenly fascinating?' Mum asks.

'Nope.'

'I had a call today,' she says, as we walk on briskly, the pushchair rattling against the pavement. 'From Mr Stubbington.'

My whole body freezes.

'Katie, I'm ashamed of you. I leave you to walk home on

49

your own because I think you're old enough. Then I find you have been going into his shop and stealing from the charity pot. What has got into you lately?' Mum turns to me, demanding an explanation.

Mr Stubbington has banned me from the shop for a week because he caught me trying to steal coins from the charity stocking. Mostly it's full of one- and two-pence pieces but there are always those tantalizing silver and gold coins stuck in the netting of the toe. When Mr Stubbington turned away to put some apples into a brown-paper bag one afternoon, I could not resist plunging my hand in to try to get a fifty-pence piece. 'This money goes to Help the Aged,' he rebuked me, wagging one finger furiously when he saw what I was doing.

I can offer no explanation. 'Unless you promise to stop stealing, I will collect you every day,' Mum threatens.

I don't look up.

'With Bells,' she adds.

Does she know what I'm thinking?

'I promise I won't do it again, Mum.'

Two girls are walking towards us. They stop and gawk when they see Bells. 'What's wrong with it?' one of them asks. I am focusing on a particular crack in the pavement. If I step on this line it will bring me bad luck.

' "It" is my daughter, Isabel. She was born with a cleft lip and palate, and your staring doesn't help,' Mum says, pushing past them. I turn to look at them and they are still standing there staring with their mouths wide open.

'What the hell is a cleft lip?' one of them asks the other.

'I'm sorry, Mum.'

'It's all right, but please don't steal again, Katie. I have enough to do, just looking after this one.'

After that, Mum and I walk home quietly. 'Hello, Bells,' I say behind the closed door, stroking her hair. 'I'll give her her tea tonight,' I tell Mum because I know she's tired. I like mushing up Bells's food. 'How are you today? Have you had a good day?' I push her into the kitchen. The guilt sits like a lump in my stomach.

8

'I'll meet you at the station,' Sam suggests, cramming in a mouthful of toast and marmalade. 'What time does Isabel's train get in?'

'Don't worry, we'll meet you back home.' I don't know why I think delaying the meeting is going to help. At some point the bomb will go off.

'You know, I'm really looking forward to meeting her. I have to be honest, I was slightly dreading it to begin with, but now I'm quite curious to know what another Fletcher sister will be like.'

'Sam, she's very different.' This is the perfect time to tell him. 'I haven't told you everything about her,' I say. 'When she was born . . .'

His mobile rings. 'Hang on a sec,' he says, answering the call. 'Yep, leaving now, Maguire . . . No, I don't agree . . . You've got to look outside the box.' He hangs up.

'Sam, can we talk?' I ask as he puts the phone back in his pocket.

He pulls a face. 'Can it wait till tonight? I'm running late.' He plants a kiss on my lips, opens the front door. 'What's the plan for *ce soir*, by the way? Because I thought you, me, a few of the boys,' he winks at me, 'could take Isabel out for a drink tonight, get her acquainted with London night life, maybe go out dancing?'

I can't take this any more, I should have told him straight away. I have a throbbing headache, a few more grey hairs, and if I don't tell him now I'll explode. 'Sam, Isabel isn't going to be what you think.'

'What?' He looks puzzled. 'What do you mean?'

'She was born with a cleft lip and palate. It's quite a common thing,' I add, when I see his alarmed expression. 'But there was an added complication because she was brain-damaged at birth. She lives in a community in Wales and it's her summer holidays, that's why she's coming to stay.' I feel as if I can breathe again. I wait for a reaction; anything will do.

Sam's face shows little expression. 'Bells? This was what you were talking to your dad about?' He's thinking out loud. 'You let me believe she was your dog.'

'I never actually said that. Bells . . . Isabel.' I shrug my shoulders. 'We call her Bells for short.'

'Right.' Slowly he scratches his head. 'Right, I should have clicked. Well, that's OK. No, hang on,' his voice rises, 'why didn't you *tell* me any of this?'

'I don't know. I'm sorry. I thought you might hate the idea

53

of her staying. And I have no choice; she has nowhere else to go. Mum and Dad are in France. My mother's not well,' I explain, hoping this will make him more sympathetic.

'Well, it looks like I have no choice either.' He frowns. 'Next you'll be telling me you have a brother in prison. Katie, I don't know what to say. See you later.'

'Don't go.' I grab his arm. 'We need to talk.'

'We had all week to talk, Katie, we had last night.' He pulls his arm away before his mobile rings again. 'Lakemore speaking,' he says. 'No, Maguire, that's *not* what I said. Are we even on the same fucking page?'

I close the door after him. I feel terrible. Sick to my stomach. I feel so guilty. I have been lying to myself, to Sam, to Bells. Why am I such a dreadful person? Why am I such a coward?

'I hope her train is early, touching wood,' Eve says in her smoky French accent, tapping my desk.

For a moment I think about correcting her English, but then I think I prefer it the way she says it. 'Thanks, Eve, if you can lock up . . .'

'Yes, yes, do not worry. I look forward to meeting your sister *demain*, I mean, tomorrow, of course.' She unpins her honey-coloured hair. I have never seen such long hair, Botticelli would have loved to paint Eve. 'My mother says it is like Rapunzel's hair, tumbling down the tower,' she laughs whenever I compliment it. 'Where are you picking up Isabel?'

she asks, tying it back up into a bun and sticking in a long hairpin with a coloured glass kiwi fruit on the end of it.

'Paddington.'

A customer comes in looking for a wedding outfit. 'Can I leave you to it?' I ask Eve.

'Yes, yes, I see you tomorrow. Please, come this way,' she says to the customer, leading her up the wooden steps to the second floor. 'I think we have just the thing for you.'

As I drive to Paddington in Sam's BMW, I make a mental list of the things I still need to do. I went to Sainsbury's in my lunch hour to buy some fish and chips for tonight. When I agreed to have Bells I called home to get an idea of what I needed to plan.

'In Wales they have a Mexican night on Monday,' said Mum, 'and they're always given fish and chips on a Friday with mushy peas. I get her the tinned peas, disgusting, I know, but Bells likes them.'

'OK, I'll do that.' If she ate, say, a baked potato on Monday, would that matter terribly? I thought to myself.

'If you don't have time to cook at lunch she enjoys the vegetable samosas that you can buy at the deli counter. On Wednesdays I think they have their Indian nights. Or is it their organic night?' Her voice trailed off. 'Anyway, darling, she loves cooking, so maybe you can do that together.'

As I listened, panic set in. I rarely cook at Sam's. Most nights we eat out, and if we want to drink Sam pays for a cab home with his company card. 'I don't like cooking, I hate the mess,' Sam says. 'I remember Mum making stock for soup with leftover chicken bones. The smell of it in the morning,' he said with a disgusted frown.

'Bells likes her routine,' Mum continued. 'It's very important to her. They eat lunch on the dot of twelve-thirty.'

'I'll do my best, Mum, but she has to fit in with what I'm doing too.'

Mum sniffed. 'She likes her Coke too, but buy her the Diet Coca-Cola or her teeth will rot. And do take her to Sainsbury's, it's like an outing for her.'

'Fine. Is that all?' My patience was running out.

'Yes, make sure she always carries her inhaler. Her asthma is much better, but we can't afford to take any risks.' I thought she would ask me then if I still smoked, but she didn't.

'Of course, Mum.'

'Thank you, Katie.' Mum seemed tired, I could hear it in her voice.

'Mum, nothing's wrong, is it?'

'Wrong? No! Just because we're taking ourselves off on holiday does something have to be wrong? Don't we deserve . . . ?'

'Sorry, Mum, I didn't mean it like that.' I was twisting the phone cable, knotting it around my finger tightly.

'I'm sorry too. I didn't mean to snap.'

I let go of the cable. It had left a deep red indentation in my finger. 'Promise?'

'I promise.'

'It's about time you and Dad had a holiday. Have a lovely time.'

'Katie?'

'Yes?'

'How are you?'

'Fine. Good.' Why is it that I always want Mum to ask me how I am, to be more interested in my life, but when she does ask, all I can do is reply in monosyllables? 'Right, I'd better go and do all that shopping!'

'I know she'll have fun with you. It sets my mind at rest.'

'We'll have a great time. Make sure you come home rested. Love to Dad.'

'Katie?'

'Yes?'

She cleared her throat. 'Do put sun cream on her face, her skin is so delicate.'

'Don't worry, I'll look after her.'

'Thank you,' she said. 'For helping out. It means a lot to your father and me.'

I sensed she wanted to say something else, so I waited for a moment, but she said nothing more. ''Bye, Mum.'

''Bye, my darling.'

The train pulls into the platform. The doors open and passengers step out in a heaving mass. The men wear grey flannel suits and carry briefcases. Some of them have taken their jackets off in this heat and loosened their ties. A pregnant woman walks past in a blue cotton dress worn with Birkenstock sandals. Another girl totters past me in high heels, pulling a neat little designer suitcase on wheels.

'I'm off the train, sweetpea,' says a man on his mobile, 'will be home in time for dinner.'

The crowds are filtering away, leaving a dull grey lifeless platform. Where is she? She can't have missed the train. I can't bear it. I walk down the platform looking into each carriage, but no sign of anyone. Then I hear a door open and see a small figure stepping out of the train. She's wearing a denim jacket covered with lots of badges, a round embroidered hat that looks more like a doily over her head, and a red football scarf. She carries a large purple bag and a couple of plastic Sainsbury's bags.

'Bells!' I say, quickening my pace towards her.

'Hello, Katie. How're you?' I'm so relieved she has arrived that I almost hug her, but instead I take her luggage. 'Well done! You made it,' I say, as we walk away from the platform, past the guard at the entrance. There's a heavy silence after the mobs of people have moved on.

We arrive back at Sam's and I show Bells around the house. The kitchen is in the basement; on the ground floor is a large airy room that looks like a smart waiting room. In here are Sam's new leather sofas and a fireplace controlled by slick silver controls; he has a dark mahogany bookcase filled with glossy hardback books that he hasn't touched. He doesn't read anything apart from the *FT*. On the second floor are the bedrooms, and a cosy room with suede beanbags and a large Stanley Spencer print. The bay window looks out on to the other rainbow-coloured houses along the crescent. If we're in, we pretty much live in this room. Sam plays poker here. On the top floor is the steam room with the old-fashioned bath. 'This is my favourite room, Bells,' I tell her.

'Sam rich?' she asks.

'Yes, he is. He works very hard.' I take her back downstairs to her room, a large bedroom with a double bed, wardrobe, a long mirror whose frame I gilded and one small bedside table with an orange and white stained-glass lamp on it. More or less everything in this room is white – the shutters, the walls, the bedspread. The only other piece of colour is the rug with great big orange and red circles on it. Bells sits on the bed, looking around. It's hard to know what she makes of Sam's house.

'What's your room like in Wales?' I ask, sitting down next to her.

'I wish you would go and visit your sister sometimes,' Mum says to me.

'She's a forgotten sister,' Dad adds.

'Not big like this,' says Bells, waving her arm around.

59

'Have small bed and television and lots of posters. Room looks out on garden and sea. In my plot of land, I grow carrots and potatoes. We grow strawberries this year too. You like strawberries, Katie?' She sticks her thumbs up at me.

'I do. We don't have a garden here,' I say apologetically. 'I think you have Mum's gardening skills. I'd kill everything! There would only be weeds in my plot of land.' She doesn't say anything.

'Now, you've got your own TV in here, so that's something, isn't it?' I point to the big silver machine with the wide screen in the corner of her room. 'You can watch the tennis. Who do you think's going to win Wimbledon this year then?'

'Agassi.'

'You cannot be serious,' I say, imitating John McEnroe.

She looks at me with no hint of a smile. I'm going to have to try harder than a poor imitation of John McEnroe.

'Shall we unpack?' I open her zip bag and out comes a medley of junk and clothes. 'Why have you got Mary Veronica's jumper?' I ask, showing Bells the nametag in the jumper, like the ones we used to have to sew on our school socks and PE kit. 'Bells, you don't have many summer clothes in here. Is this all you packed? Odd jumpers, a few T-shirts and a pair of dungarees? Oh, hang on, you have one frilly pink blouse here that says it belongs to Jessica Hall. I think I'm going to have to get you some new clothes,' I say, talking to myself rather than to her. 'You put all this away while I put the fish and chips on. Deal? You like chips on Fridays, don't you?'

'You have crinkle chips, like ones Mum makes?'

'I'm going to make homemade ones, like Aunt Agnes's.'

'Oh,' she acknowledges, and it's hard to tell whether she's pleased or not. 'How's Aunt Agnes?'

'I think she's fine.'

'Uncle Roger? He died. Poor Uncle Roger.'

'I know. Poor Aunt Agnes too. I think she gets lonely.'

'Poor Aunt Agnes. How's Mum?'

'Well, you know she's on holiday.'

'How's Dad?'

'He's on holiday too. Aren't they lucky? They're in France.'

'In France, that's right. How's Granny Norfolk?'

Our mother's mother, Granny, lives in Norfolk, hence the name. I don't know how she is, I haven't spoken to her in months. 'Look, you've got your own music system,' I tell her, trying to stop the tirade of questions about the Fletcher family.

I can hear my voice, but it's not me. I can't seem to stop talking to her as if she were ten years old.

'Anyway, you'll meet Sam soon,' I say.

Sam. I still feel nervous about him coming home. When I tried to call him earlier, his secretary said he was either 'on the other line' or 'in a meeting'. He has her well trained. 'He's really looking forward to meeting you. You'll be good, won't you?' I can't help adding. 'No dramas, right. We're going to have a really grand two weeks, aren't we?'

'No dramas,' she repeats.

'Good. Come down when you're ready.'

The chips are frying and I'm on to my second vodka. These last few days I've been counting down the minutes until I can have my first drink in the evening. Let's forget the cup of tea and go straight to the hard stuff. First hurdle is over. Bells is here, we are getting on fine, I think. The second major hurdle is Bells meeting Sam.

Stevie Wonder starts to blast out of Bells's bedroom. I run upstairs and open the door. Bells is on the bed, pinning up a poster of David Beckham, his diamond earrings sparkling.

The lovely white room is now covered in football badges and stickers with a Beatles poster stuck to the door, **SEX, DRUGS AND ROCK 'N' ROLL** written in big black letters at the bottom. It reminds me of Bells's bedroom in our parents' home. She had the master bedroom with the sink that I was envious of, and wallpaper with flowery borders. Bells didn't like the wallpaper, though, so she drew pictures of animals and pinned up posters of her favourite pop singers, Stevie Wonder, David Bowie and the Beatles. I remember she had a picture of Bob Marley on the wall too, smoking a joint. Mum did not mind her ruining the wallpaper. She wasn't strict in that sense. She let us get on with it half the time.

The entire floor is covered with clothes, joined by a tattered poetry book, a sketchpad, a small wooden case of oil paints, a collection of CDs and a photograph album. I take a deep breath and bend down to pick the mess off the floor. 'Bells!' I shout. 'Turn it down! It's so loud in here.' I climb on to the bed. 'What are you sticking the posters down with? You're not putting pins in the walls, are you?' Oh, God, she is. 'Bells, don't put pins in the walls!'

'Why?'

'It leaves a hole.'

She continues to push a pin into the white paint.

'Bells, hey! Don't do that. What did I just say?'

'We do in Wales. Mum lets me too.'

I look down at the bedspread. 'I don't care what you do in Wales, you're staying with Sam and me now.'

'Katie bossy,' she says.

I shrug. 'Bells, can you take your boots off? Sam likes you to take your shoes off when you come into the house.' She is still wearing these peculiar little pixie boots.

'Why?' she asks, and then starts to use the bed as a trampoline, while telling me that in Wales they have one in the garden and Ted can jump the highest, apparently.

'What's going on?' I hear from behind. I spin round on the bed and almost lose my balance.

'Hello,' Bells says, extending her small hand. 'You handsome.'

Sam looks at her strangely. 'What did she say?' He looks around. 'This room's a bloody pigsty.'

When Bells makes pig-like noises I want to disappear under the floorboards.

'Is this your . . . ?' He can hardly get the words out.

'This is my sister Isabel. Bells.'

'Hello, you Sam?' she says again, still offering her small pale hand.

He shakes it, limply. 'This is Bells?' He looks around the room again, despair written over his face.

I nod. 'Sam, I'll tidy the room later, don't worry.'

He stares at the posters. 'She hasn't put drawing pins in the wall? Tell me she hasn't, Katie?'

I jump off the bed, rush towards him. 'I'm sorry, I'll deal with it, honey, I promise.'

Sam puts his head into his hands.

'What's that burning smell?' he shouts above the noise, then marches over to the stereo and turns off the music, followed by the television. 'Jesus Christ, even my grandfather doesn't need the snooker on so loudly.'

'No like Sam,' Bells says.

'Bells! Don't be rude.' Thankfully I don't think he understood what she said. He's still sniffing the air with a look of disgust. 'The chips,' I yelp, and dart out of the room.

'Fucking hell, can today get *any* worse?' I hear Sam cursing as he runs after me.

*

It's been a long day when finally I make my way upstairs to bed. The chips burned and Sam hated the mushy peas. 'Who eats mushy peas anyway?' he protested.

I looked in Bells's direction and he shrugged. He attempted to ask her a few questions about the train journey. 'I haven't got a clue what she just said,' he kept on repeating when Bells was staring at him, waiting for a response. She started to hit the kitchen table with her fork in frustration, repeating her questions in vain.

'If you don't understand Bells, just pretend you do,' I tried to persuade him after supper.

I know Sam is still angry with me for not telling him about Bells and I don't blame him. What was I thinking? He has gone out for a few drinks with Maguire.

I turn off the light and close my eyes. He couldn't get out of the house quick enough.

I scream when I see a small figure silhouetted at the end of my bed.

'Bells, what are you doing?' I sit up abruptly. 'Go back to bed.' When I get a glazed response, I jump up and shake her awake.

I can hear Mum coming upstairs and then pacing down our creaky corridor in her floaty nightdress and bed-jacket. 'You shouldn't wake her up,' she scolds me, 'if it happens again, take her back to her bedroom. Bells darling, do you want to go to the loo before you go back to bed?'

'That's right,' she says, lifting up her white cotton nightie and crouching on the floor.

'NO!' Mum and I cry together. Mum starts to laugh, and so do I. And then Bells copies us, doing her mad-lady-locked-up-in-the-attic *Jane Eyre* laugh.

I feel disorientated as I turn on the light and look at my watch. It's only midnight. I shiver. I can hear both Mum and Bells now, as if it were yesterday.

The house is deathly quiet. When we were children, Bells used to sleepwalk almost every night. Mum had to put thick white bars over her bedroom window. I step out of bed and walk down the corridor, towards Bells's room. I find myself opening the door, the light glaring out at me. Mum had told me Bells still hates sleeping in the dark and that I must keep a small light on in the corner of her bedroom.

I can hear her deep breathing as she turns over in bed. She's so tiny, just under five feet tall. She looks young for her age because of her height. She could also be mistaken for a boy from behind because of her short auburn hair. Dad says he never wants Bells to grow her hair. 'You must never hide behind your hair,' he told her when she started to be a self-conscious teenager who wanted to look like everyone else. 'You look the world in the eye,' he said.

I kneel down by her bed and watch as she sleeps, absorbing each line and movement of her face. There is the familiar scar over her upper lip that crosses like two letter

Cs. She always wears three small stud earrings in her left ear; one of them is a green stone surrounded by gold.

Her hand pokes out from the duvet, the skin so pale you would not believe there was blood pumping through the veins. Gently I touch it, and it feels as soft as melting butter.

After Sam went out, Bells and I tidied her room and put the snowy owl that Mum made for her on the bedside table. Bells loves owls. Mum made me a cheetah. His name is Charlie. Bells had carefully placed her inhaler on the bedside table, along with her small photograph album that she has covered with David Beckham stickers. Mum told me she takes her album everywhere when she's away from home; it's like her comfort blanket. I pick it up and quietly leaf through the pages. By each photograph, inscribed on a small white sticker, is a precise date, time, location and description of the person photographed. There's a picture of Mum in her studio, her hands caked in clay, smiling right into the camera; there's a terrible picture of Dad with red eyes reading the newspaper; there's a picture of the water meadows where we used to walk as children. My parents live in St Cross, Winchester. There's a picture of a man wearing a purple tracksuit and football sweatshirt, holding a parrot. He has an identity card around his neck. 'Ted, 1990, St David's, in the garden, summertime.'

Bells opens her eyes and looks straight into me. I panic, thinking I shouldn't be here, but then she shuts them again. I wonder what she dreams about when she goes to bed at night. When she was little she used to have night-mares so we had to keep a light on in her room. It was a little pink light in the shape of a house. Dad said Bells was terrified of the dark as a result of all the surgery she had to go through as a baby and young child. She developed a pho-bia about anaesthetics and would scream before each injection. She didn't know what anaesthesia was, but she knew exactly what it meant. Blackness. Dad was good at talking to me and explaining. He was naturally gentle. In the end it was Emma's sister, Natalie, who came up with a solution called 'The Black Box'. We had to cut off a piece of Bells's hair – it had to be something physical rather than an item of clothing. We put the strand of hair in a box and the alternative practitioner did a kind of absent healing. Mum and Dad thought we were mad, but realized there was little to lose. Besides, we were all going insane from lack of sleep. I can still remember Natalie asking me to kiss the box. 'Gives it good vibes,' she claimed. After a few days Bells's howling at night stopped. It was like magic.

I stand up, the stillness of the room contrasting strongly with the chaos earlier in the evening. As I'm about to leave the room I hear her muffled voice.

'Nothing around me?' she says groggily.

'Nothing around you,' I whisper back, just as Mum used to reply when she was a child.

'Promise?'

'I promise.'

68

9

1989

I climb the three steps into Mum's studio. Her classical music is on in the background, just as it always is. Mum's studio is like a zoo, with the parrots, a pair of cockatoos, a zebra, a giraffe, a tiger, a lioness and a few monkeys perched on shelves, some half-finished, some that Mum calls 'rejects' because they slope too far to the right or left. Mum's a sculptor. Her last project was a camel on bended knee. A friend of hers went to the Sahara Desert and fell in love with the camel she rode and asked Mum to do a sculpture for her from a photograph. She has an entire pin-board full of postcards and letters from happy customers who have commissioned monkeys or fish, or whatever.

Mum's long table in the middle of the room is covered with jam jars filled with brushes and open paint tubes. The room has that familiar smell of white spirit, clay, chalk and dust. 'How are you, darling?' she asks, her neck craned over her work. Her auburn hair is tied back in a navy-and-white dotted scarf and she's wearing large silver hoop earrings that make her look like a gypsy.

I realize the only time I get to see or talk to Mum is either when she's cooking and the kitchen smells of garlic – Mum likes to put at least ten cloves of garlic into everything – or when she's in the studio.

'Good day at school?' she mutters, continuing with her work and humming along to the background music. Her hands are sticky from the clay. Mum, turn around, I think. Instead I walk in front of her. 'Good day?' she repeats distractedly.

I drop my satchel on to the floor. I don't tell her that I got told off yet again for wearing mascara. 'Go and wash that black goo off your face,' my boring maths teacher says again and again. Last weekend I was caught stealing black eyeliner, mascara and a block of spot cover-up from Boots, and the police came by the house to talk to Mum and Dad. It has been suggested that we need family counselling.

'Stealing isn't clever, Katie,' Dad had sighed. 'Or if you have to steal, why don't you make sure it's something better than an eyeliner? And don't get caught next time.'

'Not bad. What are you listening to?'

'*Madam Butterfly.*'

'What's that?'

'It's a cheetah.' She sits back and admires it. 'When I was about your age, my mother took us to a wildlife orphanage in Africa. I always remember this cheetah rolling on its back like a big tame cat. I was tempted to put my hand through the bars to stroke it. I would have done too if Mum hadn't pulled me away. You see, they could take a bite out of you, and more.'

I flinch. 'What do they like to eat?'

'Beavers, game birds, impala, warthogs.'

'I love its spots.'

'Did you know, the name "cheetah" comes from a Hindi word meaning "spotted one"?'

I shake my head. 'What are those dark lines by its eyes? Has your paint run?'

'Run? No! You are funny. Those are tear lines.' Finally she looks at me. 'Do you like him?'

'Him?'

'The cheetah, silly.'

'Oh, I love him. He's beautiful.'

'Here, have him, he's all finished.'

'Really?' I smile. 'But who were you making it for?'

'That doesn't matter.' She ruffles my hair and smiles. 'He's yours now.'

10

I wake up feeling disorientated. My sleep was disturbed. I feel sure I was back at home, in Mum's studio. I can even smell the white spirit. Since the news that Bells was coming to stay I've been thinking a lot about home, particularly about Mum. Yesterday, when I was working in the shop, I found myself drifting back to the time when we all went to a New Year's Eve party hosted by Mrs Kissinger. I must have been about twelve. Dad called her Lady Kiss Kiss because she thought she was very grand and did those awful air kisses with sound effects. I remember she had a face like a pug. In between bowls of quails' eggs and blinis with smoked salmon being handed around the chandeliered room, Bells lifted her velvet skirt and proceeded to pee on the carpet. You see, unless we reminded her to go to the loo she'd forget that it wasn't the done thing to do it on the floor. Lady Kiss Kiss raced over to us, saying it was her favourite carpet with hunting scenes on it. Now there was this wet patch over one of the angry warriors on horseback clutching a spear. The other guests didn't look our way. Instead they pretended to be engrossed in conversation. I had never before seen so many backs turned towards us. Dad was grateful Lady Kiss Kiss never invited us back.

Sam is still fast asleep. He must have crawled into bed at about four this morning. I slip my feet into stripy zebra slippers and put on my silk dressing gown which is hanging on the back of our door. I walk into Bells's bedroom but she is not there. She must be downstairs. I find her at the kitchen table poking the milk-bottle sculpture. She's wearing grey baggy tracksuit bottoms and a red Oxford University T-shirt.

'Careful, Bells.'

'What's this?'

'Do you like it?'

'No.'

I half smile. 'Don't say that to Sam. It's his favourite piece of art.'

'Don't like Sam.' She withdraws her hand from the sculpture immediately, as if she is touching something dirty. 'He says "F" word a lot. We not allowed to say that word.'

'You don't know Sam,' I point out firmly. 'You mustn't judge so quickly. Be nice to him, OK?'

'Don't like him,' she states.

'Bells, this is Sam's house. He has been kind enough to have you to stay. You need to get to know him. Do you want some breakfast?'

'In Wales have muesli for breakfast. Make it ourselves.'

'We need to go to Sainsbury's. Do you want to come with me?'

As we walk into Sainsbury's I watch us on the CCTV screen. Bells is now wearing her pink frilly blouse underneath a pair of denim dungarees, plus her purple pixie boots and embroidered hat. I'm wearing an orange skirt that clings to my hips, with a pale yellow top and orange beaded sandals. Bells tells me I look like a satsuma.

There's a delicious smell of fresh bread that makes me feel hungry. 'Hello, how're you?' Bells asks an old lady on a light blue scooter which has a black shopping basket at the front. 'How old are you?' She stares at the scooter, which has 'Bluebird 2' painted on the back like a number plate.

'Excuse me,' the lady says, reaching across to grab an avocado and avoiding eye contact.

Bells comes back to me with two lemons. 'I wouldn't say hello to everyone,' I tell her quietly as we move on. 'And, funnily enough, people aren't that happy to declare their age.'

Bells is picking out packets of dried prunes, apricots, sultanas, figs and rolled oats for her muesli. 'You have to have Diet Coke,' I tell her when we reach the drinks section.

'Best of luck,' I hear a man saying. I turn sideways to see an old bearded man pushing a trolley filled with oranges. He taps another man on the shoulder who is pretending to be absorbed in deciding what brand of tomato ketchup to buy. 'Best of luck,' he says again, winking. He's wearing a knitted jumper with ducks on it and a pair of black fingerless gloves. His eyes twitch when he talks and for a moment he looks at Bells and me, aware he's being watched. I look down at my feet, hoping the man won't point his fingerless gloves our way.

'A mad man,' Bells says. 'Poor man.'

'Shh, don't stare.' Swiftly I push our trolley on. Bells fills it with everything organic. The only vegetable that isn't organic is the tin of mushy peas. That's the only thing she likes in a tin, she tells me. She puts ingredients I have never even used into our trolley. She wants dried porcini, coconut milk, chillies, coriander, bay leaves, stuffed olives, sesame seed oil, fresh ginger. 'What are we going to do with all these herbs and stuff?' I ask her, slowly panicking that the bill is going to be enormous. 'You cook a lot at home, don't you?' I ask her. 'I bet they love you cooking for them.'

'Yes, they call me Queen of Kitchen.'

I feel relieved when we finally make it to the checkout desk. The queue is long and we stand behind a tall man with light brown tousled hair. Amongst the shopping in his trolley are a packet of crumpets, runny honey, a ready-made lasagne for two, mini Magnums and a bottle of red wine. The kind of food I normally have in mine. Bells taps him hard on the arm. 'Hello.'

I look down at my feet.

He turns around. 'Hi,' I hear him say, and briefly look up. He's wearing glasses, a white T-shirt and dark jeans.

'I'm sorry,' I say, drawing in breath.

'Hello.' Bells whacks him hard on the arm now and then holds out her hand.

'Bells! I'm sorry,' I say, wincing in sympathy. He manages a pained smile as he rubs his arm and stretches out his own hand to Bells.

'You like Beckham?'

I'm sure he's wondering if he heard right, and I nod. If you can imagine talking without being able to touch the roof of your mouth with your tongue, that's what Bells sounds like. It's easier for me because I have learned her language since I was a little girl.

'Yes, I think Beckham's great, and Posh Spice too. I can see you love him,' he intimates, looking at the football badges on her dungarees.

'You have children?' she goes on. Oh, please, stop talking.

'Really?' He smiles.

'You have children?' she asks, urgently now.

He watches her intently, trying to work out what she just said. 'No, I don't have children,' he replies, and I nod, as if to say, Well done, you got it right. 'Well, I hope not.' He pulls a crooked smile.

'How old?'

'Bells!' I say, exasperated. I want to blindfold her and put a scarf around her mouth too.

'It's OK,' the man says, beginning to pack his food into bags. 'Twenty-nine.'

'My sister, Katie,' she announces, thumping my arm. 'I staying in London.'

He tells her that that sounds like fun. As he speaks I can't help thinking that if he brushed his hair, took off his glasses, fattened up a little . . . he could really be quite attractive.

'You want cash back?' the assistant asks him.

'No, thanks.'

'Nectar card?'

He digs into his pocket and produces a few cards. As he hands the right one to the girl he turns to look at me again. It's strange but I feel as if we have met already.

''Bye,' he says, finally.

'Yeah, 'bye,' I say, still trying to put a name to his face.

''Bye-bye,' Bells adds.

The man turns around once more. 'By the way, I'm really thirty-four! I find it hard facing up to my age first time round.' I laugh as I watch him walk away.

Bells asks the woman serving us how old she is. I suppose it's better than asking her how much she weighs, I think desperately.

'Excuse me?' she says.

Before she has time to ask again, I tell her once more not

to ask strangers personal questions, especially their age. 'Let's get our food and go. I'm sorry,' I apologize to the checkout girl.

'It's fine,' she says.

I push the trolley brusquely towards the exit door. 'No, don't say anything,' I say sharply each time I think Bells is about to approach someone else.

'No!'

'Don't even think about it!'

'In the car!'

I put the keys in the ignition and breathe a sigh of relief that we made it out of Sainsbury's in one piece, that no one chased us out, threatening to beat us up with a long hard baguette. 'This is only day one, I can cope with this, I can cope,' I mutter to myself.

God help me, I have two weeks of this. I can forget being anonymous for the next fourteen days, can't I?

11

1988

I'm thirteen years old. 'How did you meet Dad?' I ask Mum
in the car. She is taking Bells and me to watch Dad conduct
an auction. It's strange seeing her out of her work over-
alls. Today she's wearing a green dress and her hair is
pinned up with her special tortoiseshell comb. It's one of
the first times we have all gone out together. A trip to London! Normally we don't do anything. My best friend Emma
occasionally comes round, but we stay at home.

'Well, my mother had given me an Impressionist painting, so I went to Sotheby's to see if it was worth anything.
It was a bit of a mystery as it wasn't signed but it looked
like a Pissarro. I was rather desperate to sell it. I'm afraid I
was too poor for sentimentality,' says Mum, twitching her
nose.

'What was it worth?'

'A free dinner,' she laughs. 'I met your father and he

asked me out. I knew he was going to be a part of my life the moment I met him. Sometimes you can't explain it, it's just a feeling.'

'Like love at first sight?' I ask.

'Yes, I suppose it was. He was an assistant back then. He was very naughty, you know. This very lugubrious specialist was explaining that my painting sadly wasn't an original, and as he was talking your father was imitating him behind his back. He was unbelievably attractive, the sort of man who could get away with anything. I remember thinking what a big nose he had. I mean, you can hardly miss it, can you, girls? But it didn't matter, it went with his long thin face. And his eyes were so flirtatious . . .' She was getting carried away now. 'He only had to smile and his eyes were chatting you up. You'll know what I mean when you're older. I remember him giving me his business card. Christopher Fletcher. "Marianne Fletcher", I said to myself.'

'Mum, that's sad,' I sigh heavily. I can't imagine wanting to marry any of the boys in my school.

'You'll be doing the same one day. You don't want to marry anyone with a surname like Pratt, or Burk, or Fogsbottom.'

She's right. There *is* a girl at school whose surname is Smellie and she dreads the school register each morning. Bells is laughing, and this conversation is annoying me now. I turn to look out of the window.

The auction room is dark, with lots of people coming in and out. The carpet is red. I'm sitting next to a man with such a large moustache he looks like a walrus. Mum was too mean to buy us a catalogue each, so I try to lean over and look at Walrus's. I can see lots of stars scribbled on each page next to the prices.

Over breakfast Dad explained how an auction worked. 'There's an estimate for each painting and then a reserve price, which means I can't sell below that figure. I'm proud my girls are going to be watching me today,' he added, as he ate his last mouthful of toast.

The Walrus peers over at me and I sit straight in my chair. He twirls a pen in his fingers and eyes me curiously. 'You want to have a look?' he says in a heavy accent. He is a French walrus.

This feels exciting. Like when you go to the cinema and everyone is waiting for the main film to start. Everyone is waiting for my dad.

Finally he enters the auction room in his polished shoes, smart suit and tie. I chose his tie this morning. He lets me do that sometimes. He's wearing the black-rimmed glasses that make him look clever. 'That's my dad,' I whisper loudly to my French neighbour. I do think my dad is good-looking.

'Good afternoon, we have a feast of paintings here today so let's get started.' He coughs to clear his throat and I watch him intently. 'Lot number one. Sketch by Matisse of a lady's face. Who's going to start the bidding at twenty-five thousand pounds . . . ?'

The Walrus holds up what looks like a ping-pong bat.

Suddenly the bidding is fast and furious. I turn to the Walrus in amazement as he continues to put up his ping-pong bat. As the auction heats up, Mum is growing redder in the face from trying to stop Bells putting up her hand to confuse the bidding. 'Hello, Dad!' she calls out. I can hear people tut-tutting behind us and whispering, 'Why bring a child to a place like this? It's quite ridiculous.' I turn around and give the two old ladies one of my dirtiest looks.

'That's my dad!' Bells shouts now, waving at him.

I feel Mum's hand tug at mine. 'We're going,' she mutters. 'Excuse me,' she asks the person next to her. Chairs are shifted, legs are tucked in to allow us to pass. I don't want to go. I can feel everyone's eyes on us and the two old ladies nudge each other triumphantly. 'Whatever happened to being seen but not heard?' I turn around and stick two fingers up at them. The two ladies gasp and my father looks at me, disappointment in his eyes. ''Bye, Dad,' Bells is now calling out, people still staring.

In the car on the way home I scream, 'Why can't you be normal? We can't go anywhere with you!'

Mum brakes suddenly and swerves into the side of the road.

'Danger, danger,' Bells says in the back seat, laughing.

'Shut up, Bells!' I screech at her.

Mum swerves again to avoid a cyclist and goes into the pavement instead, the tyres burning against the kerb in protest. The driver behind us beeps his horn furiously as he overtakes us. 'Wanker!' he shouts out of the window. The cyclist turns around briefly and shakes a fist at us.

'Now you listen to me, Katie . . .'

'But, Mum . . .'

'No. You shut up,' she says. 'If you ever say that about your sister again, I mean EVER, you forfeit your pocket money for weeks.' She grips the steering wheel. 'It's *not* Bells's fault . . .'

'You always take her side, Mum.'

'You are very lucky you . . .'

'I am very lucky I don't have a cleft lip,' I finish for her like a robot. Whenever I'm difficult, Mum and Dad's invariable answer is to tell me how lucky I am not to have been born with something wrong and that I should count my lucky stars.

'Well, you are,' Mum says.

'You love her more than me,' I tell Mum.

'I do not,' she says wearily. 'That's not true.'

I look out of the window, trying hard not to cry.

'All I wanted to do was watch your father today with no dramas, but I see that's clearly impossible. No more outings, that's it,' she tells us with finality.

Back to doing nothing.

'On Monday we do nothing, on Tuesday we do nothing,'

Bells chants to the theme of *Happy Days*. She doesn't appear at all upset that she ruined our afternoon.

Mum lights a cigarette with the car lighter and opens the window. 'It's OK,' she mutters. 'I can cope. You can cope.'

If Bells hadn't been naughty none of this would have happened. I can feel my chin wobbling, but I'm still determined not to cry. Yet tears stream down my face now. I don't understand it. Why do I always get the blame? I might as well be the naughty one, because at least that way I would get to have more fun.

12

'What am I doing now?' Mr Vickers rubs his hands together, thinking up his next trick. We're in my shop and Mr Vickers and Bells have been playing this charade game for about five minutes. Already I'm finding it a challenge having Bells around. She likes to pretend she's a customer and unfolds Eve's neatly piled clothes. She also likes to ask customers how rich they are. 'How much money you have?' she says, almost the moment they step inside. And now . . . who is this man with giant hands the colour of a purple cabbage? His circulation is so poor that his feet, squashed into old beige shoes looking more like Cornish pasties, are also a mottled purple.

I sent Bells off to buy a baguette for lunch, and somehow she managed to pick up this man along the way and bring him back here. 'Sorry, who are you?' I asked him as he walked into the shop.

'I, er, don't want to intrude.'

'I'm sorry, who are you?' I asked again.

Finally I discovered that he is called Mr Vickers and he works at one of the local libraries. He has grey hair and wears mustard-coloured trousers with a smart white-collared shirt. What's even more peculiar about him is that he has a bump about the size of a golf ball in the middle of his forehead.

'Why funny lump on head?' Bells asked immediately.

'Oh, my goodness,' Eve said, putting a hand over her mouth. 'Bells, it might be personal.'

Our visitor looked at me for a translation. 'She asked you what the, um, lump was on your forehead?' My voice rose at the end. I was oddly curious too.

'I was, er, born with it,' he replied. 'I'm not quite sure, er, what it is . . . soft tissue or something like that.' He didn't seem too embarrassed about being asked such a personal question.

'What am I, er, doing now?' he asks her, and even Eve is joining in. He holds his hand in mid-air, fingers clenched as if he is holding on to something tightly, and starts rocking backwards and forwards, making strange noises.

'You are riding a horse?' Eve guesses, her finger resting on her lip as if she is trying to solve an important crime. She looks confused, her eyes narrowed. '*Non*, that does not explain the hand.'

I glance at the door, praying no one is going to come in.

'Shall I, er, do it again?' he asks with enthusiasm. 'I'll

give you, um, another clue,' he adds generously. 'OK. OK.' He positions himself.

Bells starts rocking forwards and backwards like Mr Vickers. It's the first time I have seen her enjoying herself since she arrived. He still makes those odd noises as he rocks back and forth. 'Mind the gap,' he announces sporadically. 'That is,' he pauses, 'er, the clue,' and he smiles at Bells and Eve.

'*Bien sûr!* You are on a train!' Eve claps.

Bells claps too. 'Choo-choo train!'

'I am on the, er, Underground at Waterloo.' He talks slowly, emphasizing every word, in between his stammering. 'I could not get a seat so I am er . . . er . . .'

Oh, good lord. Is it only me who thinks this is insane?

'I am holding on to the, er, strap.'

He is about to do another role-play and I have to say something now, I'm at breaking point. 'I'm sorry, Mr Vickers, we're busy . . .'

Eve, Bells and Mr Vickers look around the empty shop.

'Er, nice to meet you, Isabel, Eve.' Mr Vickers looks at me and nods before he leaves.

'You come back?' Bells calls after him.

When he is out of sight, Eve looks at me disapprovingly and I shrug my shoulders. This is my shop, not a community centre.

13

'I'm sorry, honey, I didn't realize it was your turn to host the poker night,' I apologize again. Sam watches me as I throw down my handbag, newspaper and house keys on the sofa. Today felt about a week long. No visit from Mr Vickers, but the thing that really gets to me is when Bells touches the clothes with her gummy fingers. Thank God most of them are black, but even so, no one wants sticky grains of sugar on their dress. Eve took her up to the box room, a tiny room off the second floor where I keep a kettle, coffee and my delivery boxes. She said she'd help Bells wash her hands. 'Hot soapy water,' I could hear my sister saying.

'You bite your nails? You should eat raw jelly,' I overheard Eve suggest. 'I will treat you to a French manicure. You would like?' Sometimes I wonder what I would do without Eve. That manicure gave me enough time to refold all the clothes.

Now Bells sits down on the sofa and opens her Magnum ice-cream wrapper, oblivious to my conversation with Sam. Sam is eyeing the sticky chocolate wrapper that is precariously close to his cream-coloured cushion. 'Why do you plonk your crap on the sofa, Katie, when there's a perfectly good table next to it?' He frowns. 'Isabel, give me that wrapper.'

'You like Stevie Wonder?' Bells asks him.

'What?' Sam squints at her.

'You like Stevie Wonder?' Bells repeats, holding the CD towards him, ice cream wobbling in the other hand.

'Not a fan,' he says. 'That "Ebony and Ivory" song he did with Paul McCartney was a pile of pants.'

So charming.

'What I really don't like, though, is junk lying around the place. It's my home, so if you could respect the rules? Good girl,' he says, avoiding eye contact. 'Wrapper, please.'

She hands it to him and he marches off downstairs to the kitchen. I follow him. I can hear the television being turned on upstairs. Bells is watching Wimbledon.

'I can't go out tonight, Sam, I have to do my accounts. Bernard was on the phone today, putting the pressure on.'

'Katie, it's strictly a boys' night,' he tells me, lifting the bin lid, throwing the wrapper in and slamming it shut.

'OK, what if I told you Kate Moss was coming over this evening?'

A slight smile plays on his lips and then promptly disappears. 'Not allowed access, I'm afraid.'

'What if I'm really quiet . . . as quiet as a mouse?'

'What's Isabel going to do then? I thought Tuesday night was your girls' night with Emma?'

'I had to cancel.' I open the fridge and look inside. Potatoes for baking are in the bottom drawer, as well as a head of organic broccoli and a bag of organic carrots. Cheese, bacon, mushrooms and a pot of olives stuffed with garlic are in the middle.

'I wouldn't hang around if you had a bunch of girls here having a Botox party.'

'I don't do Botox.'

'You know what I mean. Christ, you're pedantic sometimes,' he says, rubbing his nose.

'Sam, Bells and I will stay in our bedroom until the coast is clear,' I tell him. 'We just need to make . . . oh, shit, what does she cook on a Tuesday?'

'What do you mean? Get a takeaway. The boys will be here soon.'

'I'll microwave a potato.'

'I don't believe this!' He watches me slit the potatoes across the top, waiting for me to change my mind.

'Stop rubbing your nose so hard, Sam. You know what happened last time, it went raw at the end.'

He stops. 'You're ruining my boys' night.'

I set the timer on the microwave. 'You sound like a spoilt

brat. It's one night. I won't make any noise. You won't even know Bells and I are here.' He still looks furious. 'Is this really about her? If it were just me, would you mind?'

Sam ignores me. 'Fine. If you have to bloody well be here, can you go upstairs?'

'No! Sam, as scintillating as it might be listening to you boys, I promise I won't eavesdrop.'

He makes a disgruntled noise. 'You promise?'

'Promise.'

Bells sits on the edge of our double bed eating her baked potato. She was cross with Sam because he wouldn't let her cook. 'There's no time,' he shouted at her, and then at me. Bells was opening the fridge and cupboard doors and he was hovering behind her, slamming them shut the moment she moved away. I explained why she couldn't cook her vegetarian risotto with olives and pine nuts. 'Always cook in Wales,' she protested.

I watch her as she eats. She doesn't look impressed by the soggy-skinned potato. 'Try not to get anything on the duvet,' I whisper to her.

'Sam kill me if I make a mess,' she says.

'Shh! Yes, he will. Bells, you can sit more on the bed if you like.'

She slides a bit closer to me, but still doesn't look relaxed. 'Do you want a magazine? Look, I bought a *Tatler*.' I hold it up towards her.

Bells shows no interest.

'Or how about doing the crossword? Or we can watch the tennis with the volume off? Better that way anyway, you can't hear the players grunting.' Bells stares absently at the walls. She looks so bored. Mum and Dad told me, before they left, that she did get easily fed up when she was staying with them and often wanted to go back to Wales.

'I know it's not much fun,' I say, hearing a loud knock on the front door.

Bells puts her food on the floor. 'We've got to be really quiet now,' I remind her.

Any trace of excitement on her face evaporates into boredom again. 'Why? Bossy Katie. You like traffic warden. Where's Sam?'

'Sam's here, it's his boys' night.' I'm still smiling at that image of me in uniform with a navy hat on.

'Who's at door?'

Oh God, I think to myself. Perhaps it was a bad idea staying in.

'Davey, mate,' I hear Sam bellow, followed by a few slaps on a manly shoulder.

'Who Davey?'

'Bells, whisper. Davey works in the City with Sam.'

'Lakemore,' Davey returns in a ringing tone. 'Am I the first here?'

'Yep, you are *numero uno*. No one else here,' he emphasizes loudly. 'Come on in. Looking sharp, mate.'

I flick my pen between my fingers. I can imagine him winking at Davey now. Sam often follows a compliment with a wink.

'New Paul Smith shoes. They're the business, aren't they?' Davey says.

'Very nice.'

'Like your shirt, mate. Your missus pick it out for you?'

'No, saw it down the Fulham Road. Nice, isn't it? Look the part, feel the part . . .'

'. . . and you ARE the part,' they both finish together. 'Sit down, David, pour yourself a whisky.'

'Cheers.'

There's another knock on the door.

'Crispin, me old diamond geezer.'

'Lakemore.' Thump on the back. I can hear their shoes clicking across the wooden floor. They go into the poker-playing room. Sam turns the sitting-room into the games room, puts out the card table with the polished casino chips. 'Weh-hey, Davey!'

'Crisps! How goes it?'

'Who Crisps?' Bells asks me in an even louder voice. Perhaps she's unable to whisper?

The door knocks again.

'MAGUIRE!' shouts Sam. The door crashes open.

'LAKEMORE!'

'They all deaf?' Bells asks me, rocking forwards and putting her fingers into her ears.

'Good question,' I tell her.

'Davey, mate . . .'

'Maguire, what you up to?'

'Crispin, you diamond!'

I laugh quietly to myself. I can't tell who is talking, they all sound the same.

'You OK, Bells?' She's doodling on my newspaper. 'Give us a clue,' I suggest and put my files down. Sam has been playing poker for about an hour now, and I don't know why he worried about me listening to their conversation. Boys together are about as interesting as a night out in Slough.

'I'm gonna raise you twenty quid,' I can hear one of them say.

The chips go into the pot.

'I'll play,' one of them says, more chips going in.

'Fold,' another says.

'Are we all on for Ibiza this summer?'

'Absolutely,' one of them says.

'Yeah, yeah, yeah, absolutely,' echoes another.

'Tobes isn't coming this year, his wife has well and truly put the mockers on that.'

'D'you think he played away?'

''Course he did,' one of them guffaws.

'I wonder how she found out? Pub rules. What goes on tour stays on tour,' someone says.

Bells and I look at each other. I pull a silly face at her and when she laughs I'm taken aback by how pleased I am. She lifts her right hand, thumb pointing up, near her nose. Sometimes, when I look at Bells, I wonder where she came from. Apart from the colour of her hair and eyes she looks like no one else in the family, but her laugh is almost identical to Granny Norfolk's.

'Stupid boys,' I mouth at her, hoping to hear her laugh again.

'Very stupid,' she repeats, rocking forward with her thumb up.

I move closer to her. 'Boring, aren't they?' I whisper into her ear.

'Ha-ha!' she grunts, and almost laughs again. 'That's right. Very boring.'

'She was a right moose too,' one of them carries on. 'I said to Tobes, "Mate, you could have done better than that." Sam, who was that bird you got friendly with last year?'

I tiptoe towards the door.

'Can we go now?' Bells asks impatiently. 'I'm bored.'

I put a finger over my lips.

'Need loo,' she says, getting up.

'Boys, can you keep the noise down?' I hear Sam asking, firmly but politely.

'What's got into you, Lakemore? You've turned a bit quiet. He must be holding seriously bad cards. Where's your poker face gone?'

'I could be bluffing, Maguire.'

'You're coming to Ibiza, aren't you, Lakemore?'

'Yep.'

'What was that girl's name?'

'Er, I don't know. Cigar, anyone?'

'Scared the missus will find out?' They all laugh.

'I wasn't going out with Katie then,' Sam reminds them. 'I would never cheat on her,' he says loudly, rather overdoing it. 'Music, anyone?'

Come on, answer the question. Who did you meet, Sam? It doesn't matter, we all have a history.

'I Just Called to Say I Love You' starts to play. The boys laugh.

'What the . . . ?' Sam is clearly ejecting the CD. 'Must be one of Katie's,' he says, trying to keep his composure.

I put a hand over my mouth to try to stifle a nervous giggle when Paul McCartney and Stevie Wonder's 'Ebony and Ivory' plays next.

'Blimey, mate. What's happened to your taste in music?' Maguire roars with laughter. 'Next you'll be playing Celine bloody Dion!'

'It's Katie's,' Sam mutters.

I can hear Bells now, laughing in the loo, and then there is a flushing sound. Oh my God! I turn around and lean against the door. Bells! How could I have lost my concentration and forgotten to remind her not to flush the loo? Sam will kill me. He will kill us both.

'Lakemore? What's that sound? Who's here?'

I pull Bells back into the bedroom.

'Feeling tight, not funny, Katie.'

'We're in serious trouble,' I whisper.

'Serious trouble. Not funny, Katie.'

'No, it's not funny.'

'Lakemore, what's going on? Someone flushed the loo,' one of the boys says incredulously.

I find myself laughing now and Bells copies me. This situation is so ridiculous. Sam has got to come clean. Tell them we're here.

'No one's here, boys. Can we get on with the game?' he insists.

'Come off it!'

I frown. Yes, come off it! Are we *that* embarrassing?

'Come off it!' Bells says, stamping her feet.

'Maguire, it must be the neighbours. You can hear everything, and I mean, *everything*.'

The neighbours? Oh, for God's sake, Sam. Bells is getting restless and wants to leave the room, but I hold her arm firmly. I want to see if Sam is eventually going to confess that we're here.

Maguire walks out of the room and looks around. 'Where's the loo?'

'Straight ahead of you.'

I can hear the sitting-room door open.

'Maguire, come and sit down. Listen, who else is going to be here? I've told you, it's the neighbours.'

'All right,' he concedes. Then: 'What the hell was that? There *is* someone here!'

Bells has managed to escape my grasp and is wrestling to open the door.

'Too tight, not funny, Katie,' she says now at the top of her voice.

'Lakemore, someone *is* in your house.'

Another door is flung open and Bells disappears from the bedroom. I can see her rushing past the sitting-room, her arms flailing in the air. This should be – interesting . . .

'Who the fuck was that?' one of them bursts out. 'By the way, full house,' he adds.

Bells is running downstairs. 'Who?' Sam asks, but his voice is burdened with defeat.

'That little person?'

'With the funny boots?' another of them says.

'Sam, the game's up. Confess all.'

'I told Katie it was poker night,' he shouts, banging his fist against the table.

'But that wasn't Katie,' Maguire exclaims. 'Unless she's shrunk to half her size.'

I put my shoes on and run past them and down the stairs. 'Sorry, can't stop,' I say to them.

'Thanks, Katie,' Sam shouts with heavy sarcasm.

'Lakemore,' Maguire now says. 'What the fuck is going on?'

14

The following morning Bells is in the kitchen listening to one of her Beatles CDs, wearing her embroidered hat and dungarees again. They must be glued to her body. I have to take her shopping for Emma's wedding. I don't think I have ever seen my sister wear a skirt.

'How did you sleep?' I ask, opening the cupboard that houses the mugs and cereal bowls.

'Bored,' she says. 'You know John Lennon lived with Aunt Mimi?'

'No.' I shake my head, flicking the kettle switch on. It's a large silver kettle with a black handle, which matches the toaster.

'They were Nurk Twins before the Beatles.'

'Really?' She nods. If Bells were in the black chair on *Mastermind* her specialist subject would be the Beatles. 'If you want to go back home, you would say, wouldn't you?' I ask her, feeling ashamed that if she said she wanted to go, I'd be relieved. I can't explain it, but ever since Bells arrived

I have had this sinking uneasy feeling hanging over me like an ominous cloud. I can sense something is about to go horribly wrong again, even more so than last night. I wonder if Mum felt like this most of the time when she was bringing up Bells and me.

'If you want to go home, if you're unsettled . . .' I stop. Why am I such a bad sister? I haven't seen Bells for months. Shouldn't I want to spend some time with her?

She nods half-heartedly, chopping dried apricots and figs on the table. 'Bells, use a proper chopping board,' I tell her. 'You're marking the table.' I find her a small board. Sam bought a set of five different-sized chopping boards. 'And remember to say sorry to Sam when he comes downstairs.'

'Why?' She bangs the knife into the board.

'You know why, Bells.'

Sam comes into the kitchen and heads straight for the coffee machine. His hair is dark and damp after his shower. 'I'll make you one,' I say. 'Sit down.' I stare at Bells, willing her to apologize.

'It's all right,' he says. Clearly his bad mood hasn't left him.

'Hello, Sam,' she says, looking up at him.

'Hi,' he manages, briefly looking sideways at her.

There is a long awkward silence. 'Wasn't there something you wanted to say, Bells?' I look at her and then at Sam. Still she says nothing. 'You wanted to say something to Sam?'

'Sorry, Sam.'

'No problem,' he says. 'Just don't do it again, OK?'

That was simple enough, I think with relief.

'That was the worst night of my life!' he'd shouted at me last night after the boys had gone. Bells hadn't got far. I'd found her outside our local Italian restaurant with one of the waiters. He was wearing a striped navy-and-white apron and smoking a cigarette in his break. We went inside for a hot chocolate. I wanted to give Sam enough time to get rid of the boys before we returned. 'I told you it was a bad idea,' he continued, banging one hand against the other, 'but what do you go and do, huh? You had to wreck it by being there.'

'Sam, I'm sorry, but it's quite funny when you think about it.' He threw me another warning look. I was racking my brains trying to think of something that might ease the situation. Isn't it always a good idea to tell someone an even worse story so that they realize they got off lightly? That their ordeal was, in fact, not quite so bad? Great idea, I told myself. 'My parents once gave a dinner party for these clients who had come from America to look at Mum's sculptures,' I said. 'It was a really big deal. I mean, Mum even turned the napkins into the shape of lilies, for God's sake.' I chortled, but Sam stared at me. 'So, anyway, it was a really important business dinner.' I stopped again, as Sam looked bored. He might as well have had 'So what?' stamped on his forehead. Quickly I got to the main part. 'Anyway, we sat down to find Bells had swapped the lily napkins for sanitary towels.' I laughed out loud, but Sam looked at me with disdain.

'That's revolting, Katie. Disgusting.' He gave a short derisive laugh. 'I'm never going to live last night down. The boys will be dining out on this story for the next year. The whole City will know about it.'

'Don't exaggerate.'

'Katie, all you had to do was keep quiet. You promised.' He looked intensely hurt. 'Worst night of my life,' he repeated.

'If that was the worst night of your life, then you've led a pretty charmed existence,' I couldn't help saying.

He turned his face away from me then. 'Ebony and *fucking* Ivory.'

'Sam, don't swear! Bells will . . .'

'Hang on. Let me get this straight. *I'm* not allowed to swear in front of her, but *she's* allowed to do muck up my CDs and make me look like an idiot. Right, Katie, that makes sense. Why do you let her get away with it?'

'She wasn't doing it maliciously, it was only a bit of a game. She was bored, that's all.'

'I think she knows exactly what she's doing. She pretends to be all innocent.'

Sam is, to an extent, right. But . . . 'Perhaps if you made

a little more of an effort with her,' I suggested, my patience beginning to wear thin. 'She thinks you don't like her. That's why she doesn't like you – yet,' I added, seeing his face. He's not used to being told he's unpopular. 'She will like you, it takes time, that's all.'

This morning I watch him making his coffee in the shiny silver machine. Am I imagining it or has Sam hardly touched me since Bells arrived? We have gone from nine months of barely being able to keep our hands off each other to almost taking a vow of chastity.

Bells eats her homemade muesli, and drinks her sage tea. She starts to cough. Great. It sounds as if she might be coming down with a cold.

'What are you up to today?' Sam asks her, his head still down.

'Don't know,' she replies.

'Well, you're staying here while I go to my yoga,' I tell her. I can't quite face Bells coming with me. One woman in the class does have unfortunate body odour and Bells would no doubt tell her she smelled. 'And then we're going to my shop.'

'Great,' Sam says, but he's not listening. I can tell his mind is still firmly focused on his disastrous poker evening. 'Well, it's a nice day out there,' he carries on painfully. I look outside and it's drizzling. In fact, the weather forecast has predicted a thunderstorm later this afternoon.

Sam is trying, but I notice he can't look at Bells. It's as if he's scared to make eye contact.

The telephone rings and Sam sees this as the perfect opportunity to go. 'I'll see you this evening.' He takes his car keys off the breakfast counter and is away before I even have time to say goodbye.

15

After my yoga class, Bells and I catch the bus to the shop. The one good thing that came out of Mum rarely taking Bells and me shopping is that I learned to sew.

'Where did you get that material from?' she asked me suspiciously. It was one morning in the school holidays and I was sitting on the sofa hacking up a red curtain which I'd found at the bottom of a musty old drawer. I had made myself a pattern out of school tracing paper and found Mum's black Singer sewing machine with the foot pedal.

'I'm making a skirt,' I announced proudly.

She peered at it, did her famous disparaging sniff and then turned away, muttering, 'Well, that's very good, darling. Always good to have a hobby. I'll get you some more material.' I think she was in fact delighted that I had found something to do in the school holidays that would keep me quiet and away from the shops, and meant she could carry on working undisturbed in her studio.

Needlework and textiles were the only subjects for which I received glowing praise in my school reports. None of the other girls in my class were interested and the others would tease our needlework teacher, Mrs Hook, to the point where she would tremble with fear when we entered the classroom. She had a stammer and could never say the word 'bobbin' properly. I was her gold-star pupil. I was the one who was asked to show her work to the headmistress. Mrs Davies sat in her office with a cigarette dangling from her mouth and a necklace that looked like a golden ball on a chain hanging over her black polo neck. She was usually balancing a book in one nicotine-stained hand and stroking her pug, Bertie, with the other. She would duly tell me in her coarse gravelly voice that my kimono-dressing gown or whatever else it might be was indeed a triumph, and as a treat I was allowed to take Bertie for a walk.

I started to make all my own clothes as my interest in fashion grew. I began browsing in all kinds of material and haberdashery shops. I couldn't afford the silks and furs at the upmarket shops, but I liked touching all the different fabrics and imagining what I could transform them into. Emma used to come with me, pretending she was interested, but very quickly her eyes would develop that glazed expression while I pored excitedly over exquisite rolls of coloured silks. My pocket money took me to the local markets where I searched for leathers to make jackets and skirts with slits in them. I became good at bargaining, negotiating prices for beads, zips, feathers and fabric offcuts.

The cheapest and quickest things to make were beaded chokers and belts out of sparkling black and gold beads which I sold to school friends. I created a small factory in my bedroom, the sewing machine kept permanently in the corner by the window, and all the money I made went into an old Nescafe tin which I kept hidden under the bed. All I ever wanted to do was own a clothes shop. I dreamed about leaving home and starting up my own business. I felt imprisoned by my family and longed to be in control of my own life, because isn't that what makes you happy, being in control?

I did not want to be financially dependent on my parents any longer than I had to be, so I left home when I was eighteen to live with my electrician boyfriend to whom Mum had taken an immediate dislike because his arms were covered in tattoos. I was longing to be independent and to step out into the wider world. There was going to be no more fear of what people thought of my family, of Bells, of our cut-off existence. I longed to start my own life and make a success of it, with or without my parents.

'No touching the clothes,' I tell Bells as I hand her a blueberry muffin wrapped in a white napkin. I'd popped into Eddie's deli to grab us some breakfast. My plan from now on is to stay out of Sam's way. I figure if I can get through the rest of this holiday with no further hiccups then we have done pretty well. Only one poker night ruined, and Sam will get over it. Eventually.

'No touching clothes.' She coughs again.

'Good.' I sit down behind my large wooden desk, which is angled diagonally across one corner of the shop. The desktop has a panel of glass covering black-and-white photographs of our latest fashion show. I remind Bells not to play with the credit card machine. 'And no asking customers how rich or how old they are, OK?'

'Yes, Katie, that's right.' Bells nods to me.

I carry on: 'And no coffee near the clothes.'

'No coffee.'

'No commenting on what people are wearing or what they look like. That poor man who had no hair, he was probably very sensitive about it. Or saying hello to customers three times. Fine to say it once,' I allow, 'but that's enough.'

She rocks forward on her feet, something she does when she's nervous or overexcited.

'What did I just say?' I test her, to make sure she was listening rather than merely repeating. Things do not necessarily compute with her, or if they do, she forgets them immediately.

'No saying hello, Katie, answering phone not to. Leave to you.' She looks over my shoulder, waves her hands.

I turn around, only to see Mr Vickers outside the shop window, peering through the glass. He's carrying an umbrella with a duck-shaped handle.

'Hello, Mr Vickers,' Bells calls. He waves tentatively.

I grab her arm in an attempt to stop her from opening the door. 'Bells, I don't want him hanging around the shop.'

She pulls away from me. 'Like Mr Vickers.'

'Bells,' I raise my voice now, 'please don't make me cross.'

She watches him walk away.

'Poor Mr Vickers. Mr Vickers nice man.'

'I know, but I have a business to run.' I can see Henrietta and her mother through the window approaching and quickly turn to Bells. 'Why don't you go upstairs and start unpacking the delivery boxes? That would be so helpful,' I tell her, pushing her upstairs as if she were a puppet. 'Clean your hands first,' I say, leading her to the sink. 'The boxes are here. These are black T-shirts.' I point to four brown boxes stacked in the corner. 'Scissors are in the drawer. If you could unpack them all before you come back down . . . Thank you.' I don't even wait for an answer.

The simple truth is I don't want Bells saying hello to them at all. I don't want her putting off my customers.

Customers come and go. I have made two good sales this morning. Henrietta bought two dresses and three tops while her mother sat on the chaise longue drinking cups of coffee, spiked with a small bottle of Baileys that she produced from her bag.

Bells has been extraordinarily quiet, I think happily to myself. Perhaps I will treat her to a quick lunch . . . I find her sitting on the floor, the T-shirts heaped around her in a muddle.

'Bells, what have you done?' I cry out, kneeling down next to her and picking up one of the black shirts with a small red heart printed on the breast line. I'd thought I could trust her with cotton T-shirts. I mean, how wrong can you go?

'Unpacking shirts,' she says with surprisingly little interest, followed by a cough. Isn't it obvious how angry I am? I open my mouth to speak, but nothing comes out. Finally, 'How many have you done?' I whisper in despair, picking up the labels she's cut out that look more like silk raffle tickets strewn haphazardly over the floor. 'People buy these shirts *because* of the labels. They're French designer labels.' I can't look at her otherwise I might hit her. 'What were you thinking of, cutting them all out?'

Bells stands up.

'Don't touch anything else, you hear me? Leave everything alone.'

'Help Katie. You said unpack everything?'

'No! Leave everything alone. If you touch one more I will be really angry. Why did you cut them out? Did I tell you to cut out the labels? You stupid, stupid girl!' I scream at her, almost in tears. I can't cope any more. Please come back, Mum and Dad. I can't do this. You're right, I am a terrible sister.

'Not stupid, Katie. Not stupid.' Bells rushes out of the room.

I stand looking at the muddle of T-shirts, too paralysed to do anything constructive. All I can do is will the labels magically to return to where they belong. I hear a door shut downstairs so try to compose myself for the next customer.

'Hello,' I say, walking towards a tall, slim man.

'Hi, I'm looking for a present, I wonder if you can help me?'

'Where's Bells?' I say out loud.

'Sorry?' he says, looking puzzled. 'Who's Bells?'

'My sister. Did you see someone running out of the shop?' I can hear the tone of my voice rising in fear.

'No, no one.' He shakes his head.

'Can you come back later?' I push him towards the door.

'Hey!' he protests, hanging back. 'I came here especially to buy my cousin a birthday present,' he explains. 'Hang on, haven't we met before? In Sainsbury's?'

'Have we?' I say agitatedly. 'Look, my sister . . .'

'The one who kept on asking me my age? I remember her.'

'Yes, she's run off.' I shut the door behind me and then realize I need the keys to lock up. 'Oh God, oh God,' I say, going back inside and grabbing my handbag from behind my desk. I plunge into it as if it were a lucky dip, hoping to pick out the right keys. Instead I can feel Bells's inhaler, which I throw on to the shop floor. My powder compact is chucked after it in frustration. Why do I always pick out everything from my bag except my shop keys?

'Look, let me help,' the man is saying. 'Where do you think she might be?'

I let out a frustrated yelp. 'I don't know, she could be anywhere. If I knew . . . Oh, where *are* they?'

'Keep calm,' he says.

If my stare was venomous I would kill him on the spot. Finally I find the right keys. Where is Eve when I need her? Why did she have to be sick today of all days? I scribble on a piece of paper 'Back in half an hour' and pin it haphazardly to the door.

'OK, here's what we do,' the man says authoritatively. 'You go across the park, I'll go on the main road, and we both head for the tube station and the shops. If you find her, whistle like this.' He puts his hand to his mouth and belts out a loud whistle. 'It works in the classroom,' he adds.

I breathe deeply. 'I can't do that, I've always wanted to.'

'Well, use a real whistle then. I'm a teacher,' he quickly explains. 'Always keep one on me for emergencies.' He digs into his black rucksack and pulls out a red plastic whistle attached to a piece of string, which he places around my neck. 'She ran off . . . what? . . . five, ten minutes ago? She can't be far away.'

'What's your name?'

'Mark.'

'Thanks, Mark,' I call after him as we turn in different directions.

*

It's damp and overcast. The park is almost deserted. 'Bells,' I shout, and keep on running. 'Bells, where are you?' I walk past a man wearing headphones. He won't know where she is, will he? He might. I'd better ask. I tap him hard on the shoulder. He pulls the plugs out of his ears.

'Excuse me, I've lost my sister. She's short, about four foot something, really short hair too.' I stare into his vacant expression, urging him to show some sign of recognition. 'And she kind of rocks rather than walks,' I persist. Still no reaction.

'Nope, haven't seen her,' he mumbles finally as he puts his music back on. I see a couple ahead of me. The girl has her hand tucked into the back pocket of her boyfriend's jeans. 'Um, hello . . . hey, you!' I run after them. They turn around in surprise. 'I'm sorry, I've lost my sister. She's short, have you seen her?' I ask with pleading eyes. Please say you have.

'What's she wearing?' the girl asks.

What's she wearing? Good question. 'A little embroidered hat and dungarees,' I describe breathlessly. When I get no response, I add, 'And some sort of football shirt with stickers on.'

'You're having me on.' The boy smiles at me. 'Is this some kind of joke? We're on some funny game show, right? *Graham Norton*?' He starts darting his head around looking for the hidden cameras.

I stare at him hard and pin my hopes on the girl. She chews gum thoughtfully and then shrugs her shoulders. 'We've only just got here. Good luck finding her, though.' As I watch them walk on, her hand back in his pocket, I realize this is one of those moments, you know, when you see someone break down and feel so lucky that it's not you. You drive on. Now I feel like the girl who's broken down in her battered old car and no one is offering to help. No rescue team, no phone, no one's that interested. I fumble in my handbag for my mobile and then realize I don't have a clue who to ring. Sam? I wait for him to answer.

'I'm in a meeting. I'll call later. Remember, I'm out tonight,' Sam finishes helpfully.

'She's run away,' I say, my eyes staring ahead. 'What am I going to do?'

'Katie, I'm sorry, but what can I do stuck behind my frigging desk? Do you want me to come and help you look for her?' he says, as if the idea is absurd.

'No, Sam. That would make you a nice person.' I hang up abruptly. I don't even know why I called him. If Bells comes back I'll tell her that it doesn't matter. What are a few labels? I can sew them back on, no one will know. Come back, Bells. Please come back. There is no one else I can call. It's like living in our own little world again, shut away from what's normal.

''Scuse me . . . she's twenty-two, four foot ten . . .' I

describe her to the next person I meet. I can't see what other people look like any more. I just want to see Bells.

'No, I haven't seen her,' he says.

WHY NOT? I want to scream at him. WHAT'S THE MATTER WITH YOU?

'I'm sure a twenty-two-year-old can look after themselves,' he mutters as he slopes off.

I call Dad though I know it's crazy. What can he do when he's not even in the country? I listen to the ringing tone, but there's no answer. He promised me he would have his mobile switched on in case of an emergency. I put a hand to my mouth and let out a long desperate wailing noise, I don't know what to do, who to ask, where to look . . .

'I've lost my sister. Have you seen my little sister?' I ask a lady sitting on a bench reading a newspaper. The familiar sound of the train rattles in the background. What if Bells is on it?

'What does she look like, darling?' She's American.

I'm about to repeat everything I have said before, but find myself crying. It's awful, but I can't stop. I put my head in my hands. What have I done? Bells, I'm so sorry, please forgive me for shouting at you. Bells could be run over and dead by now and it's all my fault. I look up and the stranger hands me a tissue from her handbag.

'What does she look like?' she asks softly again. 'Come on, we'll find her. She can't be far.'

I smile gratefully at her. Her auburn hair, the same colour

as Mum and Bells's, is piled on top of her head with an assortment of hairgrips and she is wearing sunglasses, which is strange when it's so overcast. 'If you've seen someone who doesn't blend into the crowd, well,' I sniffle, 'that's her.'

She makes me sit down for a few moments to compose myself. I stare over at the playground where there are a few mothers pushing their children on the swings, and a couple of boys kicking a ball around. Under a tree two boys practise their boxing skills. One stands with a padded shield over his hand while the other practises his punches. I tell her about our argument. I tell her about Bells. It's surprisingly easy telling a stranger about our family. 'I'm sorry for crying,' I add.

'Don't be. Being sorry for crying is such a British thing. You're going through a traumatic time, you're allowed to be emotional. What *is* that whistling noise?'

I turn round and see Mark staggering towards us, holding on to Bells. 'Thank God,' I leap up from the bench, the relief overwhelming.

'Don't thank God,' the American remarks, her dark glasses now perched on the end of her nose. 'I think you should thank that nice young man.'

As I run towards them I can tell something's seriously wrong. 'She needs her inhaler,' Mark shouts.

I try to find it in my bag, and then remember exactly where it is.

Bells is fighting for breath. 'Her inhaler,' Mark shouts again as he lifts her into his arms.

'It's in the shop. OK, she needs to sit down,' I tell Mark, who carries her as quickly as he can to the bench. The American lady stands up to make space. Gently Mark sits her down, before letting me take over. I can feel the tightness in her chest as she gasps for breath. 'Put your hands on your knees . . . Don't let her lie down, Mark. She has to sit up and try to relax as much as possible. I'll be back in a minute.' He sits with her while I run as fast as I can across the park. I unlock the door with trembling hands and rush to pick up the inhaler. I slam the door shut and just about remember to lock it behind me.

Bells takes the inhaler immediately. I stroke her back. We watch and wait.

'How's she doing?' the American lady asks.

'If this doesn't work we'll have to call an ambulance,' I say. Please let me wake up. Please let this be a terrible dream. I take in a deep breath, waiting to see if the inhaler helps Bells.

'I'm all right,' she says.

I can feel her breathing becoming more even as I continue to stroke her back. 'You're really all right?' I say. 'Oh, God, Bells, don't ever . . . I mean *ever* scare me like that again.'

Mark tells me not to shout, that she's safe, that's all that matters.

'She could have died.' I turn back to Bells, who sits, looking tired and crumpled, with her eyes watering. 'Oh, Bells.'

I reach out and pull her close to me. 'I'm sorry. I'm so sorry for shouting at you. It'll never happen again.' I feel her arms clutching the small of my back and hold her even more tightly – the way Mum used to hold me when I was younger. So tightly that I thought I would stop breathing.

'Mark's right. You're OK, that's all that counts.'

I pull the duvet over her.

'Tired,' Bells says, turning on to her side.

'Get some rest. I'm going to make you your favourite supper. What would you like to eat? Remember, it's me cooking,' I add, smiling.

'Why you hate me?' she asks.

'What?' Should I pretend I didn't hear that? I draw her curtains.

'You hate me.'

'Oh Bells, that's not true, I don't hate you.' I turn off the main light and shut the door behind me. Outside I lean against it, catching my breath. I feel winded by her question. Bells is no fool, she could hear how hollow that sounded. I can't keep on talking to her as if she's ten years old. Pat her on the head and hope she won't ask me any more difficult questions.

Bells screams then. 'Too dark!'

I rush back and turn on the light.

I kneel down beside her and make my voice like his. 'I'm sorry, Bells. I forgot. That was stupid of me.'

'That's right, Katie. You don't write me,' she says. 'Mum writes me. Dad writes me. You don't.'

I'm about to say something along the lines of no one writes letters any more, only Mum and Dad's generation, but then I realize how pathetic that would sound. She's right.

'You don't visit me.'

'No, I don't,' I say.

'Why?'

'I don't know, Bells.' I try to explain, but I don't even know where to start. 'I don't hate you, but I hated watching you in the park. I was so scared. If anything had happened to you, I would never have forgiven myself. I hated seeing you so vulnerable. I do care. I'm sorry for shouting, and . . .'

'In Wales cut labels,' she mutters.

'Oh, God, I don't care about the labels any more. And I will start writing to you, I'd like to.' I realize as I say this that I can't make an empty promise. Bells deserves more than that.

'Mark's nice man. Nice man.'

I smile. 'He is very nice. I'm so sorry, Bells.' Without thinking I kiss her forehead and softly touch her cheek. 'I don't hate you. I could never, ever hate you.' I want to tell her that I love her but I don't feel I deserve to say it. Instead I stand up to draw her shutters and turn off the overhead light. The small stained-glass lamp in the corner of her room is on this time.

'Nothing around me?' she asks.

'Nothing around you.'

'Promise.'

'I promise.'

'Thank you, Mark, thank you so much,' I tell him as I make us both a hot drink in the kitchen. I asked him back to Sam's place as I felt it was the least I could do. Also I wanted to know how he had found Bells. I'd thought he would say no, that he had to get on with his day, but to my surprise he agreed.

'Is she all right?' he asks with concern, turning away from the milk-bottle sculpture.

'I think so. I ran her a bath, that seemed to relax her.'

Mark tells me he found Bells waiting at a bus shelter. She was clearly in an agitated condition, but everyone at the stop was doing their best to ignore her.

I feel such a failure as I listen to him recall the drama, realizing Bells is having a miserable time with me. She wanted to see the bright lights of London and the most gripping thing we have done together is go to Sainsbury's. Now I know where I met Mark before. 'That's right, of course,' I tell him. 'You're thirty-four.'

'Yes. But you can forget that bit.' We laugh together for the first time today.

'If you hadn't been there anything could have happened,' I say. 'Thank you.'

'It was nothing, honestly.'

'No it wasn't. You don't know me, know us, you didn't have to help.'

He looks at his shoes sheepishly. 'I did nothing special. Where does Bells live?'

'In a community in Wales. My parents are on holiday so I'm having her to stay. Actually, I need to call them. Back in one minute.' I walk out with the mobile and key in Dad's number. Still no answer. I call their home number. It's their answerphone. What am I doing? They are in France. Stop this, Katie.

I walk back into the kitchen. 'Is this your place?' Mark asks, glancing around the bare kitchen. 'I like this . . . um . . . sculpture.'

'It's Sam's.'

'Oh, right.' Mark runs a hand through his hair. 'He's your boyfriend?'

'Yes.'

'What happened to Bells? I mean, what . . . ?'

'What makes her different?' I suggest, sitting down opposite him.

He nods.

I tell him she was born with a cleft lip and palate. 'My parents would visit her in hospital after each operation. Bells had to be strapped to the cot to stop her from scratching out the stitches.'

'That's terrible.'

'She was also brain-damaged at birth. A large part of her brain still works. If you tap into a subject she knows a lot about, then you're OK. But she's never been able to lead a fully independent life.'

'Is she aware that she's different?'

'Yes and no. I think she's comfortable with herself now, she's her own person, but as a teenager she wanted to be like everyone else. She hated the way she looked. Well, that's what Dad said,' I add. 'You see, I didn't really see that side of Bells because I left home when I was eighteen and she was only eleven.'

'It must have been tough for your parents.'

'Yes, it was,' I say, wondering if I have ever told them how good they were, still are, with Bells. No, I know I haven't. I've spent too much time feeling left out of the family and resenting all the energy they put into her. 'To be honest, I've never had Bells to stay with me before and I'm finding it hard. I mean, look what happened today.' As I tell him about the problems she's had with Sam, I'm surprised by how easy it is to talk to Mark. The words are flowing effortlessly, almost too much so. 'How about a drink?' I say, overwhelmed by the events of the day and in desperate need of relief.

As I open the fridge to grab a couple of beers, to lighten the conversation I decide to tell him about the ruined poker night and the switched CDs. Mark laughs.

I tell him how Bells asked a customer's husband why he had no hair, and that triggers another memory. 'When I was about fifteen we had a plumber with a wooden leg and a glass eye – Mr Curly.'

'Mr Curly?' Mark grins. 'Sounds like a *Mr Men* character.'

'One day Mr Curly was up a ladder in our kitchen when a screw in his false leg came loose and then the whole thing fell off. "Why haven't you got a proper leg?" Bells said immediately, and then started to howl with laughter while Mum and I were desperately trying to find the screw on the floor. Bells wasn't being mean, it's just her way. She says what she thinks. If she doesn't like someone, if she thinks they're boring or stuffy, she says so.'

'Good for her. Saves a lot of time.'

I smile at that. I decide not to tell Mark that Bells definitely does not like Sam.

'How old is she?'

'Twenty-two. The thing is, you can't put a mental age on Bells. Some things she's very good at, like gardening and cooking, she gets all that from Mum. But if you ask her to visualize something abstract it means nothing to her at all. When my Uncle Roger died, Bells bought some flowers and wrote in the card: *"Dear Uncle Roger, I'm sorry to hear you are dead."*'

I notice Mark has a dimple like me. Only special people have dimples, Dad used to say to me when he squeezed my cheeks.

'It's getting late,' Mark mentions. 'I ought to be . . .'

'No!' I say rather too dramatically. 'I mean, have another drink.' I pick up my mobile. 'I'll order some pizza. Bells would love you to stay for supper. You don't live far away, do you?'

'I'm near your shop actually, in Chapel Road.'

'No way! That's where Emma lives. She's a really old friend,' I add when I see Mark's blank expression. 'What number?'

'One.'

'She's twenty-nine.'

'My first fake age.' He smiles.

'Exactly. Come on, stay.' The truth is I don't want to be left on my own.

'Thanks, but I think I'd better be on my way.' He scrapes his chair back.

'Another drink?'

'Hey,' Mark says, walking towards me. 'Look, it's been a shitty day, it's not surprising you're feeling like this.' He lays a hand gently on my shoulder.

I'm thinking about Bells and what she said to me earlier this evening. 'Why do you hate me? Why don't you write me?' For the first time in years I cry, and he holds me.

'I don't think I have ever apologized so much in one day.' I say, as finally I sit down at the table with dry eyes. 'To better days.' I hold my can up towards his.

'To better days,' he agrees.

*

'Bells! Stop!' I scream.

Mum's footsteps hurtle down the corridor. 'Stop her, Katie!' Bells is towering over Mum's dog Peggy, clutching a chunky pair of black jagged-edged scissors. Everything turns to slow motion as I watch her holding the scissors near to one of Peggy's ears. She smiles as she opens the handles, Peggy looking up at her innocently. I have to stop Bells from hurting her! I try to move. The scissors are open wide, the jagged silver edges gleam. My feet won't move. I can't move. I won't stop her in time. It's too late.

'Stop her!' Mum shouts at me again.

I wake up in a sweat, gasping for breath. Was that me screaming? I take a look around the dark room. Calm down. Deep breaths, Katie. It was only a dream. Let it all go. It's all right. I sit up and hug my knees tightly under the duvet. Our bed is empty. Sam isn't back yet. Where is he? The room feels black and cold. The least he could have done was call to see if I had found Bells, to see if we were both OK. I lean over to the bedside table, turn on the lamp and hold up my watch. It's one o'clock. 'Why didn't he call, Charlie?' I ask my cheetah, who sits protectively by the lamp. 'You would have called me, wouldn't you, Charlie, even if you were busy hunting?'

When I go to bed alone I keep my mobile on the bedside table. I pick it up now and ring Sam. It's his voicemail.

I walk down the corridor and quietly open Bells's door. She's curled up in bed, looking peaceful.

I turn off the lamp and lie down again in the darkness. When I was a child I hated the darkness, just as Bells did, but I couldn't admit it to Mum. I was terrified there was a crocodile under my bed, a witch behind my door or demons lurking under the window seat. *The Owl Who Was Afraid of the Dark* was one of my favourite books. Dad used to read it to me. He sat on the end of my bed, still in his suit and polished shoes. Now I shut my eyes and try to think of something nice to dream about.

'Nothing around me,' I whisper.

'Nothing around you,' I can hear Mum saying.

I turn over on to my side. Where are you, Sam? I miss you.

I have never felt so alone.

16

Still awake, I turn my pillow over because it's getting too warm. I feel so tired I can barely open my eyes, yet my mind will not switch off. If only it could go quiet at the touch of a button.

One moment I'm worrying about Sam. What if he's so drunk he has passed out on some park bench? What if he's with another woman? No. He couldn't be. It's nearly three o'clock now. Then I am fretting about what could have happened to Bells if Mark hadn't helped find her. Bells will tell Mum and Dad about me shouting at her. Mum will be furious.

Deciding it's pointless trying to sleep, I put my dressing gown on, and walk past Bells's room. She's breathing heavily, still fast asleep. Quietly I shut her door and walk downstairs. I pray Sam has not hidden the cigarettes in too hard a place this time. Thankfully I find a pack in the cutlery drawer.

As I sit by the window, smoking, I think about home again. Bells being here has stirred up so many feelings. Why am I finding it this hard having her around? I knew it would be difficult, but hadn't anticipated such a string of dramas in only one week.

After Bells's birth Dad told me that we would get through this together. He told me that life carries on and that things would turn out fine. There are many families who go through exactly what we are going through, he said.

I had felt this overwhelming sense that I had to look after Mum. It wasn't because she was falling apart. Looking back, she was strong. I simply felt responsible for her. I planned what I could do to help. I knew we didn't have a lot of money because I'd heard Mum and Dad talking about it. Mum no longer had time to work in her studio and Dad was earning a pretty meagre salary in the auction house. So I'd go shopping with her and slip packets of orange Club biscuits and salt-and-vinegar crisps into the bags without being caught. I told Mum she did not have to give me any pocket money and she seemed touched. I said I would raise money at school by selling horse chestnuts in the playground. I wanted to help on the practical side too. I helped Mum feed Bells and dress her. This was something I could do and I enjoyed it, even if Mum pointed out to me that I had missed a buttonhole or was putting her arms where her legs should have gone. Dad was no better. He was once left to look after Bells for the day and Mum came back to find her cardigan put on all askew and her bonnet back to front. It was what Dad meant by muddling through together. It did work for a while.

I was also very protective of Bells. I knew she was vulnerable, not the same as other small children; my sister was different. I probably tried too hard. I remember insisting I should take Bells out for a walk in her pram. I said I'd only take her down our road – up the hill and back again. As I reached the top and was turning the pram around a group of boys came running along behind me, pelting water-filled balloons at one another. One of them barged into the back of me and my hand slipped. The pram started to roll down the hill, gathering speed alarmingly. Mum is going to kill me, was my overriding fear. 'Help!' I screeched to the group of boys. 'Help!' One of them stopped and turned around, the pram crashed into him and toppled over. Bells landed in the gutter. She was cut badly on the forehead and her right arm.

'How could you have let go?' Mum said, pacing up and down the kitchen. She was throwing her arms up in the air, gesticulating madly.

'It was an accident,' Dad intervened, trying to calm her down.

'An accident? We can't afford any more accidents.'

When I burst into tears Dad tried to talk to me. 'Your mother knows it wasn't your fault, she was frightened, that's all,' he said. 'When we're scared, we lash out at the nearest person.'

I began to withdraw from Mum when she started spending all her spare time at the hospital. Bells was about two years old then and I was nine. By this stage she needed a series of operations to start healing her face. Piece by piece, the doctors rebuilt the gap between her nose and lip. When the bandages were taken off, it was hard to tell the difference immediately, but slowly Bells started to look more normal.

In the school holidays, when Dad was at work and Mum was at the hospital, I spent most of my time with Emma's family. Emma's sister, Natalie, was seventeen then and I can remember thinking how grown-up she was. She was tall and slim, with long black hair dyed with purple streaks. It was so long she could sit on it. She wore Gothic clothes and her eyelashes were coated in thick layers of black mascara. I remember her constantly sucking mint imperials. To disguise the smell of cigarette smoke, I realize now.

When Emma's family was away, Miss Grimes, our local babysitter, filled in. I hated my mother for making me put up with her. Miss Grimes always wore the same old brown tweed skirt, boring lace-up shoes and flesh-toned tights that squashed down the black hairs on her white legs. Her hair looked like one of those Brillo pads we had in the kitchen sink. She wore steel-framed glasses perched on the end of her nose. It was hard to believe she lived only three doors away from us; she looked as if she came from another country. One where all they ate was cabbage.

'She is very nice, poppet,' Mum told me when I wrinkled my nose in disapproval. 'The main thing is I won't have to worry about leaving you.'

Dad loved her because she brought over steamed puddings and lasagnes for our freezer. 'She's a one is Miss Grimes,' he chuckled.

I will never forget the time she came to look after me for an entire night. Mum and Dad had taken Bells to hospital the day before her next operation.

'You always have your nose in a book,' Miss Grimes scolded me, leaning over to see what I was reading. She was knitting a sludgy-green jumper the colour of the damp rotting moss that sat on our garage roof. 'You're far too young for a book like this,' she said in a shocked voice and swiped it away from me.

I tried to grab it back, clutching the air. 'Oh, keep it then, I've already read *Riders* anyway.'

'You'll amount to nothing,' she said to the click of her knitting needles. 'You're a little piece of fluff. Your sister has a lot more problems than you, but she will be a proper person.'

I shrugged my shoulders and muttered, 'Piss off.'

She lurched forward and hit me hard on the knuckles with her knitting needles. 'I beg your pardon?' She was doing that mad thing with her eyes again. When she was cross or excited they started to roll, so all I could see was their whites.

I held in my breath; I did not want her to see that the blow had hurt. 'You look like a mad blind lady!' I told her, smiling to cover up the pain.

Before I knew it, I was being dragged upstairs and into the spare room. She pushed me inside and turned the key in the lock saying *that* would teach me. I banged on the door, I screamed and shouted, but she ignored me as she watched *Corrie*.

Miss Grimes unlocked the door the following morning and told me she was sorry. I told her she was a sad old spinster woman. When Mum and Dad returned I told them what had happened. Mum said she knew how much I hated Miss Grimes and that I would do anything to get rid of her. I looked at Dad, who was so often my ally, but he told me not to harass Mum. Couldn't I see how tired she was?

Miss Grimes continued to babysit for us, despite my telling Mum I was no longer a child. She carried on locking me in my bedroom; she even locked me in the attic once for being 'insolent'. I never forgave them for not believing me. They closed their ears and eyes to it because they had too much else to think about.

When my father became an auctioneer, his salary increased and we could afford to have someone coming in during the day to look after Bells. This was when Mum started work in her studio again, working round the clock, working, working, working. I think it took her mind off family problems and immersed her in a different world.

Her life was divided between trying to meet Bells's needs and completing commissions. It felt like she was not interested in me any more and we grew even further apart.

Bells was 'Mum's girl'. I know both Mum and Dad found her comparatively easy to live with by now, straightforward in comparison with me. Bells was 'the artistic one'; Mum encouraged her to draw, paint, write, cook – all the things she'd loved as a child and still loves. Katie was 'the rebellious one'.

'What have you *done* to yourself, Katie!' I can still hear Mum cry in that familiar despairing tone, green eyes glaring, mouth opened wide in reproach. 'How could you have been so stupid? So idiotic?' I can see her savagely untying her mucky apron which she then throws to the floor.

I had dyed my hair blue and pink, like an exotic bird. I was copying Natalie, who changed her hair colour as often as Madonna.

I can feel Mum's arm pulling mine. 'Which godforsaken hairdresser did this to you? It looks like you have pink and blue worms crawling in your hair.' By the time we were going home in the car, she was upset rather than cross. 'Why do you deliberately try to upset me all the time? Katie, what's happened to you? You used to be such a sweet girl.'

Wasn't it obvious? Did I have to get my tongue pierced next to get her attention?

I don't think Mum has moved on from describing me as the 'rebellious one'. I think she still believes that I lead this full-on crazy life in London, burning the candle at both ends. I am still the dissident.

When I think about it now, it seems almost trivial; people go through much worse things after all. But we don't forget, do we? We don't forget the smallest slight, let alone the feeling that we have been somehow abandoned. Left to play second fiddle to our own sister. It wasn't Bells's fault. I know she never set out to be the golden child in Mum's eyes, and I know how much she has gone through, but there is still a part of me that blames her for needing Mum so much. If Mum wasn't at home, she was at the hospital. Bells had speech therapy classes every week, or her eyesight had to be tested, or her hearing aid needed to be fitted. There was always some appointment to go to. I suppose I have never spoken to Bells about it because Mum has always instilled in me how lucky I am not to have the same affliction. How dare I be angry or cross when I have my whole life ahead of me?

In many ways my childhood helped me. It made me strive to be independent. Yet I'm still not truly independent, am I? I have this need to be with people; look at the way I move in with every man I meet. I want to be loved; I want to feel needed. I have this gaping hole inside me which I have tried to ignore for years, yet it will never go away. When I hear Bells talking about Mum so freely all that old anger and jealousy returns.

We were close once, there was tenderness between Mum and me.

I light another cigarette and blow a smoke ring in the air. I will never forget Mum not turning up to watch me perform the leading role in our school production of *Guys and Dolls*. I had reserved two seats in the front row, but something had 'cropped up with Bells' – the same old excuse. I pretended I didn't care. Maybe that's my mistake, I am too proud. But I can still remember how it felt when my father sat down next to an empty seat.

17

'He didn't even call me later to see if I had found her,' I say quietly down the phone to Emma. I am in the shop the following morning. Eve and Bells have popped out to buy some croissants and cappuccinos.

'NO! That's dreadful!' Emma says. 'What did you say to him?'

'Sam, a fat lot of use you were.'

'What are you on about?' He was shaving and I was talking to his reflection in the mirror.

'Yesterday!' I shout in exasperation as I pull on my work jeans, catching my finger on the zip. 'Fuck!' I suck in my breath. 'Bells went missing and you didn't even call.'

'Had she run off then?' he remarks, without a flicker of concern. He might as well have been commenting on the weather. I hurl a trainer at him. It hits him on the back and thuds to the floor.

'Jesus, Katie, what the . . . ?'

'You could at least pretend you're interested. Show a bit of concern.'

'Well, you found her, didn't you?' He turns to me impatiently. 'You know what? I haven't got time for this, I'm seeing my personal trainer in half an hour.'

I throw the other trainer at him. This one hits him bang in the face. Bull's-eye.

'NO! You didn't?' Emma gasps, and then laughs.

'I did.'

'Good for you! I hope it hurt. Then what did he say?'

'What has got into you?' he yells, touching one side of his face. 'Great, I'm going to have a socking big bruise on my cheek. Thanks, Katie.'

'Yesterday was awful,' I say, lowering my voice, but making sure it doesn't lose its angry edge. 'If it hadn't been for Mark . . .'

'Who?' There is a slight twitch of interest, at last.

'Mark.'

'Who's Mark?'

'He's a very nice man,' I point out emphatically. 'He found Bells yesterday. He came home for pizza too.' This piece of information has done the trick. At last Sam pays attention.

'For pizza? Why did you have to invite the guy back for pizza?'

'To say thank you. If he hadn't found her, I don't know what would have happened. She had an asthma attack.'

'Why did Bells run away in the first place?' Sam asks, sitting down on the bed and putting his trainers on.

'Because that's what she does when she gets upset,' I explain to him, as if he really ought to know. 'It used to happen a lot at home.' I tell him about the labels, wanting to find that Sam might in fact care a little. That he is human, after all.

'Well, if you hadn't shouted at her in the first place,' he says smugly, clicking his tongue against the roof of his mouth, 'then none of this would have happened, would it?'

There is an uneasy pause. I want Emma to say, I can't believe he said that. How dare he swing that one back at you? Anything to make me feel less guilty. 'What *did* you say?' she finally asks.

I pick up his cup of coffee which sits on the bedside table. 'Uh-oh, nervous twitch, might spill this all over the white sheepskin rug.'

'Katie, don't,' he says imploringly, 'put it down.'

I do put the mug down, as I bought that rug and I love it. Instead, I grab his watch. 'I would say this is an emergency situation, wouldn't you, Sammy? Perhaps if I pull the emergency cord?'

Sam can't watch. Instead he stands up in his jogging trousers, tight T-shirt and trainers. 'Go on, pull it, and you can pay the fucking fine. I'm late for my PT.' He storms out of the room.

I put the watch down. I feel so deflated. A week ago I was happy, things were going fine. My fashion show was a success. I hear Sam coming back and my heart lifts. He'll tell me he's been an idiot and not at all supportive.

He stands at the door and puts one hand against the wall. 'You've had your say, now it's my turn.'

'What?' I say, uneasily.

'You never told me about Isabel and now, all of a sudden,' he raises his eyebrows, 'I am supposed to be deeply concerned about her welfare? Katie, I didn't know that she runs off when she's upset. I still don't know a thing about her. I don't feel comfortable around her because *you* haven't made me feel comfortable.'

I sit in silence.

'Did you think I would go off you because of her . . . you know, the way she is?' he finishes. 'It's your own hang-up, Katie. If you hadn't been so ashamed to tell me about her . . .'

I see Bells standing behind him now in her pyjamas and football slippers and I am frowning madly and buttoning my lips together, but . . .

'If you hadn't been so ashamed of your own sister,' he continues, oblivious, 'things might have got off to a better start. OK, she's different, but so what? I was on the tube

139

the other day and there was this woman sitting opposite me barking like a dog. There are lots of Isabels around, she's not unique.'

Bells looks at me and I put my head in my hands. She walks away and Sam glances round, finally realizing he wasn't talking just to me. 'I couldn't do anything when you called because I was about to go into a meeting. I *am* at fault for not calling you back, and I'm sorry. But don't blame it all on me. Perhaps you should take a good hard look at yourself too, Katie,' he says before slamming the door behind him.

I lie down on the bed and stare up into the ceiling. Bells is now playing Stevie Wonder. Stevie Wonder is probably the only constant thing she has in her world at the moment.

The closeness we shared yesterday, the affection – well, it has all been undone in one swift blow and I'm taken aback by how much I care. I can't let Bells think she isn't important to me. Lord, oh, Lord, I feel dreadful.

Emma is now painfully quiet. Please tell me that Sam is in the wrong, I think. Yet deep down I know that there is a lot of truth in what he said. I should have told him about Bells. What was I thinking? Thankfully she does not say I told you so.

'Is Bells all right?' she asks. 'Do you want me to talk to her? Her asthma hasn't flared up again?'

'Thanks, Emma. I think she's OK but she has been quiet,'

I admit. 'Oh God, I've really mucked up. When Mum and Dad come home I can hardly say Bells has had a great time.'

'It's not too late,' she says.

'You should be telling me, "I told you so",' I laugh hopelessly.

'Yeah, yeah. I should but I won't. I'm not doing much today,' she says, as if she is brewing an idea, 'so why don't I fill in for you at the shop and you can take Bells out? Have some fun together.'

'Are you sure? You really wouldn't mind?'

'No, Jonnie is being boring and spinning records at home so I'm free. Take her shopping. Spend some proper time together.'

'Oh I'd love to. I could get her something for your wedding.'

'Great idea. I haven't even got my dress yet,' she adds.

'Thanks so much, Ems,' I say, thinking about the day ahead and how I can make it up to my sister.

'How about this?' I suggest to Bells, holding up a pale green skirt and an embroidered silk jacket. I peer at the label on the skirt. Size 12. I will have to take it up a good five inches.

'I like it.' She takes the jacket and skirt from me without really looking at them and shuffles off to the changing room. 'No come in,' she insists, pulling the curtain shut.

Next I can hear her stamping her feet in her big black DM boots. She is giving the purple pixie boots a rest today.

I turn to apologize to the shop assistant, who says nothing. Instead she looks away. Why did I bother to say sorry? What am I actually saying sorry for? I open the curtain slightly. 'Please let me come in,' I ask. 'Please.'

'All right, Katie.'

I sit down on a stool in the corner of the cubicle. 'Do you need a hand?'

'No, can do it on own. Can dress myself.'

'I know, sorry. What's that funny thing you have in your hand?' I ask, trying to break the ice between us.

She shrugs.

'Come on! Show me.'

She holds out her hand. 'You shake hand,' she says. I place my hand in hers and something vibrates against my palm, making a loud buzzing sound. 'What's that?' I shriek, shaking my hand free. 'Do it again!' I giggle. Bells laughs with me for the first time this morning. She said nothing on the bus; she didn't even say hello to the other passengers. I found myself longing for her to ask the man wearing a turban his age. 'Whose hand would you really like to shake? Apart from Beckham's and Stevie Wonder's,' I add.

'Tony Blair's,' she says, rocking forward again. 'Vote Tory.'

'You couldn't say that in front of Mr Blair,' I laugh.

'Vote Labour,' she says, sticking both thumbs up.

'I'd like to shake Prince William's,' I tell her, and watch

with fascination as Bells starts to take off her clothes. My sister's style is what you'd call the 'bag lady' look. She takes off her denim jacket, covered in yet more football badges and stickers. Under this is her bright red Oxford University T-shirt.

'On the catwalk, Isabel Fletcher now models a football shirt covered in Manchester United badges.' I lean back against the wall. 'Aren't you boiling?' I ask as yet another layer comes off. She's like a Russian doll. I'm surprised she can even walk. 'Bells, it's the summer. You're dressed for a day in Siberia.'

'Feel cold,' she mutters, extracting the next top, a holey and faintly smelly tank vest. I must get rid of it, I think to myself as I do a bit of fake snoring.

'Ha, ha, very funny, Katie,' she says, rocking forward with a smile.

I can see the shop girl's pointed toes. She peers around the curtain and immediately shuts it again when she sees me attempting to get the jacket on to Bells. It's too tight over her bosom. Bells has a heavy chest considering she's only four foot ten. Nature overcompensated. If only we could do a swap. I could give her some of my height – I'm five foot nine and a half; and she could give me some of her bosom – I'm a mean 34B.

'Do you remember when Mum used to tickle us under the arms after we'd had a bath?' I say, instinctively unbuttoning her jacket. It reminds me of dressing and undressing

Bells when she was little. 'Oh, Bells, sorry,' I say, pulling away. 'Sorry.'

'All right, Katie. You help me,' she says, nodding her head. 'You are Fashion Queen.'

I break into a big smile. 'Well, I think that jacket is too small. Do you want me to see if they have the next size up and shall we try another colour for fun?'

'No, we don't, I'm afraid,' the shop girl says loudly through the curtain. I step out and she is hovering over our changing room like a prison guard.

'Sorry? You don't what?' I ask.

'It only comes in that colour, the colour she's in.' She bites her lip and looks away. If this shop had a box room that is where we would have ended up, and I realize I am no better than this girl. She wants to boot us out of here as soon as possible so we do not put off potential customers. How sad. How truly pathetic I am.

'Really? But I'm sure I saw it in another colour.' I walk over to the rails and, sure enough, the jacket does come in a different colour. In fact it comes in about four different shades and patterns. I take another one off the hanger and walk past the girl purposefully, back into the changing room. 'Here we go, Bells.'

I hear more customers coming in. 'Can I help you or are you browsing?' a sugar-sweet voice asks them.

This jacket buttons up smoothly. I stand back and tell Bells to come out. 'You look lovely,' I encourage her. We

144

stand outside, behind a girl with honey-blonde hair. She poses in front of the mirror in pale blue jeans, holding up a black dress. Her boyfriend sits in the corner of the shop reading *FHM*. Bells shuffles forward, trying to catch a glimpse of herself. The girl moves out of the way and I thank her. Bells's skirt trails on the ground like a train. It's the right colour though because it brings out the green of her eyes. Every time I look into them I see Mum. Bells takes another step and then I hear a rip. Immediately I push her back into the changing room and examine the dress closely. There's a large rip above the hem. 'Bugger,' I mutter. 'Bugger.'

'That black dress is fabulous,' the shop girl is saying at the far side of the room. 'It's such a staple for your wardrobe, you can't go wrong.'

'Bugger,' Bells repeats loudly.

'Shh!' I say, hearing footsteps coming towards our cubicle. 'Get dressed quickly.' I look at the pile of clothes. Once Bells is ready we walk out to the shop desk. I am ready to tell the girl what happened and buy the skirt. I can mend it at home.

'Are you going to take that?' she enquires, her voice straining to be polite.

'You married?' Bells asks her. 'You have children?' She steps forward to shake the girl's hand. I can see she has her little electrical device ready. I am about to stop her, but when I see the expression on the girl's face I change my mind.

'Oh my God!' she yells and recoils as the device goes off, withdrawing her manicured hand in horror. Bells rocks forward in delight and I smile. The girl glares at us both with nothing but disdain now. 'What happened to her?' she spits, now looking directly at me. 'Is she mad or something?'

' "She",' I emphasize, 'is called Bells. If you have a question, why don't you ask her?'

'Born with poorly brain and a cleft lip and palate,' Bells says, just as Mum used to tell her.

'If someone asks, you tell them straight. You have nothing to be ashamed of,' I can hear her saying.

'Will you be taking the skirt?' the assistant demands, clearly not interested and still unable to look at Bells.

'I'm afraid it has a rip in it so, no, thank you,' I say, hardly believing that these words are coming out of my mouth. 'We're not interested in damaged goods,' I carry on, relishing every word now. The shop girl claws the outfit away. 'I'm sure there was nothing wrong with it earlier . . .'

'You could always put it in the sale,' I suggest helpfully.

'You not very nice lady,' Bells says to the girl. I walk out, holding on to my sister's arm. 'Not very nice lady,' she repeats, shaking her head. 'Katie, not very nice lady.'

'No, not nice at all.'

I take Bells out for lunch. 'No more shops, Katie,' she'd said. I order a glass of wine and a Diet Coke.

We still haven't found her an outfit but I'm determined not to give up. The main thing was that we've bonded over the nasty girl in the shop. It felt surprisingly good, taking on that girl. The look on her face! I watch Bells as she looks at the menu. She still hasn't mentioned anything to me about that conversation with Sam. I wonder how she feels now. She looked so hurt earlier this morning, so vulnerable.

Why didn't I tell Sam about her? I suppose the reason is simple. We tell friends about the things we feel comfortable with, proud of. I like to share the good times with Sam, I like the glossy world we have created together. Sam the hotshot guy in the City; Katie who runs her own business. There is little room for imperfection in that scenario. Why would I tell him about Bells when I feel so guilty that I ignore her letters, that I am a useless sister, that I resented her so much as a child for taking all the attention away from me? That I did stupid unoriginal things to turn the attention back on me? Talking about Bells brings back a lot of memories I'd rather erase. It feeds the corrosive guilt inside me. But I realize none of this makes it forgivable. Sam was right.

'Bells, about what you heard earlier . . .'

'You ashamed.'

'I am sorry, Bells, so sorry. Can we make a fresh start? You have one more week with me in London and I'd really like to make it up to you.' I realize I can't say I'm not embarrassed when Bells says hello to everything that moves;

when she asks people why they have no hair, or why they have 'only the one leg'. Most people would be embarrassed, wouldn't they? 'Bells, it was wrong of me not to tell Sam about you, I don't know why I didn't. It was one of those things you do and then wish you could rewind time.'

Bells doesn't say anything.

'Where's the thingy that vibrates?' I laugh nervously as I take her hand. 'Friends,' I tell her, but still do not feel I have said sorry properly.

I have an uneasy feeling lingering in the pit of my stomach. I start to think of all the times when people asked me at parties, 'Do you have brothers or sisters?' and I replied that I was an only child because I couldn't face the follow-on questions: Where does she live? What does she do? In the evening, when I am getting ready for bed, I say a quiet prayer to God, asking his forgiveness for denying her. That makes me feel better, that I won't go straight down to hell.

I look at Bells, who is drinking her Coke so quickly that she starts to make loud slurping noises through her straw. I am not going to look around to see if anyone is staring. But then she makes one final slurping noise which sounds as if it will blow the place down. Without thinking I do glance around, but in fact no one is looking at us. They are too interested in their own drinks and food. I order her another Coke. 'Bells, the thing Sam said about being ashamed of you . . .'

'It's all right, Katie,' she interrupts, looking at the framed poster on the wall.

'No, it's not all right. I am *not* ashamed of you, I promise you. The only person I am ashamed of is myself.'

'Why?'

'Sometimes I find it hard . . .' I don't know how to end my sentence so I start again. 'To be honest, I was dreading you coming to stay.' I don't look at her because I am scared of hurting her. 'You remind me of everything I don't have.'

'Don't understand,' she says.

'I don't feel part of our family, I'm an outsider. Look at your photo album. Pictures of everyone, Mum, Dad . . . not one of me. It's my fault, I'm the one who distances myself. I'm not blaming you, but you, Mum and Dad are so close. When you were young I was palmed off to Aunt Agnes, or stayed with Granny Norfolk, or some horrible babysitter looked after me. You needed their help, Mum and Dad had no choice, I know that, but I didn't cope with it very well.' My thoughts are scrambled. 'Do you understand what I'm trying to say?'

'Sort of. Difficult for Katie too.'

'Yes, in a totally different way from what you had to go through. I feel so guilty for feeling like this, I don't want to feel the way I do.'

'That's right. You jealous?'

'Yes,' I reply simply, realizing how perceptive she is. 'I was really jealous of you for having all the attention. I have to get over it, though, I know it's not your fault.'

149

'You blame Mum?' Bells asks.

'I guess I do. Mum's always taken on the brunt of it. With Dad it's different somehow, we've always been closer. Shall we make a pact?'

'Yes, pact.'

'That we make a fresh start?'

'Friends.' She holds out her hand, with her short little fingers and bitten nails.

'Yes, friends,' I tell her, clutching that tiny hand.

18

It's nearly six o'clock and I'm making price tags with black velvet ribbon. Eve has left, picked up by Hector, who was not at all what I'd expected: short and oily like a sardine.

Eve bought a baby chandelier for the shop today, with shimmering cut-glass drops. She also found some ivory silk cushions trimmed with black lace to decorate the cream chaise longue in the corner of the shop. Very *Moulin Rouge*. We work well together because she has a real flair for design and enjoys making the shop look lavishly aesthetic. We have similar taste, which is fortunate.

'Where's Mark?' Bells mentions again.

'Since five minutes ago, I still don't know,' I reply, watching Bells pacing the shop floor, making fists with her hands. 'Bored,' she says again.

'We'll be going home soon, I promise. Draw me something,' I suggest, handing her my notepad.

'Mark married?' she asks.

'I don't think so. Why?'

'Girlfriend?'

'No idea.'

'Pets? He have a dog?'

'Doubt it. You should have asked him.'

I wonder if Bells misses 'going out' with men. Does it even occur to her? This is when I feel guilty about envying her. There is so much she cannot have which I take for granted. I wonder what she thinks about Sam and me. She probably isn't envious when all we do is argue. She still says she doesn't like him.

'Mark nice man.'

I can see she's not going to let him slip from her mind. 'Draw me a picture of him,' I say, pleased that she grabs a pencil from the papier-mâché pot on my desk.

I continue looping ribbon through the tags. 'We going to see Mark again?' she asks as she sits down on the wooden stair and begins to draw earnestly.

'Maybe.'

Mark scribbled down his telephone number just before he left. The piece of paper is still in my handbag. He told me he was around if I needed him as it was the school summer holiday. I could call him. We could go out. Sam doesn't need to know. Mark is Bells's friend after all.

I have thought a lot about Mark and our evening together. It has been a ray of light in the last few days. 'I have a friend who has a brother,' he told me, after the tears and after I had explained how foolish I felt for not confiding in Sam about Bells. 'I had never met the brother until I went to their sister's wedding. I was the very informal photographer,' he added with a modest cough. 'I was in the kitchen with the brother, whose name was Ben, and he seemed pretty normal to me, sitting there in his jacket and tie, until he asked his father if he could have a Scotch egg.' Mark smiled. 'I thought it was strange,' he furrowed his eyebrows, 'a man of thirty-something asking his father if he could have a Scotch egg, but then I thought nothing more of it until he turned to me, quite randomly, and said that their dog should be put down.'

I laugh out loud, remembering. 'What so funny?' Bells asks as she walks over to my desk clutching the pad.

'Something Mark told me.'

'Mark nice man, isn't he?' She is doing that excited thing with her hands again, as if they're dancing together.

'He *is* a very nice man. But back to your portrait.' And I'm surprised when she sits down obediently and carries on drawing.

'I was amazed my friend had never told me much about him,' Mark continued. 'Baffling, really. I had known him for six years.'

I smile, thinking about that word 'baffling'.

Then came the awful question that all of us ask though we wish we didn't. 'And what do you do?' I was focusing on the large hole Mark had in the elbow of his navy jumper. It looked like an ancient Marks & Spencer one that needed either replacing or a good darning.

'I'm a teacher.'

'Oh yes, you said. What do you teach?'

'English and drama.'

There is something romantic about being a drama teacher, I think now, tapping my red biro against the desk.

'Really?' I asked. Why do we say, 'Really'? Did I expect Mark to stick his tongue out and say, 'No, only joking'? 'What age?' I continued.

'Teenagers. I like a challenge.'

With his tousled light brown hair which has no parting whatsoever, the small mole on the right side of his face, even the nerdy round glasses he wears, I reckon a lot of the girls would have a crush on Mark.

'I enjoy the summer holidays too,' Mark had said. 'Gives me time to do my own stuff.'

'Your own stuff?'

'I'm trying to write a book,' he confessed. 'I find it difficult working from home, too many distractions like daytime television. "At nine-ten we can show you how to make yourself look like a Hollywood actor in less time than it takes to boil an egg,"' he said, imitating Lorraine Kelly. 'There's Wimbledon too. If Henman's playing I have to leave the house, my nerves can't cope.'

He asked me about my shop. I told him about my time at art college and working for a West End theatre, designing and making costumes, followed by working for a fashion designer for three years. She went bust eventually, but taught me a lot about the business. Bells had come downstairs by then in her pyjamas, clutching her photograph album. He turned his attention to her as I made a salad. They talked about the tennis, Mark said he had the hots for Sue Barker. He asked her about football. I couldn't help noticing the ease between them. Bells was laughing with him and at one point she stroked his arm affectionately.

Mark looked at all her pictures slowly. 'Who are they?' he asked.

'Mary Veronica, Ted, in Paris,' Bells said proudly. I went over to have a look. Mary Veronica and Bells were standing outside a café with their thumbs up. Ted was in the middle with his arms crossed. 'We climbed Eiffel Tower,' she told us.

'I would love to do that. Now, who is this? She's very beautiful.'

'My mum,' Bells said. 'That's my dad. That's Budge, he plays for my football team.'

'Katie, how come there are no pictures of you?' Mark asked, sounding surprised.

I clear my desk. It's late and I want to go home. Today I popped out of the shop to post some letters and found myself hoping I might bump into Mark.

Well, he knows where I am and where the shop is too. 'Let's go, Bells. What do you fancy doing tonight?'

'Sainsbury's? Cook tonight, organic night.'

I pull a face. 'Let's grab a takeaway.'

'Mark likes Sainsbury's.'

Good point. 'What do you fancy cooking?'

Bells and I are sitting like plum puddings on the sofa, sharing a tub of toffee ice cream with a slice of chocolate biscuit cake and watching the old black-and-white film *Titanic*. Earlier Bells cooked us a wild mushroom and aubergine risotto. She showed me how to prepare the aubergines, slicing them and sprinkling them with salt, while telling me that we had to leave them for half an hour before cooking them.

There was no sign of Mark at Sainsbury's, just the same old man with his trolley of oranges, wishing everyone the 'best of luck'. Bells tells me she has watched this movie at least one hundred times.

'About to hit iceberg.' She claps as she leans forward and laughs outrageously.

'The wallies! Bells, it's coming, it's coming!' I sit forward too.

'Rewind,' she says. I pick up the controls and rewind. I hear the front door shut and Sam coming upstairs. For a second I'm actually disappointed he's back.

'SMACK!' Bells cries out. Sam stands at the door, shakes

his head and walks out. I follow him downstairs to the kitchen. He sits down at the table, which is covered with a baking tray, a greasy butter wrapper, tin of cocoa, digestive biscuits and a bag of sultanas.

'Sorry,' I say, quickly beginning to clear up the mess. 'We made a chocolate biscuit cake.' I walk past him and put the dirty bowl, licked wooden spoon and tray in the sink.

'Katie, I'm sorry. I'm behaving like an idiot.'

I turn around and lean against the oven. 'Yes, you are. We *both* are. I'm sorry too. I was scared. I feel responsible for her, but I shouldn't have taken it out on you. Everything you said, me not telling you about her,' I scratch my forehead, 'you were right.'

'Take a long hard look at yourself, Katie,' he imitates himself.

I sit down next to him and Sam slides his fingers in between mine. 'We are OK, aren't we?' I ask.

'I think so. 'Course we are. Come here.'

'Katie!' I hear Bells shouting.

I pull away from him. 'Coming?'

'No,' he says awkwardly. 'I'll clear up this mess.'

'Sam, Bells won't bite.'

'I've seen *Titanic*.'

'So have I. Bells has seen it a thousand times!' I laugh, wanting him to change his mind. 'We'll clear up later, Bells loves washing up.'

'Hot soapy water,' she says as her hands plunge into the

foamy basin, a look of extraordinary delight on her face. However much mess Bells creates, she always tidies up after herself, preferring not to use the dishwasher. She makes her own bed because that's what they do at home. She cooks her own meals. And even though her room is full of posters and music and looks like a car boot sale, it's an organized chaos. She knows exactly where everything is and gets cross if I move anything.

'Go,' he says, acting like a boy who doesn't get the attention he deserves.

All the tension between us returns, but I don't want another argument. I leave him in the kitchen.

'Katie,' he calls after me.

'About to hit iceberg, Katie,' Bells tells me again. 'Katie, watch.'

I sit down with her. 'The wallies! What do you call them, Bells?'

'Wallies.' I watch her face light up as she stares at the screen, her laugh infectious.

'SMACK!' We laugh together, before Bells presses rewind.

19

I flick the kettle on. Sam has already escaped from the house. His alarm clock went off so early that I thought it was still the middle of the night.

'Morning, how are you, Bells?' I yawn. 'Sleep well?'

'Bored.'

'You're bored? What do you expect to be doing at seven thirty in the morning?'

She shrugs. She is wearing her grey baggy tracksuit with her red Oxford University T-shirt which now has chocolate stains down the front. 'I need to put some washing on,' I say flatly, still trying to wake up.

I open the blind and squeeze my eyes shut. The sun streams through the window. I stretch my arms out above my head and let out a great big sigh. Bells continues to eat her chopped apricots and figs quietly, occasionally prodding the milk-bottle sculpture. Stevie Wonder plays in the background. Poor old Stevie never has a holiday. I want to turn him off, it's too early for 'I Just Called to Say I Love

You'. Déjà vu screams at me. We get ourselves so tied up in a routine that we spin round and round like an old pair of socks in a washing-machine cycle. Wake up, go for a run, eat breakfast, go to work, come home, go out, go to bed. I'm not complaining, I like my life, but sometimes I don't stop to think. I'm like a robot.

I'm going to skip my run this morning and instead make myself a bacon sandwich for breakfast with lots of tomato ketchup. Go on Katie, be wild! I make an even bolder step by deciding I will take two days off in a row. I'll see if Eve minds being on her own. I think she likes being in charge.

'You and me are going out today,' I tell Bells.

'Where? The shop?'

'No, it's a surprise, you'll see,' I say, trying to hide my own excitement. 'Get dressed quickly. Look at the sun, Bells. It's a beautiful day.'

She fidgets with her hands, as if she is conducting her muddled thoughts.

'Upstairs!' I tell her again. 'Your dungarees are in the airing cupboard, I washed them for you, and it's hot today so wear something cool. Don't wear five vests!'

'Where we going?'

'It's a surprise.'

'Can Mark come?'

I dig into my handbag and give her the piece of paper, now crumpled, with his number on it. 'Let's ring him,' I say.

*

I feel a tiny twinge of guilt for not being at work again, but it disappears when I see Bells. She rocks forward, tapping her hands together. After queuing for an hour and a half we are finally standing in our glass capsule, propelled one hundred feet into the air and surrounded by tourists. Mark wasn't at home. I was ridiculously excited by the thought of seeing him again but also a little relieved there was no answer. It's nice to spend time with Bells, just the two of us.

'Not moving?' Bells jitters. 'Broken down, broken down!'

'We are moving, I promise. Apparently we're moving about one quarter of a metre per second,' I tell her, putting Sam's binoculars around her neck. 'Take a look.' I stand close behind her. She smells of Persil and lime. 'You can see all of London from here, Bells,' I say, pointing to different landmarks. 'Doesn't that make you feel tiny? Like an ant.' She's breathing deeply. 'There's Big Ben . . . the Houses of Parliament . . . look, you can see Buckingham Palace where the Queen lives. Isn't it incredible?'

'Yes, Katie, yes.'

Bells stops looking through the binoculars and puts her hands behind her head, rocking forward again, then turning to face the other way. I sit down on the bench in the middle of our pod and stretch out my legs, the sun beating down on my face. I'm wearing my black-and-white spotted sundress with flat-heeled white leather sandals, and my hair is scooped up into a loose ponytail. The freckles across my nose have come out in their full glory.

'*¡Mira! ¡Mira!*' shout the Spanish group sharing our capsule, running over to where Bells is standing. She flaps her hands, getting caught up in their excitement. '*¡Mira!*' They point into the distance. Bells looks in their direction and then looks at me and then turns to them again. They run to the other side in a stampede frenzy and she follows them.

A Japanese couple ask me if I'll take a picture of them both and they link arms as the flash goes off. Bells rushes over to me and they offer to take a picture of us. Bells is clapping her hands against her thighs now, then she runs to the side of the capsule and calls to me, 'Look, Katie, look! London. Where Sam's house?'

'Turn round for a second,' I say, asking the Japanese man to take our picture quickly before she runs off again.

Bells and I are lying on a pale yellow checked rug in St James's Park, looking up into the clear blue sky. We have finished eating our picnic: vegetable samosas and a Diet Coke for Bells, a Pimm's and a packet of Marks & Spencer sushi for me, and two large chunks of chocolate biscuit cake.

'There are no clouds, Bells. Just clear blue sky like the sea.'

'No fluffy clouds,' she echoes. 'In Wales we have sea.'

'Do you miss Wales?'

'Yes.' She tilts her head. 'No. A bit.'

'What do you miss?'

'Miss Ted.'

'Who's Ted?'

'My friend.' She laughs mischievously, restlessly kicking her legs and knocking over the cups.

I lean on my elbow and look at her. 'Really? So Ted's the lucky man. You've kept that very quiet. You're a dark horse, Bells.'

'A dark horse,' she laughs back at me. 'Ted my friend. Ted has parrot like Grandpa.'

'Are you happy there?'

'Yes, Katie, yes. Sometimes sad.'

'Why sad?'

'Miss home, miss Mum, Dad.'

I bite my lip, surprised by how much I want to be added on to the list now. 'I'm sure they miss you too,' I tell her. 'Let's give them a call, tell them we've been up in the sky.'

I take the mobile out of my bag and punch in the numbers. Their phones are both switched off. I knew this would happen. They're hopeless. I should have insisted Dad or Mum give me the Walters' number. Why wouldn't they? 'Not there,' I tell Bells. 'How often do they call you in Wales?'

'One time a week.'

They've called twice since she has been staying with me, yet each time have sounded oddly distanced. Why won't this nagging feeling that something is wrong go away?

'Tell me more about Wales. What do you do all day?'

'Go to college Monday.'

'What do you do there?'

'Learn respect.'

'Respect?'

'Towards other people,' she tells me. 'Learn health and safety too.'

'What's all that about?'

'In kitchen. Fire rules and safety.'

'Oh, right. That's important when you're the Queen of the Kitchen, isn't it?'

'That's right. Me the Queen.'

'Do you enjoy college?'

'Yes, love college.'

'What else do you do?'

'I go to football club each week, watch my team play. Watch Budge play. Budge very handsome. I cook. Ted and I make stuff, weave and paint, we watch football videos. Clean room, make beds.'

'Are you on a rota system? You clean and make the beds one week, Ted the next?'

'Yes, that's right, Katie, that's right. Rota.'

'Do you want to clean my room and make my bed?' I ask her with a smile.

'Very funny, Katie!'

I realize how little I know about Bells's life. I know a tiny fragment from her childhood and that's about it. I've never wanted to be involved, but now . . . 'I can see why you get bored with me.'

'Sometimes bored, that's right, Katie. You marry Sam?'

I look away. 'How did you learn to cook so well, Bells?'

'You marry Sam?' she asks again, quite insistently.

'I can't see myself marrying anyone, not yet anyway. Bells, you're not burning, are you? We'd better put some cream on, just in case.' I dig into my basket for a tube of sunblock. 'Sit still.' I apply it gently to her forehead and cheeks. She doesn't flinch. Her skin is as pale as a china doll's and soft as cashmere. As I look at her, it's hard to believe she's twenty-two, only seven years younger than me.

'What you looking at?'

'You,' I say, wiping the chocolate crusts from the corners of her mouth before dabbing a large blob of cream on her nose.

'Not funny, Katie,' she laughs with me.

'Ha ha, Bells. I think it's *very* funny.'

Bells and I sit on the bus and it's rush hour, the traffic is as slow as a slug. After our picnic we went shopping. In a charity shop we found Bells a pair of red shoes with clover-shaped patterns embroidered on to them. In other stores, if there was no one helpful, we walked away. Why should they get my money? In the end, with the help of a lovely shop assistant, we found a dark red-and-gold Chinese dress with a jacket for Bells.

'You like it?' she asked the girl.

'I love it.' The girl beamed at her, kneeling down and

adjusting the hem. 'I think it's dead stylish, you are going to be the belle of the ball.'

I thought my heart might burst as I watched Bells looking proudly at herself in the mirror, her outfit finished off with the shoes she'd bought. I found myself wishing Mum could see her looking so pretty. When Bells was out of earshot I thanked the girl.

'For what?' She looked almost put out. 'It's my job.'

'You know what I mean,' I said.

She nodded. 'I've had more fun today than during my whole time here. And I've been working here for over a year!'

I bet you that nice shop assistant goes home tonight and tells her flatmate/boyfriend/whatever that she managed to find a really great outfit for a slightly unusual customer.

'Pull my finger,' Bells says. I turn and look at her dubiously. The moment I pull it she sticks out her tongue and bursts into laughter. The grey-haired woman sitting opposite stares at us strangely and then returns to her paperback.

'Pull mine.'

Bells leans forward to touch my finger.

'Bad luck, missed,' I exclaim, withdrawing my hand.

She laughs and the woman opposite stares directly at Bells with cold blue eyes. I want to tell her to stop staring. When I was much younger, I hated people staring at Bells in the supermarket or on the street or at the bus stop. I know I'm guilty of wanting to hide my sister, yet am surprised by how much it still angers me when people are rude or stare. Who are they to judge anyone? I shift in my seat. She is still looking at us. It makes me feel uncomfortable, but at least Bells doesn't appear to notice, or does she? Mum and Dad used to tell strangers what was wrong with her. Dad always explained to me, 'It puts them at their ease. It's normally fear or ignorance that makes people stare. You have to work hard to reassure them. It shouldn't be like that, but that's the way it is.'

'Oh, dear.' I shake my head solemnly at Bells. 'Too slow, miss a go.'

'Not funny, Katie!'

'Pull my finger, come on.' She misses again. 'Sorry, if you snooze, you lose.' That's an expression of Sam's. I doubt he meant it to be used in exactly the same context, however. 'Shit, this is our stop!' I grab our bags and Bells follows. 'Mind the step.'

I wish I'd said something, I think to myself, as the sour-faced woman bristles and looks down at her book.

Bells points animatedly to each tray behind the counter – couscous with pine nuts and peppers, carrot cake with a whipped orange and butter icing, warm ciabatta bread with olives or spinach, rice cakes with garlic. We buy some ginger to make a sticky ginger pudding 'like the one Mum makes,' she tells me. I buy some pistachio nuts, fresh bread and olives. Emma's coming over tonight especially to see Bells.

'You think Mum eats nice food in France?' Bells asks me.

'I reckon she's eating like a queen and she doesn't even have to do the washing-up.'

Bells rocks forward. 'No hot soapy water?'

'I'm not going anywhere near those chillies,' I tell her when she asks Eddie for three red ones. 'The last time I chopped them I forgot to wash my hands, picked my nose, and boy, did it kill!' I laugh. 'Sam almost had to ring for a doctor.'

'Not funny, Katie.' She comes forward and touches me briefly on the shoulder.

'No, it wasn't!' I carry on, still glowing from her touch. It's the first time she has initiated affection, and it makes me feel as if someone has wrapped a warm soft towel around me.

'It was supposed to be a romantic evening and I had to spend the entire night with my head in a bowl of cold water.'

'That's disgusting, Katie,' says Eddie. 'Is that all, girls?' I had forgotten he was there. He's wearing a short blue apron that shows off his hairy legs, finished off with brown sandals and socks.

'You wearing anything under that?' Bells asks him.

'Wouldn't you like to know?' he replies, winking at her.

'No, I'd prefer the table in the corner, please . . . um, say about seven-thirty . . . yep, thanks,' I hear Sam muttering as Bells and I come into the kitchen. He puts the phone down. 'I'm taking you and Isabel out tomorrow evening, for her last night in London,' he announces proudly.

'Are you?' I look at him strangely, wondering what has suddenly brought all of this on.

'I am,' he declares, and looks at Bells for a response.

'Where are you taking us, then? Bells, did you hear that? Sam's taking you and me . . .' I am tempted to add 'the two bad smells', '. . . out on the town.'

She nods.

Sam looks disappointed. 'We're going to my favourite restaurant. They have the best wine list in town.' He clicks his tongue against the roof of his mouth. 'And the best steak.'

'Bells doesn't drink,' I can't help saying.

'Don't eat meat,' she adds.

I feel bad for sounding ungrateful. 'Sam, that's a lovely idea, thanks.'

'Thank you,' Bells murmurs, turning Stevie Wonder on.

Sam and I go upstairs. 'I have had such a lovely day,' I tell him, sitting down on our bed and kicking my shoes off.

'Really? At work?' He lies down next to me.

'No, with Bells. We went on the London Eye, had a picnic, went shopping and Bells bought an outfit for Emma's wedding. I really feel like I'm getting to know her.'

'What d'you mean, getting to know her? She's your sister.'

'Yeah, but what I mean is . . .'

'I'm going to the gym tonight, want to come?'

'No.' I shake my head. 'You go.'

'I need to buy some more trainers,' he's muttering. 'Remember, we're going away for the weekend when Bells leaves.' There's a book on hip hotels on his side of the bed which he now picks up, turning to the marked page. 'I booked the Moroccan Suite, Katie. Look at it, it's beautiful and we need to get away. *Look* at this place, honey.' He points at the picture again.

The hotel bedroom looks like a mini-paradise. A four-poster bed with white linen sheets, pale blue shutters, and creamy blue tiles in the bathroom. Tiny windows looking out on to the gardens. It is very tempting. 'It looks nice . . .'

'Nice? I don't do "nice", Katie. I do "amazing". The place ticks *all* the boxes. I mean, even Madonna has stayed there,' Sam boasts.

I smile. 'You are . . .' I'm about to say 'a sad name-dropper', but then stop myself, realizing that he's being completely serious. Normally, am I impressed by all of this? Yes, I suppose I am. All I want to say to him now is, Who cares?

Finally he finds his trainers in his gym bag. 'Check out the spa and beauty room,' he continues, gesturing to the picture in the book of a woman being massaged. 'You can have a seaweed wrap, apparently it gets rid of the build-up of toxins. You girls are funny. Right, got to run.'

He stands in front of the mirror to make some last-minute adjustments to his hair. 'I'm looking forward to having this place to ourselves again.'

'Um . . . me too.'

'No offence to your sister, nothing like that, but, well, you know what I mean.'

She touched my arm today and it felt wonderful, I want to shout. You should have seen her expression when I took her on the London Eye. It was one of pure joy, and I was responsible for that. We played silly games on the bus and it was fun fooling around with her. Today made me feel alive. I want to tell all of this to Sam, I am aching to tell someone; but I don't think it will mean anything to him.

Only a few weeks ago I was telling Emma how much I was dreading Bells coming to stay. Now I want to say how stupid I've been, how *wrong* I've been. I can't wait to tell her all about our day together.

Sam kisses me, bringing me back to reality. 'In a few days it's back to you and me.' As I kiss him, all I feel is dread. The prospect of waving goodbye to Bells leaves me feeling hollow.

20

'When are you, er, going home, Isabel?' asks Mr Vickers. He was walking past the shop and Bells had rushed out to greet him.

'Tomorrow, catch train from Paddington. Do your funny thing,' Bells demands.

He looks at me nervously. He doesn't do his impersonation of a man on the train, holding on to the bar, which I know he'd do if I weren't there.

I clear my throat. 'Mr Vickers, would you like to stay for a cup of tea?'

This question sets him in a spin. 'Er, er . . .'

'Stay, Mr Vickers,' Bells says.

'How very, er, kind, er, of you. You are so very kind. Yes, please.'

I leave them downstairs while I go to the box room. Eve nipped out to get some milk; she'll be back in a minute. I make the tea and take it downstairs, only to find Mr Vickers parading about in front of Bells. He appears to

172

transform himself into a confident comedian when he is performing in front of an audience. 'Who is, er, this?' He clears his throat, puckers his lips and places his large purple hands behind his back. 'These plants look very interesting, well worth talking to.'

'Don't know. Who?' Bells punches his arm for an answer.

'Hello, Mr Vickers,' Eve says, as she returns with the milk.

I hand him a mug of tea and a chocolate digestive.

'Thank you so much,' he repeats. 'Do you, er, know who it is?' He looks at each of us in turn.

'I did not see you do it properly,' Eve says. 'Can you do it once more?'

He looks flattered by the attention and prepares himself again, putting on a distinguished voice, his hands clasped behind his back. 'These plants look very interesting, well worth talking to.'

'Oh, my goodness,' Eve says, jumping up and down, 'I know who you are, I know this voice.'

'So do I! Prince Charles,' I leap in before her.

Mr Vickers's face breaks into a smile and I find myself smiling back at him. His eyes look grey and weary, as if they have seen too much nastiness in the world, but when he smiles his entire face changes. He has an innate goodness, like Uncle Roger, a face that would never tell a lie. 'Er, yes, you are right, er . . .'

'Katie. Call me Katie.'

'Another one!' Bells claps her hands.

'What is your, er, favourite hobby?' Mr Vickers asks her.

Bells looks at me. 'You like cooking?' I suggest.

'Cooking,' she repeats.

He thinks. 'I have one.' He picks up his biscuit and takes a bite. 'Delicious, just the right consistency.' He licks his lips. 'Well, after much ruminating and cogitating I think the . . .'

'I know,' I burst out.

'*Masterchef* man,' cuts in Bells. 'I know!' She is jumping around.

'Loyd Grossman,' I finish.

'Er, correct.' I notice his stammer returns when he is not performing.

'Another!' Bells demands, just as Henrietta and her mother walk into the shop. They gawp at the strange party around my desk drinking tea.

'Do stay, Mr Vickers, and finish your tea.' I smile politely at him. 'My bank manager came round,' I tell Hen and her mother, signalling to Mr Vickers. 'It was so kind of you to come and see me personally,' I add, smiling at him.

That wipes the looks off their faces.

Bells, Sam and I sit in the corner of the restaurant looking at the menus. I take another sip of my vodka and tonic, and start to crunch a large piece of ice.

'Don't do that, Katie. It's bad for your teeth,' Sam says twitchily. A couple enter the restaurant. He casts his eyes in their direction and he visibly relaxes when he registers that he doesn't know them.

'Hello, Katie.' Bells holds my hand and the vibration goes off loudly. We both laugh.

'What *is* that?' Sam furrows his brow. Bells holds out her hand towards him. 'Um, the waiter's coming over, do it later, yeah?' he mutters.

'I'd like the chicken, please,' I tell the smooth-haired waiter when he stands at our table with his pad poised.

'Chicken?' I feel someone kick me under the table.

'Sam, that hurt.'

'Katie, I'm here to spoil you and Bells. We can eat chicken any old day.' He looks at the waiter as if to say, Women, hey! Can't take them anywhere. 'What are the specials?'

'We have salmon, or the smoked haddock risotto is very popular. I would also recommend the medallion of pork.'

Sam closes his menu smoothly. 'Thank you, but I think I'll go for the beef en croûte, please.'

'Certainly, sir, a popular choice,' the waiter affirms. 'How would you like it cooked?'

'Rare, please. You can't beat top-class beef.' Sam looks at me again. 'Choose something more adventurous, Katie.'

'But I love chicken, Sam.' I don't like the sound of my voice, a whimpering pathetic little sound. The kind children make when they say they don't want to eat their carrots and peas.

He smiles at me as he touches his chin. 'Kitty-kins, you're

a funny little mouse sometimes, a creature of habit.' He scans the menu for me. 'How about the scallops?'

'Yes, you're right,' I say. 'The scallops would be lovely.'

'How about you, Isabel?' he asks.

Bells has been noticeably quiet. She looks awkward. Perhaps she is quiet because she's leaving tomorrow?

'You have chips?'

Sam's face drops and now I kick him under the table. 'Yes, I'm sure you have chips, don't you?' I ask the waiter.

'Of course.'

'Why don't you have the homemade beef burger with chips?' Sam says.

'Bells is a vegetarian,' I say yet again. Does he never listen?

He raises his hands in a gesture of apology. 'Sorry I spoke,' he mumbles.

'Bells, why don't you have the vegetarian lasagne, with chips on the side?'

It worries me how quiet she is. Is she nervous about catching the train tomorrow?

'Can choose my own food,' she shouts, banging her elbow against the table.

'Bells, I'm sorry,' I say. Sometimes I slip into talking to her like a child and I have to stop it.

'Would like risotto,' she states.

'You order the wine, Sam.' I push my chair back and it hits the wall. 'There's no space! Is this the only table they had?' It feels like we have the children's table in this dark corner.

'Afraid so.'

'Really? But there are tables outside. It's warm tonight.'

He rubs his nose. 'Let's stay here, shall we?' His mouth begins to twitch too. 'So, what have you two been up to today? Your last night, hey, Isabel. Bet you're dying to get home.'

I know Sam is trying, but he just irritates me.

'Mr Vickers said goodbye. I like Mr Vickers, nice man.'

'Mr Vickers? Who's he now? I'll just check I ordered the right wine.' Sam swiftly changes the subject. I look ahead and see a vaguely familiar man joining the group in front of us. Sam is now lifting the menu to shield his face. His mobile rings. Still holding on to the menu with one hand, he picks his phone up with the other. I talk to Bells and Sam excuses himself, darting through the doors that lead downstairs to the loos.

After five minutes he still hasn't returned.

'Bells.'

She holds out her hand again and the buzzer goes off.

I touch her arm. 'Be back in a minute.'

'Oh, mate, this is a nightmare,' Sam says.

I stand at the top of the stairs, then quietly tiptoe down a couple and lean over the banister far enough to allow me to see him. Sam is by the cigarette machine, his back to me, one hand leaning against the wall. He laughs. I bet he's talking to Maguire.

'It's Isabel's last night and I seriously, I mean seriously, mate, need to get back in the good books with Katie. I've avoided them as much as I can.' Sam is silent; he must be listening to something very profound. 'Too right, Maguire, hopefully more action between the sheets when she's gone. Jesus, it's been like the Gobi Desert!'

I open my mouth and close it again.

'I tell you, mate, when she told me her sister was coming to stay I didn't expect this.' He pauses as he listens. 'Yeah, yeah, yeah . . . absolutely.' He paces the floor. 'Too right, Maguire. This isn't what I signed up for.' Pause. 'Yeah, I'll see how it goes. I mean, I do love her. At least, I think I do, and I know she's crazy about me.'

Who does he think he is? I want to hit him so hard, or better still put him in the stocks and throw rotten eggs at him, in front of Maguire and all his work colleagues.

'Look, mate, better go and butter them up . . . Back to my post, yeah, you know how it is.'

The food still hasn't arrived when Sam returns. 'Sorry about that,' he says, 'a client. I had to take the call.'

On the surface I remain calm, but the pit of my stomach is a seething knot of fury. 'Really? Who was it?'

'No one you'd know, honey. All very boring stuff.'

'What did they want?'

'What's with all the questions? It was a guy from work,

that's all. Crikey, Isabel, your sister can be a pain, can't she?' He laughs, hoping Bells will follow.

I watch Sam and can tell he is still preoccupied with the group in front of us.

'Do you know those people, Sam? You keep on looking over?'

'Tell you what, Bells. Why don't we eat outside, hey?' He gets up and takes his jacket.

'Look.' I smile sweetly at him, pressing a hand against his arm. 'Our food's arriving.'

Sam grimaces as he sits down again.

'Lakemore?' a man calls across to him then. 'It *is* you! Good God,' he bellows.

'Hi,' Sam says, trying to sound surprised, his cheeks burning with colour. The stout man with glasses comes over to our table. He is small and round, with curly brown hair and sideburns. I wait for Sam to introduce us, but after a second-too-long gap do it myself. 'Hello, I'm Katie.'

'Yes, sorry, this is Katie. Katie, Colin Lucker.'

'Hello, Katie, wonderful to meet you.'

'Hi, Colin.'

'Hello,' Bells says, holding out her hand.

'Hello, er . . . ? Now who might you be?'

'This is my sister, Isabel,' I tell him.

'Bells,' she corrects me.

'Hello, Bells.' Colin shakes her hand. 'Oh, my, what was that?' He laughs curiously.

As I'm about to tell him Sam says, 'Isn't it hilarious, Colin? She's a funny one is our Isabel.'

'Better be getting back to my table.' He shuffles back a few steps. 'Nice to see you again, Sammy boy. We must catch up soon.'

'Who was that, Sam?'

'My old boss,' he says, cowering behind the menu again and taking another large gulp of wine.

'Really? What a coincidence. We could join them for coffee.' The knot is unravelling in its own way. 'Mr Lucker?' I call out.

'Christ, Katie. Leave it, will you?' Sam snaps.

'Er, yes?' Colin Lucker answers tentatively.

Sam now kicks me so hard I don't dare to continue. 'Sorry, Colin, we'll leave you to your dinner, please ignore us,' Sam says to him cheerfully. He turns back to face me. 'What's your problem?' he asks in a low whisper.

'You,' I reply. I didn't want to say anything, not on Bells's last night, but I can't help it. I lean closer towards him. 'I heard everything you said on the phone just now. Everything.'

Sam runs a hand through his hair. 'What?' he says.

'This isn't what you signed up for, is it?' I try to look discreetly at Bells.

'Hello, Katie,' she says, holding out her hand.

'Sorry, Bells. Not now,' I say, turning back to Sam.

'Don't know what you're on about,' he mutters. 'I was talking to a client.'

'Don't lie!'

'Don't lie!' Bells repeats.

'You were talking to Maguire!'

'To Maguire.'

'What is your sister going on about?' he says to Bells, trying to keep his composure.

'Sam. I heard.'

'Well, you shouldn't have been fucking eavesdropping.'

'Sam said F word,' Bells laughs.

'Bells!' both Sam and I say together.

'You having pudding?' she asks me.

'I'm pretty stuffed.' He waves a hand at a waiter.

'I want a pudding.'

He allows Bells a quick chocolate brownie. While she is still eating he grabs his jacket from the back of the chair, tells me he's going to pay the bill and that we need to be ready, by the door, in five minutes. Sharp.

Sam sweeps round the corner in his BMW.

'Slow down!' I insist from the back seat as we hurtle round another corner. I press my foot on an imaginary brake.

'It's all right, shut up. These cars are designed to belt along.' He puts his foot down even harder.

'Not funny, Sam, not funny.' Bells is grappling with her seatbelt.

'Bells, don't take the belt off,' I tell her.

I hear a click just as her door swings open and nearly hits a lamppost.

'Jesus!' Sam shouts. He grabs Bells's floppy jumper and pulls her in, one hand anchored firmly on the leather steering wheel.

'Pull over!' I am shouting, turning from Bells, to the road, to Sam, to Bells again. 'Sam, STOP!'

He pulls over swiftly, the tyres burning against the pavement, and turns off the engine. Thank God no one was driving behind us.

'Not funny, Sam. Not funny,' Bells berates him.

'Christ Almighty,' he repeats, his head in his hands and almost weeping. 'My new car.'

'But you nearly fell out of Sam's car, Bells. Promise me you won't do it again.' I lift her feet on to the bed.

'Too fast, Katie.'

'I know.'

'Was scared.'

'So was I, but you could really have hurt yourself.'

She is still quiet.

''Night, Bells, sleep well.' I turn off the main light.

'Nothing around me?'

'Nothing around you.'

'Promise.'

'I promise.'

21

I stand on Bells's bed and take down her Stevie Wonder poster. The Beatles poster is pulled off the door. I open her wardrobe and take out her Chinese wedding outfit.

We fold her baggy jumpers, shirts and holey vests together. They go into the zip bag along with the medley of junk, including the buzzing device, her CDs, notepad, photograph album, box of paints and the football badges.

'Do you want to wear these . . . or these?' I hold up her large black boots and the purple pixie pair. Today she's wearing a black T-shirt I gave her from the shop with a little silver star in the middle, which is sadly hidden by her dungarees on top. She decides to go for the pixie boots.

Her large purple zip bag is finally packed; there is only one Stevie Wonder CD we can't find. 'I'll send it on to you, promise.'

Bells doesn't appear too bothered. She tells me she will take the sheets off the bed, like they do at home.

"Bye, Isabel,' Sam says, standing at her bedroom door in

his jeans and leather jacket. 'It was great to meet you. Come and see us again.' He looks relieved as he scans the room, seeing it clean and clutter-free. Back to his normal routine. Nothing out of place; CDs in their correct boxes; the kitchen surfaces positively sparkling. I'm going to miss Bells's meals. What do you do in a kitchen if you don't cook, Sam?

'Thank you, Sam.' Bells goes forward and shakes his hand.

'It's a pleasure. No problemo.' He looks pleased that she thanked him without any prompting. 'Katie, I'll see you later.' Sam and I didn't say a word to each other last night. By the time I had said goodnight to Bells he was asleep on the sofa, so I left him there. I told him this morning that we needed to talk. Now he walks away and minutes later I hear the door shut.

'Right, ready to rock 'n' roll?' I ask her, and put a hand over my mouth. Without thinking I say things that Sam would say and I don't like it any more.

Bells says goodbye to her bedroom.

I take her bag and shut the door behind us.

'Passengers going to Haverford West need to change at Swansea,' says the loudspeaker. People are bustling past while Bells and I stand at the information desk waiting for Fiona, one of the staff in Wales, to meet us. She is going to accompany Bells back home. She should be here by now; the train leaves in ten minutes.

'Got your ticket?'

'Yes, Katie.'

'What does Fiona look like?' I am scanning the crowds. Perhaps we're in the wrong place?

'She's fat.'

'Bells!' I laugh at her.

'Like partridge.'

'Eddie and Eve would love to see you again, you'll come back, won't you?' I would love to see you again, that is what I should be telling her.

'Very nice people. Would like to see Mark again.'

'I know, me too.' I still think about Mark and what he did for us. We didn't manage to meet up again, and now that Bells is going, I have no excuse to ring him. Yet it's hard to believe I'm never going to see him again. Was he only supposed to come into our lives for that single brief evening? 'If I do see him, what message shall I give?'

Bells rocks forwards and backwards. 'Will he marry me! Here's Fiona!' Bells waves her hands in a flutter as Fiona waddles towards us in a checked skirt and white blouse with a frilly collar.

'Hello, I'm Katie.' I shake her hand.

'Hello,' she says. 'Hi, Bells. How are you?' Her voice warms up. 'How was your holiday? Mary Veronica has missed you very much, she got back yesterday.' She takes Bells's bag and I walk behind them. 'We'd better be quick, I'm running late, aren't I? I thought we were meeting at the ticket desk?' She turns briefly to me.

'No, I'm sure we said . . .'

'Never mind, Katie, all is well. Was it fun?' she continues.

'Yes, fun,' Bells says. Fiona marches us on to the correct platform. I won't have time to say anything now, I panic to myself, feet pattering along to keep up. I've had all of this morning to tell Bells that I would like to visit her, that I have enjoyed the last few days so much, but I haven't said anything. 'Got your ticket?' is about the sum of it.

'Went on London Eye,' Bells says. 'Saw all London.'

'How marvellous,' Fiona says. 'It sounds like you've had a smashing time.' She turns to me. 'Thank you, Katie. We'd better get on, the train leaves in a couple of minutes.'

I look at the big clock, the seconds ticking by.

'We want to make sure we're near the buffet car,' Fiona says, stepping up on to the train. Bells follows her. 'Say goodbye to your sister, Bells.'

NO! I want to shout. This is not how I imagined it would be. I want to say goodbye properly.

''Bye, Katie, 'bye.' Bells stops on the step and tries to turn round.

'Stand away from the door,' the conductor instructs as Fiona is stowing Bells's bag in the luggage rack.

'Isabel, be careful. Mind the gap. Get right inside,' Fiona orders.

''Bye, Bells,' I call. She turns and waves at me. ''Bye, Katie. Thank you for having me.' I watch her and Fiona taking their seats. Bells sits by the window, Fiona next to her. Bells looks out of the window and waves again. She hits her hand against the glass. The conductor blows his whistle.

'Hang on, don't go!' I push past the conductor and press the red button to open the automatic doors into their carriage. Fiona is about to say something but I don't let her. 'I want to say goodbye to my sister, properly,' I say, swallowing hard.

'Hello, Katie,' Bells says.

'Hi, Bells,' I say, my eyes beginning to fill. 'I . . .' Don't lose it now. The other passengers start to sigh around us. 'Excuse me,' the conductor says, 'unless you are travelling to Swansea, can you please get off the train?'

'Get a move on!' a boy jeers, pelting a tennis ball towards me. It hits Fiona on the forehead instead, making Bells laugh. 'Some of us are in a hurry.'

I wince. 'Fiona, I'm sorry, did that hurt?'

'Well, it did, rather.' She sits in a more upright position.

'Push off!' another person says. Normally passengers are so buttoned up they don't say a word to one another. Why is it that today everyone is being so vocal?

'Quiet. She wants to say goodbye to her sister,' says the passenger opposite Fiona and Bells. I smile at him gratefully.

'Yeah! Let her stay and say goodbye nice and proper,' adds another.

Even Fiona smiles at me now. 'Come on, quickly, say goodbye.'

I lean across and kiss Bells clumsily on the top of her embroidered hat. My handbag bashes into Fiona's large stomach. 'I'll come and see you, and I'll write, I promise. Will you come back to London too?'

'Yes, Katie, yes.'

I dare to make one final move before I am hurled off the train. I kiss her on the cheek. ''Bye, Bells. I've loved having you to stay.' I dig into my bag and find the photograph the Japanese couple took of us on the London Eye. I made a copy for myself on Sam's computer. 'I thought you could show your friends? Maybe put it in your album.'

'Yes, Katie, I will. Loverly photo. Thank you, Katie. Thank you.'

The conductor rolls his eyes at me as he finally blows his whistle. I jog along the platform to keep up with the moving train. Bells waves at me and I wave back, tears running down my cheeks. ''Bye, Bells. 'Bye.' I wave one last time.

I stare ahead, not knowing what to do next. I straighten my dress, flick back my hair and take a deep breath. You walk away and your life carries on, I tell myself. I half laugh. At least I told her. I could have let her go without saying anything, but I didn't. I told her how much I'd enjoyed having her around; I feel we have made a start. One tiny part of my family has come back to me.

I walk away from the quiet of the empty platform and back into the hustle and bustle of the normal world.

22

The house feels eerily quiet as I walk inside. I go downstairs to the kitchen and expect to see Bells sitting in the corner eating her homemade muesli and prodding the milk-bottle sculpture. I give it a prod for her. I want to see some of her clutter in the room – a cookbook, an empty Diet Coke can or a baking tray lying on the table. Instead the kitchen table is smooth and clean. I even miss Stevie Wonder playing in the background. It's almost as bad as when Mum's classical music stopped being played at home. I turn the radio on – anything for some noise. I have to get ready for work, yet am unable to get myself into gear. Finally I walk upstairs and then up the further flight to our bedroom. I can't help looking into Bells's bedroom once more. The room is now back to a stark white again. I'm about to pick up the lamp from the corner of the room but then decide against it. It can stay there. I like it.

I take a long shower. As the hot water blasts against my face I turn my mind to Sam. What am I going to do? Is it time to call it quits? But if we do split up, where am I going to live? Isn't it time I thought about buying my own place? I'm nearly thirty. What's stopping me?

I have always lived with boyfriends, avoiding the responsibility of a mortgage. Every penny I have earned has gone into my business. I have drifted along in my twenties, focusing mainly on my career and going from one unsuitable relationship to another. If I go back to the beginning, I lost my virginity to Scott when I was eighteen. He was the electrician with tattooed arms. I met him while I was studying for my A levels. We went out for six wonderful months. I moved into his bedsit. Mum accused me of using our house as a hotel. 'You only come home to do your washing and have a free meal,' she said. I was permanently hungry going out with Scott because all we could afford to eat were cornflakes, cornflakes and more cornflakes. It was exciting when we discovered we could make a new meal out of Frosties and cream, like a *crème brûlée*.

Next there was Alex, a singer and guitarist who toured the country playing gigs. I was at art college in London and quickly moved in with Alex to avoid student accommodation. His flat was more like a hole but that didn't matter. I loved telling Mum that I had landed on my feet. Look at me in London, I wanted to shout. I have a boyfriend, a home, and I have my place on an art course.

Things petered out with Alex eventually. The next boyfriend broke my heart by sleeping with my flatmate, Fran.

He was training to be an architect. He was intelligent and decent, the last person I could have imagined cheating on me. I made a promise never to let myself get so hurt again. So after that I had a series of easy, let's face it, lazy, relationships. Look at the one before Sam. He was always abroad working, so in reality I was leading a single life. Emma says it's better not to be in a relationship than to be in one that's going nowhere. Better to go alone than be badly accompanied, she says. I know Sam isn't exactly one of her favourite people. . . I wash my hair, the shampoo lathering in my hands. If he and I split up, I lose this place and the convenience of living so near to the shop. I'll miss the steam room, too. I mean, who else has a steam room?

I laugh at myself. Come on, Katie, those aren't real reasons to stay with someone. What about love and commitment, kindness and passion? What about caring for someone so much that I'd put their welfare before my own? Would I die for Sam? I did love being with him until two weeks ago. Whatever his faults, he has his good points too. He has gone out of his way to book this weekend for us. He's taking me skiing this Christmas. He is confident, successful, he can be charming. I love our secret dances in the kitchen. When we first met he made me feel like the only person in the room. He is supportive of my work. Look at the way he organized my fashion show at his client's house. If someone had told me then I would be considering splitting up from him I would have laughed. How can so much change in two weeks? Will I regret it if I act rashly?

Maybe we need to talk, I mean *really* talk about *real* things. For instance, I want to know more about his family. I'd like him to tell me about his father. If we stand a chance of staying together we have to be honest with one another and share more. I know I'm very much to blame as I started the whole charade off by not telling him about Bells. If we do break up I will miss our lifestyle. But is that enough for me any more?

I lock up the shop, but I don't want to go home. Bells gave life to Sam's house and now it's back to being a show home. I find myself going to the bar across the road and ordering a drink. Half a bottle of wine and an hour later my mobile rings and Sam's number appears in the box. I ignore it. He tries to call again, but I let it ring.

If you could write the script of your life, what would you write? It's another cliché that Sam throws at me from time to time, but at least this one does have some meaning. I would not be sitting here with nothing but failed relationships trailing behind me. Yet I can do something about it, I tell myself. I pick up my mobile and am about to ring Emma. Then I put it down. I know what she would tell me, and isn't it about time I made a decision like this on my own? I need to stop limping along in no-man's-land. Of course I know what I have to do.

*

It's late by the time I make it back to Sam's. He's sitting on the sofa reading the *FT*.

'We need to talk,' I say, walking over to the window.

He puts the paper down. 'If it's about last night, let's leave it, hey? It was a load of bravado, Katie. You know what I'm like with the lads, especially Maguire. I didn't mean any of it.'

I'm not even sure how much I care about it now. I don't feel any anger or betrayal. I don't feel a thing. 'I've been thinking about this weekend . . . maybe we should cancel it. I think we've got a few things to sort out.'

'Sorry?'

'The hotel? I don't want to go,' I say quietly.

'You're joking, right?'

I shake my head.

'The room's booked. There's no way I'll get a refund at such short notice.'

He is unreal. 'Don't you want to know why I don't want to go? Sam, this can't go on!'

'What can't go on?' He slams his glass on to the table. 'This is about last night, isn't it?'

'Yes . . . no . . . I don't know. Come off it, you probably did mean what you said. This isn't what you signed up for. When we started going out, you knew nothing about my family. Well, now you do. I come with Bells. Also, I know nothing about yours. Why won't you tell me about your dad?'

'There's nothing to tell,' he exclaims, exasperated. 'He's a workaholic, I never see the guy, what else is there to say?'

I frown with frustration. 'Where do you see us going?'

'Oh no, don't do this, Katie.'

'Where are we heading?' I persist.

'I thought we were having a great time, having some fun. Clearly,' he huffs, 'I was under the wrong impression.'

'We can go out, go to fancy hotels and expensive restaurants, go skiing this Christmas, we can do all of that for another year or so, and then what?' I raise my voice. 'What next?'

'We wait and see. Jesus!' He stands up and faces me properly. 'Why are you so neurotic all of a sudden? What's your problem? What do you want? A ring on your finger?'

'Don't be stupid.'

'Well, what then? I thought we were happy the way things were.'

'But what about the future?'

'Bollocks to the future. Seize the day, I say. Worry about tomorrow,' he pauses, thinking, 'tomorrow.'

'If we're not right for each other we're wasting our time.'

Sam ignores me. 'We're going to that hotel, it's all booked,' he says, his tone overbearing. 'We need this time together. Can I have the nice fun Katie back, please? Where's she gone?'

'Sam, you meant what you said last night,' I now say with

conviction. 'You couldn't hack Bells, and the two weeks were pretty much a disaster.'

'It wasn't that bad, was it? I thought we got on fine. Anyway, she's gone now.'

'I'm not getting through to you at all, am I?'

Sam stares at me, confused.

'What do you care about, Sam?'

'Look, you're not my flipping shrink. You've changed. Ever since Bells came to stay everything has changed.'

I nod, realizing he's right. 'You're a good friend, Sam,' I say, knowing even that isn't true. Once we part I can't imagine meeting him for coffee. What would we talk about? 'We've had some good times, but . . .'

'No way,' he says, cutting me off. 'Uh-oh, no way.' He gets up. 'I think you should go.' He walks past me and out of the room. 'You can stay tonight, but I want you out by tomorrow. It's over.'

I don't shout or scream. I feel only relief. 'Done and dusted,' I say quietly to myself. '*Capisce?*' I sit down on the sofa and stare out of the window. Sam gave nothing to me, and I realize I gave nothing of myself to him, something I have been doing for too long.

I key in the number and Dad answers immediately. They are due to come home in two days.

'Bells left today,' I tell him.

'You had a good time?' he asks, catching his breath.

I tell him about her stay, sensing he's only half listening. 'Can I have a word with Mum?'

'Katie, we have to go . . .'

'Hang on! How are you both? I tried to call you the other day . . .'

'Katie, I can't talk right now.'

'What's wrong?'

'Listen, I'll call you later.' And he hangs up.

I key in the number again, but it's switched off now.

I sit staring at the telephone. Something is clearly not right. What's going on? Why are we such a dysfunctional family?

Why can't we talk?

23

1990

Bells, Mum, Dad and I are sitting in a circle in a pastel blue-painted room, a plastic clock ticking in the background. The chairs were arranged like this when we arrived. I look around. This place reminds me of hospitals. It has that same clinical feel to it, the air tangy with disinfectant. Why are we here? All I did was steal a few eyeliners and records by Adam Ant and A-ha. I didn't even want them, the As were the closest to the door, that's all. Is that really so bad?

Mum looks uptight, legs firmly crossed along with her arms. Dad is tapping his knees hard, as if they are a pair of drums. Mum leans across and slaps his hand. 'Stop that,' she orders. Neither Mum nor Dad has said much since we arrived. Mum picked me up from school. At least I missed double physics.

'The Fletchers. Would you like to go in, please,' the

receptionist told us and pointed to the door with Family Clinic written on it.

Mum looked frantically at all the other miserable-looking patients waiting for their appointments before pushing Bells and me through the Family Clinic door with alarming speed. Dad joined us here, out of breath, complaining that he hadn't been able to see his last client at work because of this bloody session we were about to have. Bells is the only one who looks happy to be here. She is flicking through a *Woman's Realm* that she found on a table in the corner of the waiting room.

The door opens and a small man limps into the room. He is so skinny his grey trousers are held up by a shiny black belt. He carries a file labelled 'Fletcher Case'. He shakes Mum's and Dad's hands and smiles briskly at Bells and me. 'Hello, I'm Simon Shackleton,' he introduces himself. He is wearing a gold watch; black hairs sprout from his wrist to either side of the strap. I wonder what's wrong with his foot as he pulls up a chair to join our circle.

'What's wrong with your leg?' Bells asks immediately. 'You broken it?' If I'd asked like that I would be told off for being nosy.

I watch his mouth twitch as he smooths his thin brown hair across his forehead. 'We haven't come here to talk about my leg, now have we?' He smiles at Mum and Dad and they smile awkwardly back. 'I tend to arrange the chairs like this. It brings everyone close together,' he says.

I watch Simon Shackleton as he peers at the first page of our file. It looks far too big for a family that doesn't do anything most of the time. Are our problems really that bad? He closes the brown folder and looks at me. 'Katie, can you tell me a little bit about your family?' He leans back in his chair. For such a puny little man his voice is surprisingly bold and authoritative.

I look at Mum and Dad, who shift in their seats. 'They're all right.' I shrug. 'I don't know what else to say, really.' The plastic clock appears to be ticking even more loudly in the background. Mr Shackleton's eyes are focusing hard on me. After a lengthy pause he says, 'Well, perhaps I should make it a bit more specific. Why don't we go around the circle saying the things we like and find, let's say, *difficult* about each member of the family? It's an excellent way of seeing where the main problems lie. Maybe I should start with you, Mr Fletcher?'

Dad sits up and clears his throat. 'I love my family,' he states. 'I'm not going to pick out their bad points.' He shakes his head and sinks back in his chair again.

'Ah, so there are bad points?' Mr Shackleton twitches his bony nose.

'No family is perfect. Are you telling me yours is?' Dad's voice rises in indignation as he sits up again. Mum puts one hand on his thigh. Dad looks over at me and smiles sympathetically. It's a smile that suggests he is sorry for what he is about to say. The ticking of the clock is getting louder. I can hear the pages of Bells's magazine turning over and over. Finally Dad says, 'I do wish Katie hadn't got into trouble because then we wouldn't be here. We were doing fine until this.'

Mr Shackleton takes some more notes. 'Please go on, Mr Fletcher.'

'Katie has always been a good child. She has had to cope with a lot, help look after her sister Isabel and so on. I'm sure you are aware of the medical history of our younger daughter.'

Mr Shackleton nods. 'I am.' He taps the file.

Bells looks up from the magazine. 'Can we go?' she asks.

Mum tells her to be quiet. She had explained in the car why we were coming here today but Bells has clearly forgotten already.

'We are aware that it hasn't been easy for Katie. She has had to grow up quickly, fend for herself more. Katie's a great girl,' Dad continues. 'This is a phase, nothing more. I'm sure there are other families who need counselling a lot more than us.'

'Mr Fletcher, I am sure that is the case, but every family has their issues . . .'

'Exactly,' pounces Dad. 'We're no different. Do you counsel every family who has the odd hiccup, Mr Shackleton?'

'Mr Fletcher, I don't think you can call this a hiccup exactly. Stealing should be taken very seriously.'

'No like this man,' Bells says.

Mr Shackleton doesn't appear at all offended by her remark. I look at Dad. He has managed a smile. I am sure he wanted to say exactly what Bells just has. Part of me wants to reach across our circle and hug him.

'And I am sure you would agree with me that it is best to address this problem now,' Mr Shackleton intones.

Dad turns to Mum, begging her to help him out.

'To go back to what you asked us to do first, Mr Shackleton,' Mum says. 'I do find Katie, at times, difficult. She's very like I was at that age. Headstrong. She does things to cause a reaction. I think a lot of young girls do. It was very foolish of her to steal, but . . .'

'Why are you only going on about me?' I cry out then. 'I'm not the only person in this family. What about Bells? She never gets told off, she's never to blame for anything. Everyone just laughs, don't they? It's all one big joke when she does something naughty. But when I do something bad the police are knocking on the door.'

'Don't like it here,' Bells moans, kicking her legs restlessly. 'Want to go home.'

'It's not quite the same, Katie, and you know that only too well,' Mum points out calmly to me, although I can tell she is desperately trying to keep her voice in check. 'Mr Shackleton, is it really necessary for Isabel to come to these sessions? She doesn't understand why we're here. This is really to do with Katie, isn't it?'

'There you go again,' I screech. 'It's only ever *my* fault.'

I turn to Mr Shackleton, waiting for him to tell Mum and Dad that I'm right, it's not fair that I am the one they are criticizing. That he wants us to talk about everyone in the family. Instead he sits back as if to let us take over. I can't stand that smug smile imprinted on his face. What do you find difficult about your family? OK, my turn then.

'I hate it when you don't pick me up from school,' I tell Mum. 'I stand there at the gates waiting and all the other parents say to me, "Doesn't your mother know it's the end of term?" You look different too, in your painting stuff, it's embarrassing. I wish I could board there like some of the other girls. And I hate it that you didn't bother to come to my sports day. I had practised every lunch hour and after school, and all the parents were there except you. I won first prize for the high jump.'

'That was nearly three years ago, and I came to it.' Dad hunches forward defensively, now actively taking part. 'That's not fair, Katie.'

'Darling, it's OK, if this is how she feels.' Mum rests a hand on his. 'We need to listen.'

I stare at her again. 'I won the art and needlework pupil of the year award, not that you care!' Each week the school puts up the best drawing, painting or something someone has made, and I had won the most times in the year. Dad's face did go soft with pride when I told them that but Mum didn't say all that much.

'Now, that's out of order, Katie. Of course I care. Stop

feeling so sorry for yourself.' She looks pale. 'I'm sorry if I didn't say "Well done" enough or come to your sports day, but you have to understand your father and I only want what is best for you. And I do care,' she repeats. Is that water gleaming in her eyes? Real tears? 'We work hard so we can send you to one of the best schools and now we need to work doubly hard to make sure we can send Isabel to one of the top schools in the country next year.' Mum and Dad have spoken to me about this. They want to send Bells to a specialist school where she will be with others like herself. She will be taught all the normal things like reading and writing, and do arts and crafts, things like that.

'I'm afraid that sometimes we can't both get to your prize-givings, I wish we could, but at least one of us always comes,' Mum finishes.

'Well, it's usually Dad. You're always working, and I get bored at home. I can't even bring my boyfriends back to the house because Bells hits them in the balls. They run a mile. When they can,' I add.

Mr Shackleton straightens his hair.

'You don't have a boyfriend, do you?' Dad asks.

'I don't now! She,' I point to Bells, 'frightens them off.'

'Not funny, Katie,' Bells cries out.

'We hardly ever do normal things like go to the cinema or on holiday,' I continue remorselessly, 'we never do anything. I'm fifteen! If it wasn't for Emma living next door I'd run away. I'm going to leave home when I'm sixteen any-way. Then you'll be sorry.'

Mum and Dad look at each other. Dad looks hurt. I feel bad that I said that about sports day. He did come, and he entered the fathers' races. He even won the egg-and-spoon. Mum looks upset too. Good.

Mr Shackleton leans forward. 'I think we should prob-ably call it a day there,' he says. 'I found it interesting that you focused on the things you find difficult and never on the positive. All your energy is being channelled into see-ing faults in one another, which can't be healthy. I can see Katie feels neglected, she craves attention like any normal teenager. She wants to be praised. Am I right, Katie?' He turns to me expectantly. I can feel myself turning red now. 'From this first visit, I feel you all need to spend more time together, set aside a piece of quality time each day to be with one another. Communication is the key to under-standing our own and other people's needs.'

Mum grabs her handbag and we follow her out of the door. Mr Shackleton limps after us, smoothing his thin hair over his forehead, saying we must book in another appointment on our way out and that we have already made substantial progress by talking about these issues.

We never see him again.

24

I find Sam's car keys in his jacket pocket. I walk downstairs and out of the house. Who does Dad think he is fooling? Something is wrong.

As I drive down the grey motorway, I have this surreal feeling that I am looking down on myself, that it's not really me driving. I tap the steering wheel hard to reassure myself that I am in control. I turn the radio on, and then flick the switch off, left alone in an oppressive silence with only two thoughts racing through my mind. What am I doing, driving home late at night? Am I going mad?

I pull into our driveway. Mum and Dad's car isn't there and instantly I feel relieved. My house keys hang on an old rusty silver key-ring with the initial K. I bend down to open the bottom lock but the key won't turn. It isn't locked. I turn the key in the top lock and the door creaks open. Why hasn't Dad double-locked?

'Hello,' I call out, my voice echoing in the hallway. I pick up a pile of mail, place it on the hall table. The answer-phone is on but it isn't flashing. That's strange. Surely someone has rung them since they've been away?

The curtains are drawn in the sitting room. My heart races as I walk into the kitchen. The blinds are open, the plug switches on. There are two dirty mugs in the sink. Everywhere I look tells me they never went away. I open the fridge. There's a packet of chicken, sitting in its blue polystyrene tray, curling at the edges. I read the sell-by date and it was only two days ago. There's a box of eggs, butter and mayonnaise on the top shelf.

I walk upstairs. My pace quickens and soon I'm running down the landing and into Mum and Dad's bedroom. The bed hasn't been made. Mum's moisturizing cream sits on her dressing table, along with her hairbrush and tortoise-shell hair comb. I head into their bathroom. There are Mum's and Dad's toothbrushes, and my father's old-fashioned shaving cream. I turn away, unable to comprehend what's going on. Then I hear the front door opening.

The only immediate noise I can hear is my own breathing. 'Katie,' my father says in shock when he sees me at the top of the stairs. Mum stands next to him, her pale face vivid against her auburn hair.

My panic and fear turns to anger. 'Why aren't you in France?' Dad looks at Mum but neither of them says anything. I wait for some kind of explanation. 'What's going on? Why did you lie to me?' Mum walks past Dad, down the corridor and into the kitchen. 'Dad?' I press him.

He collapses in a heap on the bottom stair, his face buried in his hands. I rush downstairs and kneel down in front of him. 'Dad, what's wrong, what's happened?'

'I don't know where to start,' he says.

'Mum,' I call, my voice splintered with fear. I lift my hand off Dad's knee and walk into the kitchen. She's opening the drawer at the end of the kitchen table, where she keeps old letters from her mother and father. She's ripping them into shreds. 'What are you doing? Mum, please.' I shake her shoulders. 'Stop it! Mum, *please*, you're scaring me. What's wrong?'

'I don't know how to tell you,' she says finally.

'Why is Dad crying?'

'Because I've just been told I have a brain tumour.' She picks up another letter at random and tears it in half.

25

I watch Dad guiding Mum down the hallway. His arm is around her waist, and she moves one of her hands behind her back so that it gently touches his.

I walk back into the kitchen and sit down. 'This can't be happening, it's not true. Tell me it's not true,' I say over and over again.

'I can't,' Dad says as he sits down at the kitchen table.

I have to compose myself. 'How could you not have told me? Why are you going through this all alone?'

'We thought we'd never find ourselves in this position. Our GP told us it was nothing to worry about.'

'*What* was nothing to worry about?'

'Your mother had an epileptic fit six months ago . . .'

'An epileptic fit? Why didn't you . . . ?'

Dad stops me. 'We didn't tell you because when we went to see the GP he dismissed it as something that happens at our age. He told us to go away, not to worry about it.' Dad walks over to the drinks cabinet and pours himself a whisky. 'Then she had another one when she was in the kitchen cooking supper. She was standing right here, in this spot, making my stupid bloody supper. Chopping vegetables.

'And then she had another and another, the medication wasn't touching it. I insisted she saw a neurologist. You know what she's like, Katie, didn't want to accept anything was wrong. When I called you to ask if you could have Bells to stay, well, we went to see the neurologist two days later. I couldn't cope with Bells and this at the same time.'

I nod. 'I understand, but why didn't you tell me then?'

'Because we still desperately hoped it was nothing, that the fits could be controlled with medication. She had the EEG and again that showed nothing untoward. She did all those other ridiculous tests, you know, told to count backwards in sevens and to follow the doctor's finger with her eyes. She felt fine, nothing seemed wrong. Then he suggested doing an MRI and we got the results today. We've been at the hospital all day.' Dad collapses back down in a chair. 'There's a tumour growing and the epileptic fits were caused by increased pressure on the brain. The tumour may have been there for years.'

I don't know what to say.

'Believe me, Katie, I wanted to tell you so much, but she wouldn't hear of it. She felt there was no point in worrying you until we knew for sure what we were up against. We were going to tell you, I promise.'

'Can't she have an operation? Have it taken out?'

Dad cradles his head in his hands, trying to block out the world.

'Isn't there anything we can do?' I ask.

'Stop, Katie, please.' He crouches down on the floor. I have never seen my father cry. I move forward to hold him, tears streaming down my face now. He clings on to the back of my top, bunching the material in his fingers, twisting and pulling the fabric. His face is pressed against my shoulder, and I can feel my top grow damp with his tears.

'I can't live without her, Katie. I can't live without her.'

I sit on the old dressing-up box which has now been turned into a window seat in my bedroom. I light a cigarette. I can hear voices in the street, they sound happy. Maybe they have returned home from the pub after another evening out. Do they realize that their lives could change overnight? That something might happen to them tomorrow that could change everything? Of course they don't. They are just like I was a few weeks ago. Blundering on in my own world, thinking that it was a catastrophe when my father asked me to have Bells to stay; thinking it was the end of the world when she cut the labels out of my T-shirts. My mobile rings yet again and finally I take it out of my bag. It tells me I have three new voice messages. I dial 901.

'Where are you, and where's my fucking car?' Slam. 'It's me again,' Sam bellows. I switch it off midway through this ranting. I'll call him tomorrow to explain.

I walk down the dark corridor, past Bells's old bedroom. How are we going to tell her about Mum? We have to tell her. Mum and Dad can't lie to us any more, or try to protect us from the truth. It never helps; it only hurts.

I bend over the bathroom sink, feeling sick. I open the mirrored cupboard door and stare at the various bottles and potions. There's an assortment of bottles with screw caps and yellowish pills inside. Everything looks ancient. I pick up one bottle, dated 1974, and throw it into the sink. I pick up all the bottles in turn, there are so many – for stomach pains, chest pains, headaches – but none to help me sleep.

I stand in front of the mirror, the one where I used to stand and pray to God as a little girl to give me blonde hair and blue eyes. 'I know we aren't close, but I want her back. Dad needs her. Bells needs her. I need her. Oh, dear God, please make Mum better.'

'Katie.' Dad strokes my back, his voice calm.

'I can't sleep, Dad. I'm so scared . . .'

'Shh.' He puts an arm around my shoulders and walks me back to my bedroom.

I light another cigarette. Dad hates me smoking but he doesn't say anything. He sits down on the other end of the window seat. 'If I was going to start smoking, now would be a good time,' he says, taking off his black-rimmed glasses and rubbing his eyes.

I half laugh. 'Sorry, Dad, I know I shouldn't, but . . .'

'You smoke; you die. You don't smoke; you die. What sodding difference does it make?'

I inhale deeply. 'How's Mum?'

'Fast asleep.'

'Good. I can't believe this is happening.'

'Nor can I. Oh, Katie, what are we going to do?'

'I don't know.'

We sit quietly, staring out into the dark sky. 'Make a wish upon a star,' Dad says.

'Dad,' I say cautiously, 'when are we going to tell Bells?'

'Soon. Your mother and I have been talking about it.'

'I think we should call her tomorrow, tell her that Mum is unwell and that she should come home. It would hurt her so much if she found out we'd kept it from her. Mum can't go on trying to protect her, or thinking she won't be able to cope, because it only excludes her and makes her feel like she's not normal and . . .'

'Katie,' Dad stops me abruptly, 'you're right, we agree. We want her here with us. She's more precious to us than anything. You both are,' he adds.

I look at Dad. His eyes seem to be a paler blue, a washed-out version of their normal colour. He stares back at me quizzically. 'A few weeks ago you wanted nothing to do with Bells. I had to remind you that you even had a sister.'

I bite my lip. 'This is different.'

'Yes, I realize that, but you've changed. You're fighting for her.'

'I want to make up for being such a bad sister. Since she came to stay, well, we've become good friends. She's worth fighting for.'

Dad reaches out for my hand, grips it tightly. 'I'm so proud of you, Katie,' he says.

26

I wake up from a disturbed sleep. The walls see-saw around me. Where am I? It takes me a minute to recollect, and when I do my body feels heavy as I struggle to get up and put one foot in front of the other.

I find Mum in the kitchen, dressed in her tattered old bed-jacket and nightdress. She's rifling through the shelf that holds her cookery books and files. More letters are on the table, torn to pieces. She turns to me, a look of total calm on her face. 'Morning, Katie, did you sleep well?'

Confused more than anything, I tell her, 'Not bad. Mum, why are you tearing up your precious letters?'

'I don't want you and your father worrying about any of my business. The more I can get rid of now, the better.' She goes out of the kitchen, down the corridor, and climbs the two steps into her studio. 'What am I going to do with all these unfinished animals?' she asks herself. 'Take whatever you want, won't you, Katie?'

I pull a chair back and sit at her worktable. 'Mum, one of us *has* to tell Bells. I can't stop thinking about her.'

Mum agrees. 'Can you arrange for her to come home?'

'Yes. If she gets a mid-morning train I can pick her up later.'

'I'd do it, but . . .' Her voice tails off. 'I can't even drive,' she says, shamefaced. 'I feel so useless, like a toddler, your father chauffeuring me around everywhere.'

I look at her. She is pencil-thin, her cheekbones even more accentuated, her eyes large and haunting. Her bed-jacket is practically falling off her shoulders. 'It's all right. I can do it, Mum. Don't worry.'

'How am I going to tell darling Bells?'

'Dad and I will be here. We just need to be honest. Mum?'

'Yes?'

'What did the neurologist say, exactly?'

'He told me I would be in charge of my pain control,' she replies, her voice once again as calm as still water as she sits down with me.

I can't bear the idea of Mum being in pain. 'Is there anything more we can do?'

'He did say we should see someone else, in Southampton, a neurosurgeon, but . . .'

'But what?' A tiny flicker of hope presents itself. 'Let's see him.'

'Katie, the neurologist thinks it could well be malignant. I'm not sure I can stand any more tests only to be told exactly the same thing. I feel all right. Funnily enough, I can deal with this. I can't deal with your father spilling coffee all over the cream carpet, but . . .'

'Mum,' I try to slow her down, 'I don't care about Dad spilling coffee right now.'

'I can deal with this. I need to prepare myself, organize things, that's all. I don't feel ill. In fact, it's hard to believe anything is actually wrong with me. I want to enjoy the time I have left.'

I shake my head. 'Mum, you need to see the surgeon.'

'I want to go on holiday with your father. We always promised ourselves we'd go on a trip down the Nile, or else go back to Paris again. Or visit our old friends in France whom we haven't seen for fifteen years.'

'The ones you pretended to be visiting.'

'I'm sorry. I shouldn't have made your father lie. We were wrong about that. I would love to see them,' she insists. 'None of us will have changed; we'll just have grey hair.'

'You can go, you can do anything you want, but I think we should follow the doctor's advice and see the surgeon.' I lean closer towards her, my elbows pressed hard against her worktable. 'I can't live with the knowledge that we didn't even try.'

'Nor can I,' Dad says, as he walks into Mum's studio in his frayed dressing gown and leather slippers. He sits down at the table, looking more positive this morning. 'I was going to say exactly the same thing.' He's holding the piece of paper with the surgeon's name and number on it.

Dad, Mum, Bells and I are sitting around the kitchen table. Dad has made a pot of tea, but no one has touched their cup.

How are we going to tell Bells?

When I picked her up from the station earlier this afternoon her first question was 'How's Mum?' I took her purple bag. 'She's looking forward to seeing you,' I said, unable to look her in the eye.

'How's France? They have good holiday?'

How are we going to tell her?

Mum is now wearing slim-fitting linen trousers with a white cotton shirt, her bobbed hair pulled back into her tortoiseshell clip. 'Bells, would you like some of your special sage tea?' she asks, handing her a plate of chocolate digestives.

Here we are, trying to be a normal family having tea, when everything is falling apart. Dad and Mum look at one another. It's like a game of Wink Murder, each trying to signal the other to start.

'Darling,' Mum says, looking directly at Bells, 'I wanted you to be here because I have something to tell you. I'm so sorry.' She reaches out to hold Bells's hand, but Bells won't let her take it.

'What sorry for?' she asks.

'I have a brain tumour.' The words are out so quickly that I have to catch my breath.

We all wait for Bells to say something. Anything. She clenches one of her hands into a fist and uses it to hit the other. 'You going to die like Uncle Roger?' she asks, rocking backwards and forwards in her chair. The room is utterly silent except for Bells's heavy breathing.

'Yes, I'll be joining Uncle Roger. I'm sure we'll have lots of fun up there together,' Mum says, her eyes looking upward as if to heaven. 'We'll have whisky and cherry cake parties.'

Bells stands up and leaves the kitchen. 'Going to watch *Titanic*,' she says.

Mum sits back with a look of relief. 'I'll talk to her again when she's ready. Let her watch *Titanic*.'

Dad nods. Mum takes a digestive biscuit. 'Well done, darling, you bought the dark chocolate ones.'

'No!' I shout, slamming my cup on to the table, tea spilling everywhere. 'You talk to her now. You tell her that we're going to see the surgeon, that we're waiting for the scans to be sent to him and that when they are, we're seeing him.'

Mum and Dad stare at me.

'Bells doesn't want jokes about Uncle Roger, for Christ's sake. She needs to understand. I'm fed up with none of us talking, pretending it's all normal and everything is OK, when it *isn't*.'

'Katie? Are you quite finished?' Mum asks.

We can hear the theme music to *Titanic* playing in the background.

'No, not quite,' I reply. 'I don't care if the boat's about to hit the iceberg. You go in there and turn *Titanic* off. You tell her now.'

I'm eavesdropping outside the sitting-room door.

'You scared?' Bells asks Mum.

'Yes, but I've got all my family around me.'

There's another long silence. I think Mum is comforting her. Suddenly the door opens and I move away, but it's obvious I've been listening. 'I'm sorry . . . for shouting earlier,' I say to Mum. She looks exhausted.

'You were right. Now, if you don't mind, I need to be on my own.' She touches my shoulder gently before walking upstairs. I hear her bedroom door shut before I go into the sitting room to join my sister.

27

It is the morning of Mum's operation. Dad, Bells and I are by Mum's bedside.

'I think we can do something about this,' the surgeon had said, holding the MRI scan. 'I think the tumour could be benign, I can't be absolutely sure until we operate, but I would strongly advise you to have the operation.'

'What makes you think it might be benign?' Dad asked, trying to contain his hope.

'From how it looks on the scan. It may also have a clear margin to cut around.'

'So you're saying it isn't malignant?' I asked, glancing at my father. We had been expecting confirmation, not a different assessment altogether.

'I can't be absolutely sure, but if we do nothing, we shall never know.'

I'd wanted to hug him, get down on bended knee and pray to God. Dad had held Mum's hand so tightly that I thought her bones might crack.

'Thank you very much,' she'd said, as if he had told her she could have pickle with her cheese. 'When can you slot me in?'

Now Dad sits awkwardly in the light blue armchair next to Mum's bed. I know he hates hospitals, despite being so used to them. 'It never gets any easier,' he'd confided in me. Bells is sitting next to him. She hasn't said a word this morning. The only thing I can hear is her rattling chest.

'How are you feeling?' I ask Mum.

'Great.' She clutches my hand. Besides her hospital gown, she is wearing only her gold wedding band and the plastic hospital wristband with her name and date of birth on it. Normally Mum wears her aquamarine engagement ring, watch and her two gold bracelets. Everything about her looks bare, stripped down.

'I'm ready to face it.' She breathes deeply. 'I'm so glad you're all here with me.'

Bells bangs her forehead with her fist. She stands up, sits down, stands up again and then circles the bed like a trapped animal in a cage. 'Sweetheart, will you sit down?' Mum pleads, clearly upset. Were we wrong to bring Bells here? No. We couldn't have left her at home. Besides, Mum wanted her here.

Bells grabs her inhaler from her pocket.

'I'm really thirsty. Can you get me a drink?' I ask in desperation. Dad immediately takes Bells off 'on a coffee run'.

I look at Mum. It is the first time we have been on our own today. Her green eyes are large and focused. 'Tell me about Sam,' she says. Anything to fill the silence. 'Why did you break up? Was it because of Bells?'

'In a way. I think I would still be going out with him had it not been for her staying with us,' I admit.

Mum raises her eyebrows inquisitively. 'What do you mean? Did she hit him in the balls?' A small smile lights up her face, making her eyes look less penetrating.

'No, Bells has replaced whacking men hard in the balls with swapping their CDs around. Sam wasn't nasty to her,' I continue. 'He did take us out for a meal once, but he was so embarrassed when we met his old boss at the next table. Some of it's my fault. I never told him about her properly, he didn't . . .'

'Oh, rubbish, Katie.' Mum does that familiar crow of incredulity that I have always found off-putting and heavily critical. Funnily enough, now I am pleased to hear it. 'I don't know Sam, but all I will say is that when we had Bells, it sifted the good friends from the bad. Some of them disappeared overnight; they couldn't handle it at all. Will-o'-the-wisps.'

I can't help but smile. 'Will-o'-the-wisp? Wasn't there a TV programme called that?'

'I don't know, darling, probably. Off they go at the first sign of trouble, and then – puff!' She claps her hands together. 'As if by magic they come back when it suits them. Gerald and Sue are like that,' she says.

'You're right. Sam *is* a will-o'-the-wisp.' I have this image of him disappearing from my life like a plume of smoke evaporating into nothing. He came to collect his car, told me how sorry he was to hear about Mum, handed me my post, and then he was gone. He told me he would keep in touch, but I am quite certain I shall never hear from him again.

'Sometimes you find out about people the hard way,' Mum says. 'It's often the least likely ones who become wonderful friends. There are people who are outstandingly nice, others who are mediocre and some who are bloody awful,' she concludes, as if visualizing ticking the appropriate box. 'It sounds to me like Sam was pretty mediocre. Not good enough for you, Katie.'

'We weren't right for each other.'

'No, he wasn't good enough for my Katie.' I can see she is trying hard not to cry. 'Tell me more about Bells's visit,' she says, smiling bravely.

I decide to tell her about Bells running away that wet afternoon. I tell her about my saviours, Mark and the American lady in the park. 'I was terrified. I would never have forgiven myself if something had happened to her. It was all my fault.'

'It's easy to lose your rag.' Mum looks directly at me now.

'I didn't realize what a full-time job it is,' I run on. 'Being with Bells is fun but exhausting. A trip round Sainsbury's took hours! She wanted to talk to almost every shopper.' It makes me think of Mark and how much I'd like to see him again.

Mum laughs knowingly.

'How old you are?' I imitate.

'What wrong with you?' Mum follows.

I tell her about the poker night and Mum laughs so loudly while thumping her hand against her thigh that the other people in the ward cannot help but look our way. 'It sounds like you had a very funny time. You see, it's much more fun for Bells to visit you than her boring old parents all the time.'

'We went on the London Eye. Mum, it was wonderful. Bells and I did bond, we got to know one another again. I want you to know that.' I reach into my bag and take out a letter she wrote to me.

'*Dear Katie Fletcher,*' I read out. 'I love the way she writes my surname,' I add, smiling. '*Very kind you to have me to stay in London. Very nice bedroom, lots of white. Nice house. You do that remember going to London Eye. I . . .*'

She has Tippexed a word out here.

'*I loved to go, saw all London and very loverley time with you on London Eye. Mark a very loverley man. You seen Mark? Mr Vickers too a very nice man. I am sorry I had to go, very kind you to invite me to come to London. Wonderful you. Hope not very Longtime to see you again. Nice you, very kind you, please send you my love. Thank you.*'

She has signed it in pen: '*Love, Bells. Ps Please RSVP me soon.*'

Mum rests her head back against the pillow. 'Your father knew it would be good for you to spend time together. He's a wise old thing.'

'When you're better, we'll go on the Eye. You're going to come up to London and we'll go out for lunch and do fun things. Pact?'

I wait for her to answer.

'Katie, if I die . . .'

'You won't.'

'If I die,' she continues calmly, 'you'll take care of Bells and your father, won't you?'

'Mum, don't . . .'

'You were the one who made me realize we must be honest and say what we feel.'

I nod, reluctantly.

'I need to say it while they're not here. They'll be back in a minute.' She adjusts her position in the bed. 'Your father and I were going to redecorate the house and . . . well, he wouldn't have a clue,' she whispers, leaning closer towards me. 'You'll help him?'

'OK,' I say, feeling my bottom lip quiver, just like Dad's does when he's about to cry.

'And you'll be there for Bells? You'll go to her open days and visit her at weekends?'

'Yes, I promise. All the time.'

'I'm so glad we can talk like this, that we didn't need Mr Shackleton!' Mum starts to laugh and cry in between with relief. 'Do you remember his plastic belt and greasy hair? Your father still won't talk about it.'

'Funnily enough I was thinking about him only the other day.'

Mum looks like she is gearing herself up to say more. 'But who will look out for Katie?' she says, taking my hand again.

At that moment Dad and Bells return. Dad is holding a plastic tray with two cups of coffee on it. He sits down at the end of the bed. 'How're you, Mum?' Bells asks, rocking forward.

A nurse comes to the bedside. 'They're ready for you now,' she says.

Then they will shave Mum's hair, I can't help thinking.

Bells walks away. 'Don't like it here . . . not nice here.'

'Bells!' Mum calls out. 'Please come back. Will you go and get her?' she urges Dad. 'Let's get this over with as quickly as possible.'

Dad brings her back, trying to reassure her that nothing bad is going to happen.

'Say goodbye to your mother,' the nurse says impatiently to Bells.

I give her a hard, accusing look. How could she make it sound so final?

Bells is rubbing her head and breathing heavily. ''Bye,

226

Mum,' she says finally, throwing an arm over Mum's stomach and resting her head against the theatre gown. "Bye, Mum.'

Mum strokes her hair. 'I love you. I'll see you later,' she says.

Dad is furiously writing lists at the kitchen table.

Bells is watching *Titanic*, but she doesn't make any sound when it's about to hit the iceberg.

I don't know what to do with myself. All I can do is look at the clock and watch the seconds tick by. Slowly.

Eventually the telephone rings and Dad and I move to it like lightning. 'You take it,' I say.

Dad picks up. 'She's conscious,' he is saying, clearly repeating what the surgeon is telling him. 'It certainly looked benign.'

'Bells!' I scream. 'Bells! Mum's OK!'

'Mum going to be all right,' Bells says, joining us.

'But what?' Dad asks.

I stop abruptly. Bells stands next to me. 'Mum all right,' she repeats.

'Oh, I see,' Dad says gravely.

'What? What?' I demand.

'What?' Bells follows.

Dad flaps his hand furiously to shut us up. 'OK, we'll be there right away,' he says.

28

'Go home,' Mum insists again, after I have given her some more water. 'You look even worse than me.'

I look at her. Her skin is so pale that she is almost camouflaged by the white pillow and sheets. Nothing covers her head except for a fine stubble of hair and a scar on the left-hand side of her scalp, curved like a question mark. It's two weeks after the operation. It was a success in that the tumour was benign and was taken out; but the surgery left her weak and with virtually no movement on her right-hand side. She couldn't even turn herself over in bed. Everything had to be done for her and she slept a lot of the time. None of us had had any idea that she might not be able to walk after the operation. 'What's a Zimmer frame doing at the end of the bed?' was the first groggy question she asked us. Her next concern was not being able to sign her own name. 'Mum, why are you trying so hard to write your signature?' I had asked her, watching her wrestle with the pen and paper.

'I've told you. If I'm going to be like this for ever I want at least to be able to get at my money,' she said breathlessly.

Thankfully the physiotherapy is already helping her to regain strength and mobility. She has started to get up and walk very slowly, up and down the ward. To say we are relieved is a gross understatement. It is a miracle. When I watched Mum walk for the first time, I was clapping so vigorously that the palms of my hands were burning red.

'Please, Katie, go home, darling. Take the awkward squad home too.' She is referring to Dad, who is talking to one of the doctors. She thinks he fusses too much over her. She shuts her eyes. 'I need to get some sleep. And you do too,' she adds.

When I walk into the house it's quiet. No Stevie Wonder. No Beatles. I find Bells in the kitchen again, wearing Mum's denim apron, now quite grubby with a blob of spinach down the front, her small hands encased in red-spotted oven gloves. Yesterday Dad and I returned home and she had made us a cauliflower cheese, using all the leftovers in the fridge. It was the most delicious cauliflower cheese I had ever tasted too. The day before that she cooked a courgette and asparagus quiche. She chose not to come to the hospital today. In fact she hasn't been since the morning of Mum's operation. Each day we ask her if she wants to come, but all she says is, 'Tell Mum get better.' Dad and I make a point of not leaving her for long on her own, coming and going in shifts.

'Hello, how's Mum?' she asks immediately, putting a white dish into the oven and then turning to face me. 'Mum all right?'

'She's OK, a bit grumpy and tired. She sends lots of love. Bells, wow, what are you cooking?'

'Stuffed pancakes with ricotta and spinach.' Suddenly the smell makes me ravenous. 'Made strawberry fool too. You like strawberries? Mum loves strawberries.'

'I love them. You're a star,' I tell her, collapsing into a chair. The table is littered with a cooking bowl, broken eggshells, flour, a greasy block of butter and a few bruised strawberries that haven't made it into the fool. It's a comforting mess.

'How's Mum?' she asks again, yet I know she's not expecting another answer. 'Make you drink,' she says, opening the cupboard. The bottle of vodka is laid out for me; Dad's whisky is ready for him.

She hands me my vodka, which I take gratefully. 'Bells, you really are amazing.'

Dad walks into the kitchen. 'Bells has made pancakes for supper and fixed us a drink,' I tell him and he smiles.

'How delicious. Thank you, darling.'

'I might take my drink up with me, have a bath,' I say, prising my heavy body from my seat.

'Sit down, Dad,' Bells insists, guiding him to a chair. 'Sit.'

I walk upstairs and into my bedroom. Bells has made my bed – just as she has done each day since the operation.

I find myself walking into Mum and Dad's bedroom. She has stripped that too and there are clean sheets waiting to be put on; all of Dad's dirty laundry is in the wicker basket by the door. I notice she has placed the photograph of Mum and Dad's wedding by his bedside light. Bells is like our fairy godmother. I sit down on the bed and pick up the photograph. It's funny to think she and I weren't born when that picture was taken; it was the two of them together, starting out. Mum was twenty-six when she married. At the age I now am she would have had me.

I don't even hear Bells sitting down next to me. 'Mum all right?' she presses again.

'She's fine. She wants to come home, though. She hates hospitals.' As I speak I realize that wasn't the most sensitive thing to say in front of her. 'Sorry, you more than anyone know what I mean.' I put my head into my hands.

'What wrong?'

'I'm tired.'

'How's Sam?'

'We're not going out any more.'

'Not nice, Sam.'

'He was all right.' I hold the wedding picture in front of both of us.

'Beautiful Mum,' Bells says.

'Very.' I put the photograph back on the table. 'Thank

you for making my bed, thank you for everything, Bells. You've done so much these last few weeks. Dad and I, well, we couldn't have managed without you.'

Bells rocks forward, scratching her forehead. I don't think she knows what to say or do when someone compliments her. 'In Wales, have cleaning rota,' she tells me. 'Clean Ted's room. Ted my friend.'

I smile at her. 'Ted's lucky. I want someone to make things better, Bells. For you, Dad, for me, and for Mum, particularly Mum. I want us all to be happy.'

Right now I feel my entire life is slipping away from me.

'Mum didn't die like Uncle Roger,' she says.

She's right. I know I should be feeling fortunate. Mum is going to be all right. Yet, now that we know she's going to get better, I can't help thinking about everything else. My job doesn't feel that important any more, I have no Sam – not that he's a great loss, but I do miss that feeling of security. I have no home. I'm worried for Dad. I'm worried about Mum and how we are going to cope when she comes home. I'm worried about everything; it's no wonder I can't sleep. Bells is the one ray of light. Alone, Dad and I would have been eating takeaways and sleeping on grubby sheets.

'Do you get lonely, Bells?'

'At times.'

'When?'

'Night-time.'

'Me too. Why at night?'

'Dark. Don't like dark.'

'I want everything to go back to normal. I want . . . hey, where are you going?' I smile. She's bored with me. No wonder. I stare up into the ceiling. Two minutes later I am still staring at the same spot until I feel a prod. Bells is standing in front of me with the telephone.

'Who is it?'

'Someone on phone for you.'

'Who?' I repeat, not feeling like talking to anyone. 'Is it Emma?'

'Mark.'

'Mark?' Bells has a strange sense of humour. I take the phone from her. 'It's Aunt Agnes, isn't it?'

'Katie?' I can hear in the distance. 'Hello. Katie?'

It's definitely not Aunt Agnes because it's a man's voice. 'Who is it?'

'Mark.'

'Mark nice man. Mark nice. Mark helps.'

'Bells!' I say, holding my hand across the mouthpiece. 'Why did you call him? How did you get his number?'

'Asked him to see us.'

'Oh, bugger . . .' I take my hand away from the mouthpiece. 'Hi, Mark!'

'Katie, I'm so sorry to hear about your mum.'

Hearing his voice makes me want to cry. 'It's OK, it's fine. We're fine,' I stutter.

'Bells asked me if I'd visit. I know this is weird, I hardly know you, but I'd like to. I mean, if there's anything I can do to help, or . . .'

'Bells would love to see you.' I can't believe he is on the phone. I tell him Mum is still in hospital and that they think she will be there for one more week, until she can walk independently. 'Maybe you could come when she's home?' I suggest.

'Fine. Just call me.'

'That would be great,' I say, realizing how much I would like to see him too.

After our conversation Bells claps her hands. 'Mark coming!'

'How did you get his number?' I ask again.

'Took it from bag. Had it in London.'

I can't stop smiling. Mark is coming to see us. This is so random, so unexpected. Yet, at the same time, nothing feels more right.

29

Bells and I are standing on the station platform, waiting for Mark to arrive. Things are looking up, at last. Mum climbed ten stairs at the hospital and was finally discharged. She has been at home for two days. It is fantastic having her back. The only worrying thing is that already she's trying to cook and do too much. Determined to get back to some semblance of normality, she was trying to make some homemade elderflower cordial, bent down to get a large bowl and then bashed her head against the cupboard. Her eyesight has been affected by the surgery and she often knocks or bumps into things. Dad rushed her to hospital as he was terrified she had dislodged the stitches. 'The awkward squad is back,' Mum said when the doctor told her she couldn't keep away. Thankfully it was fine, nothing more than a nasty bruise.

'Three minutes,' Bells says, looking at the flashing sign hanging above the platform.

'Two minutes . . . One minute . . . Mark!' Bells waves.

He walks towards us. His hair looks unbrushed and he is wearing the round glasses that make him look like a professor. I can imagine him wearing a white coat and working in a laboratory. Instead, he's wearing dark jeans, a pale blue striped shirt, and his face looks tanned. My face is a sickly drained colour from spending too much time in hospital. Bells hits his arm. 'Hello, Mark.'

'Hi, Bells.' He shakes her hand. She hits him again, and he gently hits her back. Then he turns to me. It's that awkward moment when we don't know how to greet one another. Hug? Kiss? Hold hands? I lean towards him, ready to kiss formally on the cheek, but he pulls me towards him. 'I couldn't believe it when I heard the news. I'm so sorry.'

'Thank you for coming,' I say, falling into his arms and not wanting to let go.

When I open the front door Mum calls, 'Darling, we're in the kitchen.' She's been longing to meet Mark. 'Is this the nice chap who helped you find Bells?' she'd asked, sensing there might be more to it.

Mark, Bells and I walk into the kitchen and are confronted by the sight of Mum, Dad and a rather plump man standing behind a trolley stacked high with wigs.

'Hello, Mark,' gushes Mum, holding out a hand. Mum loves men. I always suspect she wanted to have a son. 'Katie, Bells, Mark,' she says, examining him closely again to see if he could be potential husband material, 'this is Mr Marshall, the wig man.'

He extends one thick hairy arm and shakes our hands. 'Isn't your mother doing well?' he beams. 'All we need to do now is fit her up with a nice wig and then she'll be the talk of the town!'

Mum pats her head nervously. Her hair hasn't grown back apart from a few wisps. Dad tells her she looks like a fluffy chick.

Mr Marshall opens the first page of his portfolio. 'This is Mrs Henderson, she had a terrible time of it, lost all her hair, she did. You know that rare disease where it all falls out? For the life of me, I can't remember what that disease is called. Anyway, she was lying in the bath, she was, and when she got out, all her hair was floating in the water. It was a terrible shock. She was beside herself.'

He shows us the picture of Mrs Henderson before and after. In the after shot she wears a brown wig that looks more like a wooden salad bowl tipped on to her head.

Mr Marshall takes us through the entire portfolio and by now I am dreading what he is going to suggest for Mum.

He closes his portfolio and we all wait with bated breath. 'Now, how about this for starters?' Mr Marshall bends down and takes a wig from his trolley. He holds up something ginger and cabbage-shaped, and I am dangerously close to laughing out loud. I know Mark is too, I can feel the vibes coming from him. Mum looks horrified. Dad is speechless. Bells roars with laughter. 'Very funny,' she says. 'Ha-ha, very funny!'

Mr Marshall looks puzzled, but gamely carries on. 'This is a close match to your original colour. Shall we give it a go?'

He places it carefully on Mum's head, smoothing it over and making sure there is not a single hair out of place. He proceeds to stand back in admiration. Mum looks at Dad, waiting for a reaction. Dad looks at me. I look at Mark. Mark turns to Bells.

'You need a mirror,' Mr Marshall says when none of us utters a word. He holds up a square mirror in front of Mum. 'It looks super on you, if I say so myself.'

Mum shrieks with dismay. 'But I had auburn hair, like my daughter, Isabel.' She glances at herself again and then quickly averts her eyes.

'Mum, we can buy you some really pretty silk scarves,' I suggest. 'You don't have to wear a wig.'

We all agree, except for Mr Marshall, who looks crestfallen as Dad and I show him out with his trolley of untouched wigs.

'Thank you for coming anyway,' Dad says quietly. 'I'm sorry if we sounded rude or ungrateful, but I don't think a wig's the answer.'

'No problem,' Mr Marshall says, 'but don't hesitate to ring me if you change your mind. The wig door hasn't been totally shut, I shall leave it, let's say, slightly ajar.'

Dad and I try not to laugh again. The wig door?

''Bye for now.' He bustles his trolley out of the door.

When we walk back into the kitchen Mum pats her head self-consciously. 'It really is very nice of you to come and see us,' she says to Mark, but I can tell her mind is still on that wig.

'I think you made the right choice,' he assures her. 'A silk scarf will suit you.'

'Bet you didn't think I'd end up like this, did you, darling?' Mum says to Dad, still touching her very short hair. 'I hardly look the part, do I?'

Look the part, feel the part and you are the part, I can hear Sam chanting in front of the mirror as he shaves.

Dad steps forward and kisses the top of her head. 'I love you, no matter what. You don't ever need to hide behind your hair. What did we always say to you, Bells?'

'You look world in the eye,' she says.

'Dad used to say it all the time when we were children,' I explain to Mark.

'That's right,' Dad confirms. 'You look the world in the eye.'

30

Mum and I are watching an old black-and-white film on television, *Roman Holiday* with Audrey Hepburn. Mum's making a new tapestry cushion. She can never sit still and do nothing. Her colour is returning and her mobility improving each day with physiotherapy.

She looks pretty in a rose-patterned scarf and large dangling earrings that I bought for her. When Mark came down for the day, Bells and I took him shopping. 'They look like chandeliers hanging off your ears,' he said, when I held the earrings up to my face. It was lovely seeing him. I don't think he realized quite how much his visit had meant to us.

'Katie, you need to think about going back to London,' Mum says to me out of the blue.

'What?'

'You need to go home.'

'No way. I can't, not yet. Do you want another drink? Hot water with lemon?'

'I'll be all right,' she reassures me. 'I feel guilty, keeping you from your friends and your life.'

'That doesn't matter. God, nothing matters except you getting better.'

Mum puts her needle down and turns to me. 'You've been wonderful, but you can't stay here for ever.'

'But who's going to make you breakfast in bed and cook? Dad can't cook. No, we can't leave you, not yet.'

'I'm getting better all the time and your father is a good nurse. It's time you and Bells went home.'

'I'm not sure,' I say nervously. The truth is the idea of leaving fills me with dread.

'I'm sure. You need to start thinking about where you are going to live,' she says with concern.

'I don't know . . .'

'Katie.' Mum puts her sewing on the table. 'I can't thank you enough for everything you've done.'

'I haven't done much.'

'You have. Katie,' Mum says again, 'I've been a dreadful mother.'

I feel a rush of blood coming to the surface.

Yes, you were. You were too wrapped up in your work, you distanced yourself from me and put all your time into Bells, saving only a crumb for me. I felt invisible most of the time. I've always felt second best with you. I never seemed to be good enough; it felt like you didn't want to be involved in my life. That's what I would have said to her six weeks ago. Yet none of it really matters now.

'Mum, don't . . .'

'No! I want to. Let me.' She pauses. 'I've never been any good at saying how I feel. No better than you in fact.' She laughs painfully. 'I close up like an oyster.' Mum's voice is cracking around the edge like a broken shell. 'If I can't say it now, I'll never be able to.'

'OK, tell me.'

'I've never let myself accept that I didn't give you enough time, that you needed me as much as Bells, just in a different way. I should never have said how lucky you were not to have her problems, it was the easy way out. I didn't applaud you in your own right. But look at you now. A beautiful, successful woman . . .'

'I'm not.'

'You are. I've missed out on such a large chunk of your life, and I want to make up for it. I'm so sorry.'

'You had a difficult, demanding child. I should have realized how hard it was for you and Dad instead of thinking about myself all the time. I admire you both so much for bringing us up with no help. I admire you more than I can say.'

'It wasn't good enough, though. I'm your mother,' she says, full of self-reproach. 'If I can't look after you, who can? I know I retreated into my own world. My work became everything because it took me away from the

242

everyday grind. Then you left home and suddenly you didn't need us any more. I've carried this guilt for neglecting you all my life. I buried it in my conscience.'

Mum stands up and walks slowly out of the room. 'I've got something for you,' she says. 'Stay there.'

She returns, holding a small package wrapped in white tissue paper.

'Mum, you didn't have to.'

'Open it.' She sits next to me as I unwrap the present. It is an oval silver box with an inlay of tortoiseshell and inside is her precious tortoiseshell comb. 'My mother gave both of them to me as a wedding present.'

'I love this box, it's beautiful. And your comb . . . you always wear it.'

'Well, it seemed perfect timing,' she says, adjusting her scarf. 'Besides, I want you to have them. It's a thank you for all you've done.'

I put the box down and hug Mum.

'Why did it take us so long to talk? Why did it have to take this to bring us together?' she asks, holding me close.

31

Back to normality. Back to stocktaking, ordering from suppliers, organizing the next fashion show. Back to yoga and swimming, going out again and socializing. Back to the daily grind of London; noise, traffic, rude people pushing and barging. It is terrifying.

I have moved in with Emma and Jonnie. They rent a small house with a garden near Turnham Green, and Emma insisted I stay in their spare room until the New Year, just before they get married. Being with her has made the move far less daunting and it's ideal as they live so close to my shop and so near to Mark. I need to call him soon to let him know we're temporary neighbours.

This evening I'm going to Jonnie's parents' home near Lisson Grove for supper. Since being back in London I haven't seen that many people. Last week I went over to Sam's to pick up my sewing machine. It was the last thing I had to collect. I still have keys, so I went during my lunch hour when he was at work. His house looked exactly the same, not that I had expected it to change. Everything spotless and in the appropriate place. It didn't look like I had ever lived there. I put the keys through the door. ''Bye, Sam,' I said. As I predicted, he hasn't been in touch since he heard the news about Mum.

As I wait in the sitting room for the taxi, I look at Emma and Jonnie's engagement photos taken in Battersea Park. They are in black-and-gilt cardboard folding frames. They remind me of those cards I used to be given with the end-of-year school photographs. *'The entire photograph was ruined because Katie decided to pull up her skirt and show us her knickers,'* Mum would read out. She always waited for an explanation, but I was sure I could see a small smile trying not to surface. Just thinking about home makes me miss it. It's ironic. All I wanted to do was leave home when I was a teenager. Now, it's the only place I want to be. I felt safe there, harboured in a cocoon. I felt needed.

The day I left, Dad and I stood quietly on the platform waiting for my train to arrive, both locked in our own thoughts. I was thinking about being a child again, climbing on to the train with my shiny red suitcase to see Aunt Agnes, and Dad waving goodbye as the train started to move.

'I don't want to, I'm not going,' I said as the train approached.

Dad smiled as he brushed a strand of hair away from my eyes and tucked it behind my ear, like he used to do when I was young. 'You have to go.' He opened the door and helped me in with my luggage. 'Mum and I will be fine on our own.'

Bells had left the day before. She was happy to go back. She missed college, her friends, her football and her normal routine. I hadn't missed anything, and that scared me. 'Who's going to cook for you, Dad?' I called out as the train slowly started pulling away.

He waved his hand at me. 'I'll manage without Bells, don't worry.'

I laughed. 'No more secrets, ever!' I shouted out of the window. 'We tell each other everything, good and bad. Great or bloody awful!' Strange the way our family does this. Dad and I had what seemed like an eternity of time waiting on the platform together, and now that I was actually going, the words were tumbling out.

'Everything,' he agreed.

'Promise?'

'I promise.'

We blew kisses. Dad's figure quickly faded into the distance. He was the only person left standing on the platform, still waving, until he was out of sight.

I open one of the photographs again. Emma is sitting down, Jonnie behind her with his arms wrapped around her shoulders. She's wearing a red dress that contrasts with her cropped dark brown hair and brown eyes. He's wearing a pale blue shirt to go with his blue eyes. It's all very colour-coordinated and grown up. The doorbell finally rings and I put the photograph back on the mantelpiece.

Emma hands me a large glass of wine. Perfect. Jonnie leads me into the sitting-room. 'You must meet my parents,' he says. They are standing expectantly by the fireplace. 'Mum, Dad, meet Katie.'

'Call me Will.' He is a big beefy man, so it's forgiven that I nearly laugh out loud when I hear his soprano voice.

'Call me Hermione.' Jonnie's mother steps forward to shake my hand. She must come up to about my waist. She looks like a little mouse and is wearing these peculiar multicoloured pointed shoes that curl up at the toes like the end of a gondola.

'What do you do, Katie?' he enquires, wide-eyed and smiling. I am still trying to keep a straight face. Emma did tell me that Hermione was a pain, but why didn't she warn me about that voice? She must have known how I'd react.

'I own a clothes shop,' I tell him.

'Oh, how interesting,' he squeaks, touching his navy V-neck jumper with both hands.

Think of a sad story, sad story, I'm telling myself as I look at them both goggle-eyed.

'What's it called?' Hermione chirps enthusiastically. 'I know someone who works in fashion. She gets to travel abroad to Paris. I think she works for Gucci or Givenchy, something like that.'

'Well,' I cough, 'it's called FIB.'

'Fib?'

'It stands for Female In Black.'

'Oh,' she says, her voice heavy with disappointment. 'I think black is so dreary, all you young things wear it,' she comments, scanning my outfit. I am wearing a soft black rounded-neck jumper with sequins edging the cuffs. I get distracted as Jonnie hands me a plate of mixed nuts, and winks at me.

'So, you're living with Jonnie and Emma, I gather?' Hermione has lost all interest in my career, then.

'Yes, that's right,' I say, and then add, 'For the moment, that is,' when I can see from her face that she is faintly dismayed. 'Until I find my own place.'

'You're not married then, Katie?'

'No,' I say, and feel compelled to add, 'not yet.'

'Oh, what a shame,' peeps Will, his big moon face looking downcast.

'No, not a shame. I'm only twenty-nine!'

Hermione's mouth shrivels like a prune. 'But you young people wait for so long. I married Will when I was twenty. I had three children by the time I was your age. You're all the same. I mean, look at Jonnie, he took his time,' she grumbles.

I am tempted to say she probably had to marry her husband quickly before he changed his mind and did a runner.

'What do your parents do?' she continues.

'Well, my father works at Sotheby's,' I tell them.

Hermione graciously acknowledges this, saying it must be a very interesting job. I can almost see her conferring a tick of approval. 'How about your mother?'

I clear my throat. 'My mother's recently had a terrible time, she had a brain tumour.'

'Oh I am sorry. How awful for you all.'

'It was awful, terrible . . . but she's OK now. She got through it, she's doing well,' I tell Hermione proudly. 'It will take a good six months to a year before she gets back to normal totally, but she's very lucky. We all are.'

As I say it, I can hardly believe it's true. Mum pulled through. I can see her now, sitting at the kitchen table, her brightly patterned red-and-gold silk scarf coiled around her head, reading out to Dad how to cook a fish pie for their supper. 'Flake the fish, darling,' I can hear her repeat because Dad is chopping it instead. He can only really cook scrambled eggs.

'Isn't she brave,' Hermione comments.

'Yes, she is. She took a risk having the operation, but to be honest, she had no choice.'

'Well done her,' Will chirps.

'Do you have any brothers or sisters?' Will's mother enquires hopefully.

I take one more glug of wine to brace myself for the question that I know is coming next.

'A sister.'

'Is she married?'

'No.'

'Stop being so nosy!' Jonnie calls from the kitchen. 'She thinks everyone over twenty-one should be married. Times have changed, Mum!'

'Oh. What does she do?'

Of course she was going to ask that. Asking people what they do is a kind of nervous tic with the middle classes. 'Well, Bells is a slightly unusual case. Er . . . she was born . . .'

'Bells? Is that what she's called?'

'Sorry. Bells – Isabel. We've always called her Bells.'

'Oh I see. Why is she unusual?'

'She lives in a kind of community, it sounds like a farm, but it's not,' I add.

'She works on a farm?' Hermione creases her forehead in confusion. 'Is she a volunteer?'

'No,' I say, twisting the silver ring on my finger. 'She lives there, it's her home.'

'Right,' says Jonnie's mother, looking even more puzzled.

'It's a special home for . . .' I pause, thinking of the correct way to word it, 'people with disabilities.'

If Hermione was in one of those hamster wheels that roll around the floor, she'd be spinning out of control by now. 'You mean, she's retarded?'

'No,' I say stiffly. 'No, she's not. She is Bells. Our Bells.'

'Oh dear, oh dear. What a shame,' Will pipes up.

'Poor, poor thing.'

'She is not a poor thing,' I voice defiantly. 'She's wonderful. She's a terrific cook, loves her music and football. There's nothing she doesn't know about the Beatles or Stevie Wonder. She has this magical sense of humour, too. Bells is her own person, and if you told her she was a poor thing she would hit you hard in the balls.' I want to take back the last bit but it's too late. Jonnie roars with laughter; I hear Emma choke and then let out a snort. I look at Will and Hermione but their expressions are still pitying. They aren't even listening.

AND I HAVE CANCER OF THE BOWEL, I want to shout, pointing to my cigarettes regretfully, but bite down on my lip hard. When I start to envisage Bells hitting Will hard in the balls, I have to try hard not to laugh.

Until other guests arrive, I change the subject by talking about the photographer Emma found for the wedding. Has Hermione seen the picture of the chocolate cake she has chosen which will be garnished with white flowers? What is the mother-of-the-groom going to wear? I am going to design and make Emma's veil. Hermione tells me she loves winter weddings because that's when she got married. All fun, pretty things to talk about.

'What's a pretty girl like you doing on her own tonight?' my taxi driver asks as he turns on the engine. Emma bundled me into the cab because she's staying with Jonnie and his parents tonight. 'Do you have a boyfriend?'

This cab driver is very forward, isn't he? 'I have one, thanks,' I hiccup, deciding it's much more fun to lie. 'I'm afraid I can't talk too much about it, though,' I say, crouching forward into the space between his seat and the front passenger one. 'A bit complicated. Wouldn't want it making headline news. We have to leave separately, too risky otherwise with the paparazzi.' I sink back into the padded leather seat and hiccup once more. 'Oops, sorry 'bout that.'

'I don't believe you, man,' he laughs. 'Should I be getting your autograph?'

'OK,' I concede. 'I'm on my own. I've just split up.'

'I knew it,' he exclaims. 'I can sense things. Oh, that's sad. Too bad. I missed my wife when we split, you know what I mean?'

'I'm a bad picker of men. What's your name?'

'Fourque.'

'For what?'

'Fourque,' he says and proceeds to spell it out. 'F for Freddie, O for orange, U for umbrella . . .'

'Well, Fourque, I pick men who are no good in the end. My second-to-last boyfriend was a commitment freak, and my last one was shallow.'

'You pick the vermin?'

'What?'

'Vermin. That's what I call all those people who aren't

any good. There are a lot of them out there, you know what I mean? You have to be careful.'

'Vermin! I like that. I have this picture of ratlike people scurrying around with red flashing lights to show they are hazardous.'

'Yeah, rodents, man,' he laughs with me.

'Rodents!' I shout out of the window, feeling the fresh cold air blast my face. Thing is, I wish they did have red flashing lights. You see these well-dressed nice-looking people around, but half of them are probably vermin too. I wish you could tell them apart.

'What about you now?' I ask, sitting forward again.

'What about me? Well, I want to make it in the music world. I don't want to do this for the rest of my life,' he says, pointing to the steering wheel. 'I have an interview next week. It's like my chance to do something I've always wanted to do. You have to take it, don't you? You know what I mean?'

'I know *exactly* what you mean,' I say with certainty. 'Life is way too short to waste it. Whoah, slow down, stop here.' I want to buy another bottle of wine from the off-licence.

I clamber out and pay him through the front passenger window. He smiles at me and his eyes light up like fairy lights. 'Will you pray for me to get the job?' he asks. 'And I'll pray for you to find the right man.' I find myself nodding because I like him. 'Stay away from the vermin,' he adds.

*

I head into the off-licence and stare at the various bottles of wine in front of me. In the end I take any old one and totter to the till. 'Thank you,' I say, clutching the carrier bag. 'Have a fine day!'

'Katie?' I hear.

I stop and turn round. I know that voice. I tilt my head at him. He's wearing a cord jacket and holding a bottle of water and a large packet of barbecue-flavour crisps.

'Mark.' I smile, unable to conceal my delight at seeing him.

'What are you doing here?' he asks.

'I live here.' I explain I am staying with Emma temporarily.

'That's great. How are you? And how's your mother?'

'She's not here.' Why did I say that?

Mark looks at me strangely. 'I have to pay for this, hang on a sec. Don't go anywhere.' He delves into his pocket to find some notes and loose change.

I tell him I'll wait outside and do a quick drunken skip on the pavement. This is turning out to be a much better evening than I thought. Hallelujah!

We walk home, me cursing that we'll be there in thirty seconds. Why can't we live at least a mile away?

'When did you get back?' he asks.

'Five days ago. I would have called but I've had so much to do in the shop, a lot of catching up, you know what it's like. I'm sorry, I should have . . .'

'Don't worry, I understand. Well, this is me,' he says, standing outside a black door with two steps leading up to it. 'But I'll walk you home.'

I don't budge an inch. I can't let him go. I like him too much. I'd wanted to call him, but lost my nerve without Bells as an excuse. I need to pluck up the courage now. What have I got to lose any more?

'Can I come in? Let's crack open this bottle of wine.' I stride on ahead, up the steps.

He grabs an arm to steady me. 'Don't you think you've had enough?' he asks, amusement in his tone.

I frown at him disapprovingly.

He gives in.

Mark's flat is small. His bike leans against the corridor wall. We go into the sitting-room and I collapse into a soft sofa.

'I'm going to put the kettle on,' he tells me as he walks out of the room. 'Do you want a coffee?'

'What do you do?' I start talking to myself. 'What do you dooooo?' I can hear Mark laughing in the kitchen. Five minutes later he comes back with two mugs. I peer into my coffee. 'It's Saturday night, Mark. I've been terrorized all evening by Jonnie's parents. Believe me, I need a proper drink.' I kick a wine glass on the floor at my feet. 'Oops! What are all these wine glasses doing?'

'Doing?' Mark grins. 'They're having a party.' He takes his jacket off.

There's an open bottle of white wine on the coffee table in front of me. I pour some into the nearest glass, spilling a little over the edge. Mark picks up the other glass that is precariously close to being kicked over. I can smell his aftershave. He's wearing a soft white shirt. All I want is to nuzzle into his shoulder and have a proper man hug. 'This place is a bit of a tip, isn't it? Did you have a party tonight?'

'I had a few friends over.'

'You had a few friends over,' I repeat, followed by a large gulp of wine. 'You know, Mark, it really is dandy to see you.'

'Dandy?' He laughs. 'I like that word.'

'You English teacher, you. D'you think it's fate, Mark, the way we bump into one another? There I am, at the off-licence, and – poof! We bump into one another, just like that. Or you living so close to Emma and me moving here, right next door to you. It's meant to be. Has to be.' Mark raises one eyebrow.

'I've always wanted to do that!' I peer closely at him, my mouth hanging open. 'How'd you do that? Can you roll your Rs . . .' I flop back against the sofa like a rag-doll.

He rolls his Rs and then abruptly stops. 'This is a pretty strange evening.'

'D'you know, I think it might be destiny, Mark. D'you believe in destiny?' He looks unsure. I lift myself up off the sofa to walk over to his music machine and look through his CDs. '*My Fair Lady*? Oh my God, you're gay. Haah!' I sigh deeply. 'It makes sense.'

Mark looks bewildered now. 'I'm not gay, it's a school CD. We're putting on a production this year.'

'What's all this paper?'

Mark stands up abruptly and takes it from me, shuffling it back into order. 'It's my book.'

'Oh. Shall we dance?' I twist around and Mark catches me, releases the glass of wine from my hand and holds me still. He could let go of me now, I think. He's going to kiss me. 'Look, I think you need your bed,' he says finally. 'Do you want me to take you home?'

'Do you want me to go home?' I ask coyly, trying to be seductive. 'You know, you're very attractive, Mark. You're such a nice and lovely man. There's something about you.' Is he laughing at me? 'What! I mean it, Mark. Don't look so worried, come here.' I close my eyes for a second, in anticipation of a kiss.

'Katie.' I feel a hand shaking my arm. 'Oh, shit, Katie. Wake up, Katie, please. Wake up.'

The words are echoing around me but I ignore them as I fall into a deep blackness.

32

I wake up the following morning on a sofa with a rug over me. I attempt to move. My head! I hold it heavily in my hands. I groan. My mouth feels like a sewer. I summon all my strength to sit up, pulling the rug with me. Where am I? There's a glass of wine on the table in front of me and the smell of it makes me feel sick. I'm still wearing my clothes from last night. My neck creaks when it moves. It's too painful sitting upright. This is a bad dream. My head hits the pillow again. The last thing I remember vaguely was drinking stewed coffee. I shut my eyes and go back to sleep.

I am woken up abruptly by cramp in my arm. Quickly, I fling off the hairy tartan rug and stand up, shaking my arm about. The wine glasses have gone. I look around me once more, trying to piece together the events of last night. Papers and books overflow from a desk and a tall silver lamp with long spidery legs stands to one side of a computer. There's a white-painted shelf holding even more books and a small television in the corner of the room. Sam would have a breakdown if his place looked like this. I pick up a glass of water from the floor and drink it steadily. Next to the glass is a packet of white pills. There's a scrap of paper on the floor with a torn-off ring-binder edge.

'Gone for a run, back soon, Mark. PS. These are for the sore head.'

Mark. I saw Mark last night! Of course I did. Where did I think I was? I start pacing the floor, knocking over a white plastic bowl. This is embarrassing. Did he think I was so drunk I was going to be sick in this during the night? Obviously he did.

He'll be back soon. How come I stayed here? I remember meeting him, but staying over? Why can't I remember that? I sit and think hard about what we talked about last night. Mark must have gone for a long run. I bet you he's hoping I'll be gone by the time he gets back. He's probably having brunch with his friends, telling them that I crashed out on his sofa last night. I rub my eyes. Try to remember, Katie. My head feels cobwebby. What I could do is run back to Emma's and Jonnie's, have a shower, get myself looking decent and return to say thank you for . . . what? I'll figure that out later. That's a good plan, Katie. Desperately I try to kick myself into action, but nothing is happening. I hear the distant bang of a door followed by a key turning nearby. My heart jumps again at the thought of seeing him. I sit back down and attempt to look relaxed.

Mark comes into the room clutching a bottle of water and a newspaper. His face looks fresh and squeaky clean. 'Good morning.' He smiles as if he has won a premium bond. Why does he look so happy? 'How are you feeling?'

'Fine!' I lie. I wait for any clue as to why I found myself on his sofa.

'Really? You look terrible.'

I laugh and admit, 'OK. I feel dreadful. I feel worse than I look and that is saying something.'

'I bought us some breakfast. Well, lunch really. I've already had a bit of cereal. Stay for brunch, shall we say? I'm not going to take no for an answer so come into the kitchen when you're ready.'

I pat my greasy hair self-consciously. Look the part, feel the part . . . Oh, shut up, Sam.

'Have a shower, if you like.'

My God, he is offering me a shower. Next he will be offering me his toothbrush. How has this happened? I rub my head. I remember Will and Hermione clearly from last night. Then I bumped into Mark and we drank some more wine and coffee. I am sure nothing else happened. Convinced, in fact. He wouldn't have left me on the sofa, surely? I would have woken in his bed. 'Mark,' I call, making my way to the kitchen.

I find him at the stove frying bacon. I love the smell of bacon and toast. I sit down, suddenly starving.

'Mark, what were we talking about last night?' I ask tentatively.

'Nothing much.' He's wearing those black-rimmed glasses that remind me of my father's.

'I wasn't talking crud?'

'Crud? I love your turn of phrase. I particularly like "dandy".'

'Dandy? What was I saying last night?'

'I can't really remember,' he says, the corners of his mouth turning slightly upwards as he pretends to be absorbed in cooking.

'Come on,' I gently encourage. 'You can remember, I can tell.'

'All right then. You said it was dandy seeing me, and then you conked out.'

I put a hand over my mouth. 'I'm sorry. How lame am I?' I lean my elbows against the table. 'I feel so ill,' I groan. 'Was I really so drunk I couldn't make it five steps back home?'

'Yes, pig drunk.'

'Pig drunk?'

'I tried to lift you . . .'

'Oh God, I haven't been to the gym in a while . . .'

'Katie, I didn't mean that. It's just deadweight is heavy.'

I think I would rather be called overweight than a deadweight.

'Look at you, you're stick-thin.'

'I eat like a horse but I run on my nerves. I've got my mum's genes.' Mum. I must ring today and see how she is. 'She's thin too, but we both have round curvy bottoms,' I add proudly.

Mark raises an eyebrow as he scoops the bacon from the pan and puts it on the kitchen roll. The grease settles on to the white paper with hens lining the edge. He turns to me with the spatula in his hand. His pale blue shirt collar is sticking up rigidly, and he's wearing that navy jumper with holes in the elbow again.

As we eat our bacon sandwiches and drink coffee and orange juice, Mark asks me about Sam and why I'm not living with him any more. 'Katie, you've got a bit of orange stuck on your tooth,' he points out. I censor the story. I don't tell him exactly why; I don't mention what Sam said in the restaurant; all I say is that the relationship had run its course. Mark nods thoughtfully. He knows I'm cutting the story down to make it simple. 'I'm sorry. Is there a chance you can get back together?'

I shake my head. 'There is nothing left to say. I pick rodents.' I smile, slowly remembering the cab drive home.

'What?' Mark has that baffled look again.

'Never mind. What are you doing today?'

'I've got to finish my book. Deadline is tomorrow.' Mark looks at his watch. 'In fact, I must go soon.'

I feel a sharp twinge of disappointment. I have enjoyed eating breakfast with him. It seems like an extension of my night out and I don't want to go yet. 'Your book? Don't you write from home?'

'Sometimes. I've rented out this tiny office space because I find it easier writing away from here.'

'That sounds like a good idea. And then it's going to be sent to publishers, is it?' *'Do you believe in destiny?'* I gulp hard, feeling a flush of red creep up my neck. Did I really say that?

'Yeah, it's frightening letting it go out into the lions' den.'

'I can imagine. I like reading. My headmistress inspired me to love it. By the time I was fifteen I had read all of Tolstoy, Emily Brontë and Jane Austen. I wish I could write. What's the book about?' *'Do you think it's fate, Mark, the way we bump into each other?'* I sink further into my seat.

The doorbell rings.

Mark picks up the entryphone. 'What a surprise,' he exclaims. 'I thought you weren't coming down until tonight?'

'Oh my God, you're gay.' I don't know when to stop, do I? Oh, well, what does it *really* matter, I try to convince myself. He's probably flattered by the attention.

'Are you going to let me in?' I hear from outside the flat.

'Sorry.' He presses the entry button.

'Who is it?' I ask casually.

'My girlfriend. She lives in Edinburgh.'

'Oh, right, that's nice!' A deep thud of disappointment hits the bottom of my stomach. 'Right, I should go,' I say, trying to sound like I have a busy day ahead.

A tall girl with light brown hair held loosely in a pony-tail walks into the kitchen. She's wearing jeans and a tailored jacket. She steps forward to give Mark a kiss. 'Hello, you,' she says and they briefly hug. 'Surprise! I decided to catch an earlier train. My work can wait.'

Mark coughs. 'Jess, I'd like you to meet Katie.'

'Oh, hello.' She swings round in surprise. She smiles uncertainly at me and I can tell she's trying to work out why I'm in Mark's kitchen, dressed in a black evening top, with heavily smudged black-ringed eyes.

'Right, I'd better be off,' I say.

'Mark, sorry, but who . . . I mean, what's going on?'

'Nothing is going on. I've told you about Katie,' he assures her. Then he looks at me. 'Sorry, but I told Jess about your mother, I hope you don't mind?'

'Oh, you're Katie,' she exclaims with some relief. Then bites her lip and looks at me closely again. 'How is your mother?' she asks slowly, her eyes narrowed. She is obviously still trying to work out why I am in Mark's kitchen.

'She's much better, thanks.' But Jess isn't listening. I could have said any old thing.

'What exactly is going on?' She stares at Mark hard. 'Is there something you're not telling me?'

'I should go,' I say.

'Did you stay the night?' she asks me coolly.

'God, no!' I blurt out.

'Well, could you explain to me what you're doing here?' Her voice is calm but there is an uncomfortable edge to it.

'Well, I did stay here, but obviously not in the way you think I did.'

'Jess, this is ridiculous,' Mark says. 'Katie's a friend.'

'Ridiculous? Is it?' she queries, still remaining remarkably cool and not taking her eyes away from mine. I want to go home.

Mark makes Jess sit down at the table next to me, and pulls up a chair for himself. 'Katie and I bumped into one another last night at the off-licence. I walked her home, I wanted to find out how her mother was. She came in for a drink – and you were so tired, weren't you?' He gestures towards me.

'Really tired,' I say.

'Then she fell straight to sleep on the sofa.'

'Straight to sleep,' I repeat.

'That's it, I promise,' Mark concludes.

'I'm sorry, Jess, I can see how this looks, but Mark was being a good friend, that's all.'

'So nothing happened,' she says, more of a statement now than a question.

'Nothing,' Mark and I say together.

'Look, Katie slept next door.' He leads her into the sitting room.

'Mark, if you're lying to me, I couldn't bear it,' I can hear Jess saying in a low voice, as she knows I'm only a room away. 'I'd rather you told me now.'

'You know I wouldn't lie to you,' he reassures her. This is the perfect time to make my escape. It's clear they need to talk about this, and I don't think I'm helping by hanging around.

I edge my chair back, trying to be as quiet as I can. I open the front door. 'I know it might look suspicious but I swear nothing happened,' Mark is saying.

Gently I shut the door behind me.

I walk home, slowly.

I see the empty stretch of road ahead of me. Thank God I'm outside the flat; I'm too hungover to deal with this.

The shock of Jess's arrival is now replaced with a nagging sense of disappointment that Mark has a girlfriend. *You know, you're very attractive, Mark . . . there's something about you . . .*

I have made a complete fool of myself! Oh well, I think, kicking a stone across the pavement. What did I think would happen? Break up with Sam and then fall predictably into the arms of Mark, who is, of course, the complete opposite to Sam, single *and* the answer to my dreams? For God's sake, Katie, this isn't a Hollywood movie.

'Hey, why did you go without saying goodbye?' I hear. I turn and see Mark racing towards me on his bike, his typescript balanced between the handlebars. He comes to an abrupt halt and the script flies on to the road, scattering into a hundred sheets.

'I'm sorry, I shouldn't have stayed last night.' I bend down to try and retrieve the paper. I reach out for one of the sheets and the wind blows it in the opposite direction so I end up clutching air.

'Shit . . . bugger . . . shit!' Mark curses on his hands and knees. 'I knew I should have put it in a bag.' He is desperately grabbing sheets of paper. One floats off into the middle of the road.

We laugh helplessly. I don't feel it's the right time to ask what the book is about as I pick up the pieces of paper and dust them off.

'You weren't going to say goodbye?' he mutters, scooping the remaining pages off the road.

'I need to get home, out of these smoky clothes.' I smile at him. 'Is Jess OK?'

'She's fine.'

'I'm sorry. I didn't mean to cause any trouble. Shouldn't you be with her now?'

'I have to get this to someone, it won't take long,' he says.

'I don't blame her for being suspicious, I would be.'

'We know nothing happened so we have nothing to feel guilty about.'

I nod.

He stands up and I stand up with him. He grabs his bike and follows me. 'Well, this is me.' I stand outside a red door with bits of paint flaking off it. 'I'll see you soon.'

Mark doesn't say anything. ''Bye then.' I turn the key in the door, aware that he still hasn't gone.

'Katie?'

'Yes?'

'I should have told you – about Jess, I mean.'

'Don't worry, it doesn't matter,' I say, though every part of my voice says it does.

'I'd like to see you again. There's no harm in us meeting for a . . .'

'Coffee?'

'And a sticky bun?'

I smile. 'You know where I am.'

'Great. Friends?'

Ouch! That's painful. Did he think he had to say it so I wouldn't make a pass at him again?

'Friends,' I say, wrapping my shivering arms around myself for warmth. I watch him as he pushes off on his bike, the script back in position in between the handle-bars. He uses one hand to wave at me from behind. It looks dangerous to me.

'Good luck with the book!' I call out. I want to shout, 'Be careful!' but don't want to sound like his mother.

33

The house is modern, down a steep drive. Mum warned me how steep it was and that I must leave the car in gear. I have bought my own second-hand car and love it. It's small, silver, shiny and fast. The next thing I need to do is look for a flat to rent.

My legs are stiff and aching from the long journey. I would have arrived at least half an hour ago, had it not been for getting lost along the endless winding narrow roads that all looked the same and seemed to lead nowhere. There are no signs outside Bells's house, it really was a stroke of luck that I spotted a tall man wearing a tracksuit, with a bright blue jumper and an identity card around his neck, motioning me into the drive. I recognized him immediately from Bells's photograph album.

'Hello, I'm Ted,' he says, holding out a large hand which I shake. He has curly brown hair and bright blue eyes that almost seem to pop out of his head with enthusiasm.

'Hi, Ted. I'm Katie, Bells's sister.'

'Hello, Bells's sister. Welcome to Wales.'

A tall man with dark hair walks out and says hello too, asking me how my journey was. His name's Robert. He is one of Bells's 'key workers'. He leads me inside, down a long corridor, past a pin-board that gives details of the events of the month, and into the kitchen. 'Isn't the weather remarkable today?' Ted says, following closely behind. 'They said there would be lots of rain, but we haven't had a single drop.'

'Ted is fascinated by the weather,' Robert mentions with a dry laugh. 'There's nothing he doesn't know about weather fronts.'

The kitchen's a soft yellow, the colour of primroses, and kept immaculately clean, not a spot of dirt or clutter anywhere. I like the feel of the place immediately. There are glass doors behind the long wooden kitchen table which open out on to the terrace and garden. 'What a lovely house,' I acknowledge, looking around the room.

'We like it,' Ted says proudly.

'Bells will be down in a minute, she heard your car arrive. Would you like a tea? Coffee?' Robert stands ready at the kettle.

'I'd love a tea, thanks.'

'You haven't been here before, have you?' he asks.

'No.' There's no accusation in his tone at all, but I can't help but feel a heavy sense of guilt that up until now I have shown no apparent interest in where my sister lives. 'I want Bells to show me round.' Above the larder fridge is a black-and-white photograph of her wearing her dungarees, standing over a wheelbarrow filled with cooking apples. She's smiling with her thumbs up. Robert can tell I'm looking at it.

'She's a great girl, Bells,' he comments. 'She's always doing something. She can't sit still, can she, Ted?'

'Never,' he says. 'Bells and I go to college together. Every Thursday we go. We learn all kinds of stuff, like art and writing, and I'm learning to dance too.'

'Really? What kind of dancing?'

'Ballroom dancing.'

There's another photograph, on the other side of the room, to which Ted leads me. He is large with broad shoulders. 'Guess where I am?' he says. I peer closely at the photograph. I can see Bells dressed in an Elvis outfit, strumming a tennis racquet as a guitar. Ted is behind her, wearing what looks like a shiny all-in-one outfit, with enormous fake sideburns. He's playing the drums. 'There you are!' I say, pointing.

'Groovy, huh?' He laughs. 'It was my birthday party. Everyone had to dress up as Elvis Presley. Bells and I formed a band together. We called ourselves the Gold Fishfingers.'

'Really groovy.' I smile back. 'Why the Gold Fishfingers, though?'

'Well, I love fishfingers,' he replies simply, as if I really should have known, and walks out of the kitchen.

'How's your mother?' Robert asks me.

'She's doing well. She gets frustrated because she still can't drive, but Dad is so patient with her. He sets her tasks, like putting photographs into albums and other things you never normally get round to doing.'

Robert sighs with relief. 'We were so worried, you know.'

'Has Bells talked to you about Mum?'

'No, no,' he says, shaking his head. 'She wouldn't do that.'

I'm dying to see her so I ask if I can go upstairs, but then she walks into the kitchen. She's dressed in a pair of tracksuit bottoms and the black T-shirt I gave her with the silver star on it. 'She's wearing it in your honour,' Robert says, winking at Bells.

'Hi, Bells.' She walks towards me. I'd like to hug her, but Bells doesn't really do hugs. Instead we shake hands and then she hits me affectionately on the arm and I hit her back.

'That's right,' she says.

I pick up my bag. 'I brought you some olives and cheese biscuits, and Eddie asked me to give you this ginger cake.'

'Eddie at deli.' She rocks forward and takes the bag of food. 'Thanks, Katie.'

Bells leads me upstairs. A large DO NOT DISTURB sign is stuck to her door, along with lots of peeling football stickers. Her room is small, with a single bed in the corner, and unlike the kitchen there is no space in here which hasn't been filled with paintings, stickers, posters, CDs and newspaper cuttings. I have to tiptoe in between a painting on the floor of the Union Jack flag and a poster that reads in red pen, *Come on ENGLAND*.

There's the familiar poster of Bob Marley smoking a joint, and the one of the Beatles, both of which she pinned to the walls of her bedroom in London. I sit on the edge of her bed. Her inhaler sits on the bedside table, together with her photograph album and a mug of tea.

'How's Mum?' she asks, sitting down next to me. Her chest is wheezing. She picks up her inhaler.

'She's much better.'

I stand up and walk over to her window. I catch a glimpse of the sea. 'Bells, wow!' I sigh. 'What a view you have. It's beautiful.'

She stands close behind me, breathing heavily. 'You like sea?' she asks, clearly pleased that I'm impressed.

'I love the sea. It makes me want to move out of London,' I say, turning to her. 'Come on, let's go for a walk.'

It's warm, but as Ted predicted, there are some dark threatening clouds hanging over us. We walk across the pale sand. I bend down and pick up a handful, letting it sift through my fingers like grains of sugar. Bells walks ahead of me. 'Do you swim in the summer?' I ask, catching up with her.

'No, too cold.'

After walking a long stretch of the beach I ask Bells if we

can sit down for a minute. It's so peaceful here, looking out to sea. There isn't another soul in sight and the only sounds we can hear are from the seagulls.

'How's Dad?'

'He's all right. A bit tired from Mum bossing him around.' I gently nudge Bells.

'That's right.' She nods thoughtfully. 'Poor Dad. How're you?'

'I'm back in London, staying with Emma.'

'How's Emma?'

'She's fine. Getting ready for her wedding.'

'How's Sam?'

'I don't know. I haven't seen him. Did you get my last letter?'

'Yes. How's Aunt Agnes?'

After Bells and I have discussed every friend and member of our family, we start walking back. She continues to show me around her home, and I can tell how proud she is by the way she points out everything. This is her territory; her world that I am entering. The sitting-room has a piano.

'Ted plays piano,' she tells me. 'Poor Ted,' she adds, striking a key.

'Why poor Ted?'

'Very lonely, has no family.'

Bells would hate to be called 'poor', but I have noticed how often she refers to other people in that way. It must give her a sense of security, feeling better off than the person next to her.

'No one visits Ted,' Robert says. He rests one hand on the door handle. He must have overheard us. 'I've worked here for twelve years and Ted hasn't had one visitor,' he reflects. 'You wouldn't think it could be true but some families leave their children here. Dump them.'

'That's terrible,' I exclaim, deeply shocked. It makes me realize how together my parents are, how strong they have always been. They would never have rejected Bells, it wouldn't even have occurred to them. It also makes me realize just how much I do not want to be lumped in the same category as Ted's family – the sister who never bothered.

'I know. It's the pits,' he agrees, tapping one foot against the floor. 'Everyone loves Ted, they don't know what they're missing out on. He looks after us all.'

'Ted champion on trampoline,' Bells adds. She is looking at the collection of videos next to the television.

I turn to Robert. 'So you've worked here for twelve years? That's pretty good going.'

'Yep, and I haven't had one solitary day off.'

'No way!'

'Well, maybe one or two, but I love it. My father worked here, so it runs in the family. I don't know what else I'd do.'

'You could do with a holiday, though, couldn't you?'

He smiles. 'Yeah, I suppose, but I'm not sure where I'd go.'

'You seen *Trading Places*?' Bells asks me.

'I love that film,' I say. Robert and I walk over to join Bells, and I look over her shoulder at the DVDs. 'Oh, wow, *Tootsie*, that's my favourite!'

'Very funny, *Tootsie*,' Bells agrees.

It's now three o'clock in the afternoon. Bells and I have tea and some chocolate digestive biscuits, and then I drive us to the local football club. She's now wearing a football shirt and her red Manchester United scarf wrapped snugly around her neck. Her team are playing a match late this afternoon, she tells me excitedly. We enter the clubhouse. There are a couple of men sitting at the bar.

'Hello, Budge,' she calls out. 'He's captain,' she tells me, her breathing intensifying. 'Hello, Paul. Hello, Budge.' She punches each one in turn. They turn round and hold up their hands to give her a high five. Bells's hand barely covers the palms of theirs.

'My sister, Katie,' she tells them. They briefly look at me and say hello.

Budge is very good-looking. He has dark brown hair and dark eyes that match. 'Hi,' I say back, but I can see I have lost his attention already.

'Bells, you're going to watch the match today, aren't you?' he asks, pulling at her scarf. He starts to uncoil it and she laughs furiously, saying it's tickling her. I can see her blushing.

''Course she is,' says the other one. Another army of men

walk into the clubhouse. They take it in turns clapping Bells on the back.

'How you doing, Bells?'

'How's our favourite mascot?'

'Bells, good to see you.'

'We've missed you,' Budge adds.

'I tell you,' one of them says to me, 'we need Bells back on the pitch. She's our good-luck charm.'

I'm about to say something when a beefy man, who looks like he works out in the gym seven days a week, sweeps in from behind and gathers her up in his arms. They all cheer and I join in. He puts her on to his shoulders. Bells is laughing and clapping her hands. 'Come on, St David's,' they chant like a tribe. I have never seen her look so happy, nor so at home anywhere. I stand back, letting them pass me. They're filing out now and on to the playing field.

'Katie,' I hear Bells call. 'You coming?'

I drive back to London early the following morning feeling happy. Bells's team won, 2–0. I watched the match, spending most of my time asking her, 'Are they allowed to do that?' I need to get up to date on the rules of football, clearly. After the match, I drove Bells home and found a crowd of people in the kitchen. I met Mary Veronica, a girl called Jane, another man called Alex, and Ted was still in the kitchen, looking after everybody. He said Bells was going to cook for us all. She made one of her famous vegetable roulades and, to follow, we had chocolate mousse. Bells opened her tub of olives and passed them around. Mary Veronica hated the taste and spat hers out. They turned some music on, Stevie Wonder, of course.

I can now put faces to names; I can imagine what she does on a Saturday afternoon. I can see her being picked up like a trophy and carried on to the football pitch. I can hear her laughing and clapping.

I can see her cooking in the kitchen.

The different nametags in her clothes make sense to me now.

I can see her when she picks up the phone in the corridor, in front of the pin-board.

It didn't feel sad leaving because I know Bells is in the right place. It's not perfect, nothing is, but it's her home. We've made a pact that I'll see her once a month and phone her every Sunday and Thursday night. I know how important it is for Bells to have her routine. 'Promise?' she said as I left.

'I promise.'

34

I'm sitting at the kitchen table flicking through one of Emma's many *Brides* magazines. Brides with flashing white smiles and pearls the size of quail's eggs stare out of the pages at me. Emma will look nothing like them, I hope. I can overhear Jonnie and her next door talking about the wedding. They're getting married in London, at St John's Church, Hyde Park. Double-decker buses will take the guests from the church to the reception at the National Liberal Club.

In fact, Emma can't stop talking about the wedding.

Should she choose Selfridge's, Harrods or Peter Jones for their wedding list?

Should their invitations be modern or traditional?

Should they invite friends' girlfriends and boyfriends?

'If I invite Josh, I'll have to invite Rebecca too, but I hardly know her,' she is saying. 'And what about their children? I really don't want kids there!'

I realize how much I need my own space.

Why do I feel so flat? It's been two weeks now since I saw Mark. For some reason I'd imagined he might pass by or call . . . but nothing.

I picture him on his bike again. I wonder what his book is about. Crime? Thriller? Love story? Science fiction? It could be an autobiography. Perhaps he's had a fascinating past. I imagine the cover, a picture of Mark set in a square border, the title, *Mark's Journey*. I laugh at this idea. I feel a lot more interested in everyone else's life at the moment. *If you could write the script of your life, what would you write?* I hear again, but this time it's not in Sam's voice. It's my own.

I march into my bedroom and pick up my sketchbook. I'm not sure what I would write but I know I want to start sewing again. Since splitting up with Sam, I've had more free time and I want to make the most of it. Maybe I want to take life less seriously too. No more writing lists of what I want to achieve by the end of each decade. Sam did those – he wanted to retire by the time he was forty. I just want 'to be'.

With renewed enthusiasm, I decide to go for a Sunday walk with my sketchpad. I could buy a coffee and people-watch. I need to get ideas about what people want to wear. It's cold outside, but the autumn sun is warm. I put on my blue and red poncho over my dark jeans.

Jonnie looks relieved when I walk into the room. 'What are you wearing?'

'It's the latest fashion.' I twirl around for him.

'Where are you off to, cowgirl?' he asks.

'Out. For a walk.'

Jonnie is not good-looking. If you analyse his features they are in fact quite ugly. Two crooked front teeth, a long chin, and he's too thin because he works too hard. Yet when you put it together with his blue eyes, dark hair and his sense of fun, he is one of the most attractive people I know.

'Jonnie, we have to carry on with the wedding list,' Emma insists, her face crumpled with despair.

Jonnie pulls a desperate face. 'See you later.'

I sit down by the café window with my cappuccino and gaze ahead. It's mid-morning and a few people are out. A girl walks past in a long dark brown skirt with ruffles around the bottom. She wears brown boots and a cream-coloured wrap-around cardigan. I sketch the overall effect. Tassels and fringes are back in, I notice, when I see yet another young girl walk past in a layered skirt.

As I sketch my mind keeps wandering. I'm not in the mood. I'd rather write to Bells.

Dear Bells,

I loved visiting you last weekend and seeing your home. It meant a lot to me. I'm only sorry I haven't visited before. I still think about the view from your bedroom window. You're so lucky to be able to look out to the sea every morning. That would put me in a good mood.

I thought Ted was lovely, tell him I look forward to seeing him dance at your open day. I also loved the football – are your team playing this weekend? If they are, I hope they win! Mr Vickers pops in for tea almost every day now. Eve and I miss him if he doesn't drop by. He helps himself to biscuits and makes his own pot of tea.

I forgot to tell you, but Mark asked after you. I saw him the other night. In fact, I made a real fool of myself and drank too much, silly Katie. You're right, Bells. He is such a lovely guy, but he has a girlfriend so boo hoo. Anyway, next time you come to London we should make a plan to meet up.

I stop writing for a second, and think about what Mark said to me the last time I saw him. I can still see him standing at Emma's front door. I pick up my mobile. 'Just wondered if you wanted to meet up for that coffee and sticky bun?'

My pen flies across the page as someone taps me from behind. 'You gave me a shock!' I say, retrieving my pen.

'Sorry.' Mark smiles, leaning over me. 'I was waving at you from outside, but you looked so serious. You're not writing your will, are you?'

'Mark!' I cover the page, the way I used to if I thought

someone at school was trying to cheat and steal my answers.

'What are you doing?'

'It's only a letter. To Bells.'

'Can I add something?'

'No!' I shut my sketchpad firmly now. 'You can write your own!'

'Bells is right. You are bossy. You *are* a traffic warden,' says Mark, making me smile.

'I'm glad you called,' he continues.

'Give us a cigarette,' we hear an old man in a raincoat asking in the doorway.

'You scrounger,' says a younger man who's about to walk inside. He digs into his pocket and finds a cigarette for the old man. 'There you go.'

'You have a lighter?'

'Bloody hell! What has this world come to?' Now he lights the cigarette. 'Anything more I can do for you?' he calls after the old man, who is now limping off into the distance, sucking his stick of nicotine. 'Polish your shoes, buy you a drink,' he mutters to himself as he walks over to the counter.

'I love people-watching,' Mark remarks. 'It's even better if I'm sitting in a hot country, drinking beer.'

'If only. Any news on the book yet?' He's wearing that navy jumper with holes in the arm.

He lets out a long frustrated sigh. 'No. My agent says it

needs more work. If you want instant gratification, don't be a writer.'

'You never told me what you're writing?'

'Just a fantasy adventure story,' he says modestly. 'It's for children and adults.'

'Am I sitting opposite the next J. K. Rowling?'

He grins. 'In my dreams. I've always loved books, since I was a child. I'll never forget my grandmother reading *The Adventures of Uncle Lubin* to me.'

'What's it about?'

'You don't know it? You must read it. Uncle Lubin looks after his young nephew Peter, but one day a great Bagbird swoops down,' Mark does the actions, 'and whisks the child away. Uncle Lubin has to find him. He travels round the world and up to the moon in his floppy hat and striped stockings. Uncle Lubin has a dream that he sees Peter under the sea, flanked by mermaids, and he's safe. When he wakes up he is distraught to find himself alone. Uncle Lubin never gives up, though, and in the end . . .'

'Don't tell me!' I bang my hand against the table. 'He rescues Peter?'

'Yes, sure.' Mark looks disappointed by my reaction. 'But it's more than that. It's about the human spirit and enduring love. It's about never giving up hope. I wish I still had that book, I don't know how Mum could have lost it.'

'Have you read *The Old Woman in the Vinegar Bottle*?'

Mark shakes his head.

'It's about this woman who lives in a vinegar bottle. She has a little ladder to go in and out by,' I wiggle my fingers as if climbing an imaginary ladder, 'but she grows discontented.'

'I'm not surprised. Living in a vinegar bottle doesn't exactly sound enthralling.'

' " 'Tis a shame, 'tis a shame," she grumbles, and pictures herself in a little white house with roses and honeysuckle growing over it, pink curtains, a pig in the sty. A fairy passing by feels sorry for her. "Well, never you mind," she says. She tells the old woman to go up to bed and turn around three times in her bottle. "When you wake up in the morning, you'll see what you will see!" When the old woman wakes she's in a room with pink curtains and she can hear a pig grunting outside.' I do the sound effects. 'What's wrong?' I am put off from telling the rest of the story because Mark is looking at me in a strange way.

'Come on, tell me what happens next,' he insists.

'Well, the old woman is delighted but it never crosses her mind to *thank* the fairy. The fairy goes east and west, north and south, and then comes back to the old woman, knowing how pleased she will be in her little white house. "Oh! 'tis a shame, so it is, 'tis a shame. Why should I live in a pokey little cottage? I want to live in a red townhouse and have a little maid to wait on me." "Well, never you mind," the fairy says.'

' "When you wake up in the morning, you'll see what you will see," ' Mark finishes for me.

'Next she wants to live in a house with white steps and men and maids waiting on her. Then she wants to live in a palace. "Look at the Queen. Why shouldn't *I* sit on a gold throne with a gold crown on my head?" The fairy grants her wish, but when she returns to hear the old woman complaining that the crown is too heavy for her head, she gives up. "Why can't I have a home to suit me?" the old woman moans. "Oh, very well, if all you want is a home to suit you . . ." the fairy says wearily. The old woman wakes up and finds herself back in the vinegar bottle, where she stays for the rest of her life.'

'Serves the old woman right.'

'I remember that story so well, Mum read it to Bells and me. What about your family?' I ask. 'I've been so wrapped up in my own dramas that I know nothing about you. Are you close to your parents?'

'We've had our moments. I felt I'd let my father down when I told him I didn't want to be a lawyer. My brother emigrated to New Zealand and became a sheep farmer, Dad couldn't understand where his genes came from. I was his last chance. Law is in his blood, his father was a lawyer. Jess is a lawyer too, so that helps. Dad especially loves her. My Scottish lass, he calls her.'

So not only is she good-looking and bright, she is also like family. Bugger. 'How did you two meet?'

'At school, funnily enough. In Edinburgh.'

'Why were you in Edinburgh?'

286

'One of my father's first jobs was there, and my parents loved the place so much they decided to move permanently. I think I am about one-eighth Scottish by now.'

'So you've been going out with her for a long time?'

'Only six months, but it feels like longer,' he adds, and I can't tell whether that's a good or a bad thing.

'How come it took you that long to start going out?'

'I don't know,' he says, his voice clipped and considered. 'We kind of fell into it. We went on holiday with a group of friends and that was it. We were worried it might affect our friendship, but it's fine.'

Fine? Fell into it? That was it? Mark's vocabulary lacks a certain passion. Where's the romance? Where are the fireworks?

'I guess it's true,' he says with a sense of defeat . . . or am I reading too much into his voice?

'What?'

'Somewhere along the line, girls and boys can't just be friends. At some point . . .'

'You don't believe that rubbish, do you? Come on. We're friends, aren't we?'

'You're right.'

'Are you happy?'

'Am I happy? Well, that's a difficult question.'

'With Jess, not in general,' I say, hoping that I am not being too nosy.

'She's one of my closest friends. She's always been there

for me. It's funny, though,' he shuffles his chair in closer, 'she's intelligent, but if you ask her where Guatemala is, she doesn't have a clue.'

I sit, frozen. 'Africa?' From his expression I see I'm wrong. 'America? Of course, it's America.'

'North or South?'

'Er, South? No, North.'

'It's south of Mexico, next to Honduras, and not so far from Panama.'

'Shut up, clever clogs, we can't all be geography wizards.'

'Which direction is north?'

'Shut up!'

'How did we get on to Jess?'

'We were talking about your parents. They wanted you to be a lawyer.'

'Oh, yes. It's all about approval, isn't it? You want them to be proud, whatever you do.'

'I admire anyone who teaches, I couldn't do it. Is your father proud of you?'

'I don't know,' he shrugs. 'I think so.'

'He should be.' I smile. 'You see, if you were to die tomorrow – God forbid,' I add, touching his arm briefly.

'Thanks.'

'I'm sure your father would be saying, "I wish I'd told Mark we were proud of him." I would never have forgiven myself if Mum had died and I'd left so many things unsaid.

I felt so hard done by when I was little because she was always in hospital with Bells, but look at people who have no proper homes or divorced parents who screw them up. Emma says she sees people . . .'

'Don't start saying how much worse off they are than you,' Mark says, disgruntled.

'Well, they are.'

'Look, we never really go around thinking like that. There's always someone a lot worse off than you, sure, but if someone said to you, "Think of the starving children in Africa," every time you came to them with a problem, you'd want to pelt them with frozen peas.'

I laugh. 'Why frozen peas?'

'I couldn't think of anything else. What I'm trying to say is, each problem, each situation, it's all relative. OK, you had a damaged relationship with your mother, but if someone tells you they don't get on with any of their family, mother, father and all six sisters and brothers, and that you should count yourself lucky, does that really make it better?'

'I've never thought about it like that. You should become a counsellor.'

'That'll be fifty pounds, please. See you next week?'

'Yes, please.' The scary thing is I mean it too.

We sit quietly for a few minutes watching people go by. It doesn't feel awkward saying nothing. It feels peaceful.

Eventually I break the silence. 'Do you have any unusual characters in your family?'

'How about the grandmother who kept a lion under her bed?'

I laugh. 'Well, I'm glad it's not just our family then.'

From the corner of my eye I can see a girl walking by outside, wearing a baseball cap on back to front, a black bra, black vest, a black miniskirt, a small backpack and black knee-length platform boots. A group of young friends walk past and I hear them laugh at her mockingly, but the girl marches on.

'You see that girl?' Mark says.

'You can hardly miss her, can you?'

'She looks a bit weird . . .'

'Shocking outfit.'

'Fine, all that's true, but she's far more interesting than the other girls who look like clones of each other.'

I look at the backs of the three girls, each with dyed blonde hair, all roughly the same height, and all wearing baggy trousers, skin-tight tops and trainers.

'She'd be the one the author wrote about. Eccentric, unusual, out-of-the-ordinary characters make the world go round,' Mark says. 'God, life would be boring without them.'

When Mark leaves, I finish my letter to Bells and then go to the newsagent's to buy copies of *Vogue*, *Tatler*, *Harpers & Queen* and *Glamour*.

Two weeks later I have made myself a suede coat with a

soft lining. I have also been working on my designs and compiled a portfolio. I'd love to have my own label in the future; it's something to work towards. 'I've bought a Katie Fletcher top,' I can hear someone saying. I've been people-watching constantly, looking around various shops in my lunch hour and seeing what's out there. I've been working late in the evenings after I close the shop too. It was time to change my image as well, so I went to my Spanish hairdresser's, and he made me 'feel like a different woman', as he put it. He cut and layered my hair in the front. I like pulling it back into a short neat blunt ponytail. It feels symbolic of a new start on so many fronts, most importantly with Mum.

And, even more impressive, I have bought a pair of luminous purple goggles and a black costume and have been swimming each morning before work.

I have even stopped smoking.

I like the new Katie Fletcher.

35

'Jonnie, who was that?' I call. It's the evening and I'm about to go to bed.

'Don't know, he hung up again.'

I walk into the sitting room. Emma and Jonnie are watching television.

'He?'

'Well, the only person I can think of is Sam,' Jonnie suggests.

'Possibly,' I say. To my surprise, Sam has called a few times, saying he wants to meet up, that we need to talk, but I can't see the point. I told him we should accept it's over and no hard feelings. 'You sound different. Are you seeing someone else?' he demanded. 'Sam, I've been at home looking after Mum,' I said wearily. Maybe I should meet him and be done with it.

Jonnie studies my expression. 'There's nothing going on between you two still, is there?'

'Nope.'

'Is it safe to talk about him now?' he asks.

'Quite safe.'

'Well, I always thought he was a bit of a tosser.'

'Jonnie!' Emma hurls a cushion at him.

'It's fine, honestly.' I shrug. 'If you look the part, you feel the part . . .'

'. . . and you ARE the part,' we all finish, and laugh.

'How about, "You have to think outside the box"?'

'I liked "done and dusted",' Emma says now. 'I always thought you could do a lot better,' she admits finally, and then pauses as if unsure whether to say whatever is on her mind next. 'Like this Mark person?'

'He's just a friend. Anyway, he's going out with Jess.' I change the subject. 'Right, need to put the rubbish out, it's bin day tomorrow, isn't it?'

'It is,' Jonnie confirms. 'Bin day. What an exciting fast-paced world we live in.'

I wobble out of the front door with two black bags. I am tempted to go for an evening walk; I might bump into Mark. Since that Sunday morning, nearly a month ago, he and I have been out many times. I often go round to his place after work and we have a drink together. We made spaghetti bolognese the other night and watched one of Bells's favourite Dustin Hoffman movies, *Tootsie*. Last week Mark shoved a note through the door: 'Sticky bun & coffee tomorrow?'

It's a Monday night, he should be in. It's only ten o'clock.

I feel like some company, that's all. As I knock on the door to his flat I hear his bike outside and now he's coming through the front entrance. His face looks pink from the cold night air and he's wearing a bright yellow strap across his coat, which he pulls off when he sees me.

'Hi.' He rubs his hands together. 'How are you?'

'I'm fine. I was putting the rubbish out, then I thought about you.'

'Charming! Want to come in?'

'Love to. Where have you been?'

'School. God, I'm tired,' he says as he walks into the kitchen. I follow him. 'We're rehearsing for *My Fair Lady* and there's so much work to do. Professor Higgins has ducked out now so I've had to replace him with Matthew, and I don't know if he's up to the task.'

'Sit down,' I order. 'Tell me where everything is and I'll make you something to eat and drink. My turn to fuss over you.'

'Wonderful,' he sighs, taking off his boots and the bicycle clips from his trousers. 'What luck I ran into you. Mugs are in the cupboard above the sink.'

I open a cupboard and find plates and soup bowls. 'To the right,' Mark instructs. 'Coffee's in the fridge.'

'You keep it in the fridge?'

'Keeps it fresh.'

'Why do you keep mustard in the fridge?' Mark looks at me wearily. 'Sorry. Everyone's kitchen's a novelty. You like these!' I turn to him in amazement. On top of his fridge sits a packet of marshmallows covered in chocolate with strawberry jam filling. 'Emma teases me for still liking these. She told me they're the sort of things mothers put in packed lunches and that I should have grown out of them by now.'

'Well, she's missing out then, isn't she? I love them, could eat a whole pack at once.'

I am delighted to hear this. I make two cups of coffee and Mark eats a toasted cheese sandwich. 'Katie, I have a big favour to ask. I was going to come and see you about it tomorrow.'

'This sounds serious.'

'Jess can't come to *My Fair Lady*. Obviously, as great as our production is going to be, Edinburgh's a bit too far to come for a school play. So . . . I was wondering if you would come with me instead?'

'Really?'

'Yes. What do you think?'

'Have you asked Jess?'

'I will, but I'm sure she won't mind. She knows now that we're just friends.'

'All right, if you're sure she'll be cool with it, then I'd love to. I've never been to a school play. The only time I remember Mum coming to watch me at school was when I was nine. The entire class played recorders. She tells me we were *terrible*. Granny Norfolk came too, and apparently nudged her in the middle of our rendition of "Greensleeves", saying, "The *crème* of Southampton is here tonight," followed by a squawking laugh.'

'What, a laugh like yours, you mean?'

'Do I squawk?'

'You do.'

'Thanks so much. When is it?'

'Friday night.'

For a moment I long to have something else on to make him think I have a terribly exciting and hectic social life. 'Right, fine, see you Friday. I'm going. I've had enough of you for one night.'

A school play. Do I dress smart? Casual? I opt for my black dress and the gold necklace with the medallion-like pendant. I look at myself in front of the long mirror. Since I stopped smoking I've put on a few pounds around my hips and my face looks less drawn. I put some shimmering grey round my eyes to bring out the green in them and after endless debate, decide to let my hair down.

I'm singing loudly in the street, pretending to be Eliza Doolittle.

'Shh!' Mark laughs, holding me back from swinging around the next lamppost. 'We're getting some really strange stares.'

'Who cares? You shouldn't mind what people think.'

'I don't,' he agrees.

'I've spent far too much time worrying about what others think, it's a waste of time.' I turn to him. 'I really enjoyed tonight. I think your class were great.'

'They sang their hearts out, didn't they?' he says. 'Helen really belted it out.'

Helen played Audrey Hepburn's part, Eliza. I don't want to tell Mark she nearly deafened the audience and that I wished I'd taken my earplugs. Mark stayed so intent on the performance that I didn't dare breathe in case he missed a note or a word. The real low point was when Professor Higgins tripped and fell off the stage. He was dancing with Eliza in triumph because she was finally speaking 'proper', and he stepped too far. Everyone gasped and Mark rushed to the stage as if he was acting in *Casualty*. I couldn't help watching him more than the play. What was so fascinating was the passionate interest he felt in these children who couldn't really sing. Mark was with them every step of the way. He'd screw up his face when the piano teacher hit a wrong note. There was one part where they had to start the 'Rain in Spain' song again because Eliza hit a series of wrong notes and I thought Mark was going to have a heart attack. 'We rehearsed this one time and time again,' he said in agony.

'Shh, they're doing really well,' I whispered back, reaching out to hold his hand in support. He clutched his fingers over mine. His palm was sweaty. The best part, however, was the end. Everyone stood and applauded for what seemed like five minutes. The headmaster called Mark up on to the stage and he bowed together with the cast. Bells would have enjoyed this too, I thought. She should be here. The cast bunched around him, one actor hit his arm affectionately, and another one did a high five. Mark was congratulating them all. Eliza gave him some flowers and then looked shyly at her feet. 'Who's that babe with you?' one of the boys asked loudly, pointing at me. I almost burst with pride at this point. Nearly thirty and called a babe. 'Is that your girlfriend?' he continued.

I know I blushed furiously at this point and had to pretend I needed something in my handbag. When I looked back, Mark was smiling at me.

'Taxi!' Mark shouts as we see a black cab with its yellow light lit up.

He and I sink back into the seat. I break out into another *My Fair Lady* song and Mark joins in. The cab driver is shaking his head at us.

'What's your favourite thing in the world?' I ask. 'Apart from porn.'

Mark scratches his chin playfully. 'If it can't be porn, it has to be . . . um . . . marshmallow biscuits.'

'Don't overexcite yourself.'

'Come on, you then?'

'The smell of fresh coffee and bread.'

'Skiing on a beautiful day with fresh-powder snow.'

'Going to bed.'

Mark raises an eyebrow. 'With anyone in particular or on your own?'

'On my own and having the duvet all to myself.'

'Wow, aren't we a wild pair? OK, what do you hate most in the world?'

'Rude and narrow-minded people.'

'People who look over your shoulder when you're at a drinks party.'

'I hate that!'

'The trick is to tell them you drank a bottle of gin with twenty Anadin and see if they say, "Oh, how interesting",' Mark says.

'Traffic wardens,' the cab driver shouts through. 'And people who tell me which route I should take – that gets me, that does. Think they know better when I've been driving around London for years.'

'Take a left here,' Mark says.

The driver laughs.

'Ooh, I've got one!' I burst out. 'Christmas starting in August.'

'I like this game. People who trump you,' Mark goes on. 'I tell someone I went to Vienna and they tell me the place I really ought to go to is Budapest.'

'Oh, yes, nothing more annoying.' We laugh. 'If you could change anything about yourself, what would it be?' I ask.

Mark takes too long thinking.

'I'll start,' I suggest. 'I wish I wasn't so stubborn.'

'I'm too soft.'

'You're not soft. I saw how you pulled those children into line. They respect you. You're kind, but that's different. I can be too proud.'

'I love the way you say what you think.'

'I don't, Mark, not always. Look how long it took Mum and me to talk properly. I bottle things up, stew over problems.'

'Well, I wear my heart on my sleeve. I'm too emotional. I even cried reading *Bridges of Madison County*.'

'You're a wimp. But I cried too.'

'So did I,' chips in the cab driver, clearly still eavesdropping.

'Mark.' I lean closer towards him, our legs gently brush. 'I've never noticed your eyes before.' One is tinged with brown, the other is blue. We look at each other for a second too long. I turn away first.

'Oh,' he says, 'a freak accident. I was about to score for a cricket match. I was spinning a pencil in between the guy ropes that hold up the nets for practising when it spiralled out of my hand. The likelihood of that pencil hitting me was a million to one, but . . .' he gestures to his eyes '. . . I had to have three stitches. That's why I need the glasses. It's my excuse whenever I lose a tennis match,' he says, making me smile. 'You're shivering, Katie. Here, have my jacket.'

He places it around my shoulders and I feel acutely aware of the warmth of his touch. I'm also aware we're nearly home, but I don't want the evening to end yet.

As if Mark can read my thoughts he says, 'It's still early. Do you fancy a drink?'

I nod. 'Emma and Jonnie aren't in tonight. Why don't you come over to my place?'

'Sounds good. It's a right here,' Mark says to the driver, 'and then pull in anywhere.'

Mark takes my hand as I step out of the cab. 'M'lady,' he says. 'By the way, I never said it, but you looked beautiful tonight.'

'Why, thank you, sir.' We stand holding hands, neither of us moving. 'My place, then?' I say, finally letting go.

'Whose place?' Sam is waiting outside Emma and Jonnie's front door, wearing his old leather jacket. He walks towards us.

I can see his hands are shaking and I feel almost sorry for him, standing out in the cold. He doesn't look like the confident Sam who used to stride along to the click of his shoes. He hasn't shaved properly either. 'What are you doing here?' I ask him.

'More to the point, what are you two doing together? This looks cosy.'

'Sam, it's none of your business.'

His eyes narrow as he looks at Mark. 'Who are you?'

'Mark.'

301

'Well, hello, Mark. Where have you been?'

'Look, go home, Sam . . .'

Mark interrupts, 'Well, if you really want to know, I took her to see *My Fair Lady*.'

'Katie hates musicals.'

'Well, even nicer of her to come along with me then,' says Mark calmly.

'Are you two dating?' Sam says, as if he's imagining the two of us together and it's not a pretty sight. 'Having said that, Katie's more like a nun these days. Acts like she's wearing a habit and a chastity belt.'

I don't feel so sorry for him any more. 'Sam, you're drunk.'

'Mark who loves gay musicals,' he continues, 'my ex-girlfriend's turned into a nun. So are you two together? Probably not.'

'Well, as her modesty's ensured, I'm surprised you had to come and check on such an unthreatening situation,' Mark says, taking my hand.

'Sam, it's late, please go home,' I tell him.

'It's not even midnight, Sister Fletcher.'

Mark and I continue to walk on without him. 'Do you want me to call him a cab?' Mark asks quietly.

'I miss you,' Sam cries out. Mark and I stop and look back. 'I miss you. Katie, you can't go out with someone, live with them, and then never want to speak to them again,' Sam protests. 'Why haven't you been returning my calls? I'm not going until you talk to me.'

302

I tell Mark to go on without me, that I'll call him when Sam has gone. 'If you're sure? Katie, I'll stay with you if you want?' Sam throws him a hostile look at this remark.

'Go on. I'll deal with this.'

Sam takes off his jacket and sits down on the sofa. 'I've been an idiot, you were right. Everything you said that night, about you and me not talking, about not sharing enough stuff, I've been thinking about it. I'm sorry.'

I pull up Jonnie's leather chair and sit opposite him.

'Come over here, Katie.'

'You're lucky I even let you in,' I remind him. 'You were behaving like an idiot outside.'

'I know. But I can't help it. I'm going crazy here.' He beckons me towards him again.

'I'm comfortable here, thanks. Sam, what do you want?'

He looks at me, something desperate in his eyes. 'Nothing makes sense to me if you're not around. I rattle around in that house of mine. I want you back. I'm sure we can make a go of things. We used to have fun together. Come on, what d'you say?'

'Oh Sam, too much has happened. It wouldn't work.'

'How do you know?'

'Why do you miss me?'

'I just do.'

'It's because you're scared of being on your own, isn't it?' He laughs, but I can tell he's trying not to lose his cool. 'Not true, I'm not scared of anything. I valued our relationship . . . clearly a lot more than you did.'

'Sam, you finished it,' I say, then realize he's right. It was easy walking out of his life. I haven't missed him.

'I think you and me are worth fighting for.'

'Why, Sam? You didn't call me once when Mum was so ill.' I can't keep the hurt out of my voice. 'She could have died, Sam.'

He puts his head in his hands. 'I know. I'm sorry. I've been preoccupied.'

I stare at him.

'Katie, my job's on the rocks, I could lose it. It's not an excuse, but . . .'

'I'm sorry about your job, but this is what it's all about, getting through the hard times as well as having fun together. We were great when everything was going well, but we fell at the first hurdle when life threw us a challenge. What does that say about us?' As I'm saying this I'm thinking of Mum and Dad, who have stayed together through the good and bad times because they are a team. Having Bells and me, and all the problems that came with us, brought them closer together.

Sam finally looks up at me. 'I'm no good at dealing with stuff like that . . . illness, you know, I don't know what to say. Your mum's all right now, isn't she? What can I do, Kitty, to make it up to you?'

'You don't need to do anything. It's over,' I say, more gently this time.

Sam tells me that if I don't go back to him his life will fall apart, he can't live without me. He wanted to call when Mum was in hospital but he didn't know what to say. 'My family, we never talk about things like that. My father, he used to tell me never to say sorry or be weak.' He stops. 'I'll even marry you.'

'Sam, stop this.'

'I'll do whatever it takes,' he says, gambling that this last pledge of commitment will work. 'I'll do anything. Katie? What's wrong?'

I try to compose myself. 'I don't know how to say this, I wish I didn't have to. I don't love you any more.'

'I know I was angry, but I didn't want us to split up,' he says, choosing not to hear what I've said.

'Look, it's OK,' I reassure him. 'I don't blame you.'

'It's not because of Mark, is it? Katie, you can do better than that. What's he doing, taking you to a bloody musical? You can't be serious, picking him over me?'

Just as I'm feeling truly sorry for Sam, he goes and says something like that. 'Let's not do this, Sam. We both need to move on.'

'Is it because of Bells? We were happy before she came along. I know I didn't hit it off with her, but we can work on that.'

Has he listened to a word I have said? 'No, we can't. You

can't change who you are. I've changed, things change, that's all. I'm tired, Sam. I'm calling you a cab.' I walk over to the small table by the sofa and pick up the phone.

As Sam snatches the phone from me, a glass lamp base on the table crashes to the floor. 'Look what you've done!' I shout, bending down to pick up the shattered pieces of glass. 'Just go, please,' I say tearfully. He bends down and I think he's going to help me pick up the glass. Instead he tries to kiss me. I can smell stale alcohol on his breath. I pull away, furious now. '*Go*, Sam.'

There's a knock on the door. I stand up and put the broken pieces of lamp on the table. 'Katie,' I hear Mark calling. I rush to open the door.

'Look who it is,' Sam says. 'Your knight in shining fucking armour!'

Mark pushes past him. 'I was worried.' He touches my shoulder. 'Are you all right?'

'Fine. He won't leave.'

Mark turns to Sam. 'I think you should go.'

'I don't give a fuck what you think.'

Mark opens the front door and stands there holding it.

Sam grabs his jacket and walks towards him. 'All right, I'll go,' he mutters. Mark and I briefly exchange relieved looks, but then, as Sam is about to leave, he turns around and punches Mark in the face. Mark staggers backwards, his glasses falling to the ground.

'Sam, stop it!' I scream as he is about to have a second go

at Mark. I plunge forward and grab his arm. Sam pulls away from me and proceeds to step on Mark's glasses, grinding them into the ground. 'No fucking contest.'

'Sam?' I hear Mark saying quietly.

Sam turns. 'Did that hurt?'

'Not as much as this.' Mark belts him in the stomach.

Sam holds himself steady and laughs. 'You can do better than that, can't you?'

'That's enough!' I shout at them both, stepping between them. 'Go home,' I plead with Sam. 'And Mark, leave it, OK?'

I watch Sam stagger down the steps. He looks so miserable and alone. I never wanted it to end this way.

Mark lies with his head on my lap and I rest the packet of frozen peas against his chin. 'Next time we see Sam, we can pelt these little bullets at him,' I say, remembering Mark's pelting frozen peas line.

'If this were a film, I would have pushed Sam against the door and punched him back twice as hard,' Mark says dejectedly.

'How's the hand?'

'Painful. I feel like a loser.'

'You did hit him, though. Well done.'

'Yeah, right. If you hadn't stepped between us he would have mashed me to a pulp.'

I adjust the position of the peas. 'I don't know what I would have done if you hadn't come. How does it feel now?'

'Not good. Carry on.'

'It's funny, but I was terrified of losing Sam. When Bells came to stay, I didn't tell him about her until she'd arrived. I was so nervous he'd do a runner, that he wouldn't want to know me.'

Mark sits up and turns to me. 'I remember you telling me this when we first met. That's stupid, Katie.' His tone is uncomfortable.

'I know. There's no excuse.' I can't stand the idea of him thinking badly of me. 'Bells wasn't a part of my life at all then, not until she came to stay. I only saw her as this person with the potential to put Sam off. I know it sounds cruel, but that's how I felt. I've had a lot of growing up to do. You know, he didn't even call me to see how Mum was. I would have called him whatever had happened between us.'

'What did you ever see in that man?' Mark asks impatiently.

'There is a good side to him, I promise. I know it was invisible tonight, but he's got no one, Mark. No support from his family, he never talks about his parents. There's this sadness, Mark, an emptiness. He has no real friends to confide in, only lads like Maguire. And he might lose his job. I know that would terrify him.' I feel tearful again. I didn't enjoy seeing Sam so unhappy. 'He does have a good side,' I stress once more. 'At least he doesn't pretend to be anything he isn't. I could learn from him there. I mean, who was I trying to be? Perfect Katie with her perfect life?'

Mark's tone softens. 'You shouldn't have to pretend to be anything. He shouldn't have made you feel like that.'

'It's easy to blame Sam, but it wasn't all his fault. My own insecurities were just as much to blame.'

Mark nods. 'You wouldn't put yourself through all that again, though, would you, with the next man you meet?'

'Oh no. I've learned my lesson.'

'Men aren't worth it,' he adds with his familiar wry smile.

'Thanks for coming round tonight. No one's done anything like that for me before, Mark. You're a real mate. I owe you.'

'Well, you could get me some new glasses?'

I look at Mark's glasses, smashed to smithereens; the black frames now a wonky S-shape.

We laugh. 'It's the least I can do.'

36

It's a Thursday, late afternoon, and Mark has asked me over for supper. I left the shop early this afternoon as Eve and the new assistant, Jackie, were able to manage without me. Jackie is bright and enthusiastic about her work. She also designs and makes knitwear. I'm going to sample selling some in the shop.

I sit on the stool behind the breakfast counter in Mark's kitchen. There's a pile of paperwork in front of me, his red pen scrawled across the sheets. Essays on *The Mayor of Casterbridge* with that dreaded underlined word at the end of the assignment: 'Discuss'. I swivel round on my stool and play with the gadget that adjusts the height. 'Weh-hey!' I say, sinking closer to the floor. 'I like these!'

He opens the fridge. 'No bloody milk. What do you feel like eating tonight?'

'Why don't we go out?' I suggest. Mark and I have never 'gone out' apart from that one evening when we watched the school play. Normally he cooks me supper, but I'm getting a little bored of spaghetti bolognese.

'Go out? Do you think our friendship has reached that stage?' he asks.

'I think we're ready. Did I tell you, I've seen a flat I love?'

'You're moving?' he asks, and then wonders why he's surprised. 'I forget you're living with Emma and Jonnie sometimes.'

Emma and Jonnie haven't met Mark yet. 'You have mentionitis . . .' Emma said to me the other day while we were shopping for her wedding dress.

'Mention what?' I threw her a funny look.

'Mentionitis. You talk about him all the time. When are you going to introduce us?'

Even Mum detected a change in me when I last called. 'Has it got something to do with Mark?'

'No, he's a friend, Mum.'

'Blah blah blah,' she said, followed by a sniff of boredom. 'Love comes along when you least expect it. You have to take a chance, Katie. If you like this man, tell him. If not, move on. You have to go out at every opportunity too, never turn an invitation down, because you never know who you might meet. When I first met your father . . .'

'Katie?' I hear him say now. 'You do that a lot, you know.'

'Sorry? What?'

'Retreat into your own world. What were you thinking about?'

'Um, my new place.'

'Where is it?' Mark asks me.

'Chiswick. Close to the shop.'

He leans against the counter. He's wearing the new pair of glasses that we bought together, almost exactly the same model as the broken ones. I also persuaded him to buy a pale blue round-necked jumper without holes in the elbow. 'Has the wife dragged you out shopping?' said the man in Marks & Spencer, rolling his eyes when I told Mark to try on yet another style.

'Calling Katie? Where is Katie?' Mark prods me again. 'Sounds perfect. When are you moving?'

'Just before Christmas.' I found a small two-bedroom flat to rent; I had to have a spare room for Bells.

'Shit, that's less than a month away.'

'I know. Emma and Jonnie are throwing me a Christmas-stroke-leaving party in two weeks, Bells is coming down to stay, so you'd better be around too.'

'I'll try and fit it in,' he says, and I throw his red marker pen at him.

'And Jess, is she around?'

'I'll ask her.'

'Why don't you live together?'

'What, besides the fact she lives in Edinburgh? Right,' he says, clearly keen to move on. 'Tea? Or maybe you need something stronger?'

'Tea would be great.'

'You put the kettle on, I'll get the milk and the marsh-mallow biscuits.' He picks up his house keys off the counter and walks out of the room.

Mark's mobile starts to vibrate against the table. 'Can you get that for me?' he calls, before the front door shuts.

I pick up the phone tentatively. I don't like taking calls for other people. 'Hello, Mark's phone,' I say in my best secretarial voice.

'Who's that?' a voice says abruptly. Is this Jess?

'It's just Katie.'

'Just Katie, this is Sasha Fox. Is Mark there?'

'Not right this minute.' She is terrifying.

'It's his agent, can you get him to call me back,' she says, more as a demand than a question, and hangs up.

I put the phone down and decide to have a snoop round Mark's flat. I wonder if she has news on the book? She must have. I feel nervous for Mark. Along the corridor, past the bathroom, and then three steps down and I'm in his bedroom.

It's a large airy room with a big double bed and a smooth carved oak headboard. It doesn't smell stale or of boy's socks, I'm pleased to note. Mark has shutters instead of curtains and there's a newspaper lying across the white duvet. He's reading *Life of Pi*, and next to the book on his bedside table is a silver-framed photograph. Jess is sitting on a boat wearing denim shorts and a spotted bikini, and Mark stands next to her proudly holding a barracuda. She's annoyingly pretty. Why can't she have a gap in her front teeth or unfortunate facial hair? I feel like Glenn Close in *Fatal Attraction*. What's wrong with me? I press my fingers to my temples. Perhaps I'm coming down with something? I don't think I've been quite myself lately.

I hear a door shut and run back up the stairs, tripping on the last step. I head for the bathroom, slam the door shut and flush the chain. Then I open the door casually and walk back to the kitchen.

'Who was it?' Mark asks, clutching the bottle of milk.

'Your agent.'

'Really? Ms Sucha Fox?' He grins nervously, then sits down on the stool next to me, crunching his knuckles.

'Stop it,' I say, wincing. 'That gives you arthritis.'

'Sorry.' He takes a deep breath. 'What did she say?'

'You've got to call her back.'

'Did she sound in a good mood?'

'She was a bit abrupt,' I confess.

'She's always abrupt.'

'Go on,' I say, pushing the phone towards him.

'What if it's bad news? Rejections from every publisher she has approached, saying I'm a useless crap writer?' He sits forward and puts his head in his hands. 'Katie, I've worked so hard on this book. I've had scripts rejected before, I don't know why I carry on, it's awful. It makes you feel like a fool, a failure, less than an insect. If it's a no, I'll be miserable.' He stands up, paces the room and then sits down again. 'I'm feeling a bit nervous actually.'

'I can tell,' I say, longing to hug him for his insecurity. Instead I pat his leg. 'Come on, stop being a drama queen.'

'I can't help it.'

'Look, your agent must believe in you. She would have e-mailed you if it was bad news,' I suggest.

'Good point. Although she didn't before.'

'Do you want me to go?' Please say no. I am dying to hear what Ms Sucha Fox has to say.

'No, stay,' he urges, taking the phone. 'Forget the tea, can you get me a proper drink? Right, wish me luck,' he says, punching in the number and walking out of the room.

Making vodka tonics in his kitchen, I rehearse ways to console Mark. 'It's their loss,' or, 'Did you know J. K. Rowling had masses of rejections, and look at her now!' No, that's lame. 'Did you know Virginia Woolf, Beatrix Potter, Honoré de Balzac and many other famous writers all had books self-published at some stage in their career? It's the latest trend. That could be an option.' I read that in a weekend magazine. Mark stands in front of me looking as if he's been given a parking ticket. He slams the mobile on to the table. I wait for him to say something. When he says nothing, I tell him I'm sorry and promptly hand him a neat vodka.

'What for?' He takes a large gulp of vodka. 'I've got a

deal! You're right, I can't be bothered to cook supper. We are going out to fucking celebrate!'

'No! Oh my God!' I shriek, moving forward to hug him.

He picks me up off the ground. 'I am going to be published, Katie, can you believe it?'

'Hurray!' I shout, wrapping my arms around him and laughing at the same time. He puts me down and then opens the fridge. 'We need a drink. No champagne, bugger.'

'I'll get some, my treat.'

'I can't believe it,' he repeats incredulously, circling the kitchen as if he is drunk. 'Ms Fox better not get run over by a bus or the publishers burn down or go bust or . . .'

I smile at him. 'Quiet! Back in a sec.'

I find myself skipping along the road like an excited toddler.

'You look like a cat who's stolen the cream, and eaten it too,' the man at the off-licence says.

'My friend's got a book deal.'

'Wow,' he says, taking my money. 'Tell him, many congratulations.'

Aren't people nice? I love life, I think to myself. Why do people say the British are chippy, that they don't like people fulfilling their dreams? There's not a chip in sight today.

When I return, I hear Mark talking in the kitchen. I stand there quietly and listen before joining him. 'We can celebrate when you get back . . . you don't have to do that, Jess. What am I doing tonight? Well, I think I'll have a few celebratory drinks.' I notice he doesn't say who with. He's listening to her and now he laughs. There's another long pause. His voice turns softer. 'I know, I wish you were here too.'

Of course she is the first person he wants to ring with the news. This has to be one of the biggest, proudest moments in his life and he ought to be with her, not me. Why do I feel like second-best? It only takes one phone call from Jess and – bam! Back to being Katie the good friend, someone to have a laugh with.

'Love you too,' I hear him say.

That's it, enough dreaming, Katie. Don't feel disappointed. Mark and I have a great friendship, we get on well, but that's as far as it goes. End of story, as Sam would say.

I need to go into the kitchen, have one drink and then go home. I need to accept this for what it is. I don't want to be second-best; I won't let myself feel like this. I clutch the bottle of champagne and brace myself as I walk back into the kitchen.

'Why do you have to go now?' Mark asks after one glass of champagne together. 'Come on, have another.' He refills my glass.

I push my glass aside. 'Sorry, Mark, I think I might be coming down with something,' I say vaguely. 'Emma had this twenty-four-hour sick bug.'

'What's wrong?' he asks, clearly unconvinced.

'I think I need to lie down.'

Mark touches my forehead. 'You feel fine.' He lifts my chin and holds my face up to his. 'I don't want you to go. Let's go out.'

'I'm sorry.' I put my hand over his and gently remove it. I kiss him on the cheek. 'Well done, Mark. I'm so proud of you.' I pick up my bag.

He follows me to the door and then I feel him clutching at my hand. 'Why are you really going?'

'What?' I say, unable to turn round and face him.

'I'm trying to figure out if I've done something wrong, said something, in the space of ten minutes?'

'You've done nothing wrong.'

'Then stay.'

'I can't. 'Bye, Mark.' I kiss him on the cheek one more time.

37

Sometimes I panic at night. Am I going to work in my shop for the rest of my life? Not that it's a bad life. Then my mind wanders to home. What if Mum has a relapse or something happens to Dad? Or to Bells? What if I end up an old maid? We all assume we're going to meet someone, but what if we don't? What if I end up an old lady feeding her cat fresh prawns, because I never had children and went completely potty? That could be me in years to come. It's that 'What am I doing, where am I going?' question which quietly nags me during the day but screams at me at night. When I wake up, I calm down. Mum is all right. Dad is happy. Bells is fine. I have a job. I have good friends. I know I am going in the right direction. I have so much to be thankful for.

We always want what we can't have, don't we? When I was about six I used to pray over and over again for blue eyes like Dad's. 'Your eyes are the colour of the sea,' I used to tell him as a child. After school I'd rush home to look in the mirror. They had stayed green. The colour of a murky pond, I thought. I could not understand why God didn't answer my prayers.

When Bells was born I prayed that she would get better so that I could have Mum back.

I stopped going to church when I was a self-conscious fifteen-year-old, but I still pray. Just don't tell anyone.

Mark stands at the front door, trailing his bike behind him. I haven't seen him for a fortnight. He left a message on my mobile but I didn't ring back or go round to his flat. However, I had to make contact when Bells arrived so I asked him if he wanted to come to the cinema with us tonight. Bells is staying for the weekend and will be around for Jonnie and Emma's Christmas party tomorrow evening. She wouldn't forgive me if she didn't see Mark.

His hands are covered in grime and his left cheek is smudged with oil too. His hair is even more all over the place.

'Did you fall, are you OK?' I ask. What's he doing here? It's only two o'clock.

'Nearly. The chain came off.' He grimaces. 'Clunk, in the middle of the street.'

'Hello, Mark.' Bells rushes up to him and claps him on the back.

'Hi, Bells! How are you?'

'You have car like Sam?'

'No,' he admits, almost in apology.

'Why?'

'Because I don't. Anyway, how are you?'

They hold hands and her little device vibrates. 'I should have known,' he laughs. Bells is rocking forward and clapping her hands together.

'Come in,' I tell him. He chains his bicycle to the gate and follows us indoors. His mobile rings and he takes the call.

'That was Jess, she can come tomorrow,' he tells me, putting his phone back in his rucksack.

'Great,' I reply.

Damn, bugger and shit.

'It'll be good to meet her properly,' I continue in this horrible cheery tone that I don't recognize as my own.

'That your girlfriend?' Bells asks.

Mark nods.

'You gonna get married?'

He looks at me and I titter cheerfully. 'Bells, don't be so nosy.' I can't get rid of this merry persona – ironic when I feel anything but. We go into the kitchen. All my washing is hanging on the drier next to the washing machine. Mark is standing in front of a line of my knickers and bras. There's one particularly attractive pair of grey M&S pants that have seen better days. I wish I could touch a button and they'd all disappear.

I put the kettle on. Bells hands round some fig rolls.

'Shut eyes,' she says as she holds something towards Mark. He looks at me, then back at Bells. 'Go on, don't worry, it's not a toad,' I laugh. 'Well, I don't know actually. It could be.'

'OK,' Mark whimpers. 'But I want a fig roll. I love fig rolls. The children do this at school sometimes. Made me sit on a whoopee cushion once when we had Joanna Lumley in to speak about acting. Deeply humiliating.' He squeezes his eyes shut.

Bells plants a square of mouldy cheese into his hand. It has fur all over it. From the way her shoulders are heaving up and down I can see she finds this hilarious, especially when Mark throws it back at her, shouting, 'It's alive, it's alive!'

'Mark, Bells and I have to go out in a minute, we're going to Sainsbury's and . . .'

'Sainsbugs,' Bells says, and proceeds to roar with laughter again.

'I promised Emma I'd get some food for tomorrow.'

'I'll help.'

'You look a mess, you can't go out looking like that.' Why am I sounding like his mother now? I can't bear being so conscious of everything I say and do around him.

'So what?' Mark says. 'You always say you shouldn't care what people think.'

I smile. 'Fine. Come.'

*

The supermarket is packed with shoppers and 'Jingle Bells' is playing in the background.

'Mark, what are you doing for Christmas?'

'Mum and Dad are in New Zealand with my brother the sheep farmer.'

'You're not going?'

'I can't.'

'How come?'

'It's too expensive to fly out for a week. Anyway, they're coming home for the New Year. I need to save a bit of money for next year,' he adds.

I nod. 'What's happening next year?' Mark looks preoccupied and doesn't immediately reply. 'You're not going to be on your own at Christmas, are you?' I press.

'No. I'm seeing Jess and a few friends.'

'Where does Jess live?' I realize I know the answer. Why is there this sudden need to fill the space between us?

'Edinburgh.'

'Oh, yes, of course. Edinburgh.' Why is every word I say so flat and obvious?

'Excellent,' he mutters out of nowhere, looking distracted. 'Where's Bells?' We both glance around, and walk up the aisle until we see her at the delicatessen counter, talking to the man behind the trays of olives and cold meats. He's wearing a hat with a silver Christmas star pasted on to the front. I can hear her asking him how old he is.

'Any more news on the book?' I sound like an interviewer. I realize it doesn't matter because Mark isn't even listening to me. He's watching Bells put on the man's silver-starred hat. 'Mark?' I nudge him. 'You're a world away.'

'Sorry.' He turns to me. 'I've got something on my mind.'

'That sounds serious?'

'Yes, no. I don't know. It's school, something's come up that I need to think about.'

'Anything I can help with?'

'No,' he says harshly.

'Mark?'

'Sorry. I didn't mean to snap. I'll work it out.'

Bells crashes into our trolley.

'Hey, Bells. Race you to the . . .' Mark looks at me for inspiration.

I scan my list. 'We need mini-sausages and Parmesan cheese.'

'Race you to the sausages!' Mark says as he tears off with Bells.

Mark, Bells and I are queuing for popcorn. Bells buys a barrel of Diet Coke. We're about to see Hugh Grant's latest film. 'You want Coke?' she asks Mark and me.

'Not another one?' he gasps. 'Bells, you'll have Coke coming out of your ears. I must buy some Coke shares, the industry does well out of you.'

'Not funny, Mark.'

'If I drank that much I would spend more time on the loo than watching the film,' I tell her as we walk to screen number five.

We sit down next to a young couple. I'm in the middle. Bells is laughing at the Cornetto advert. I turn to put my hand into the popcorn. Mark leans towards me and takes a handful. Our hands meet and stay there. I'm aware of every move he makes, each touch.

I hear noisy shuffling of feet. The couple sitting next to Bells are moving seats. 'Sorry, excuse me,' they are whispering as they step over people's feet. I am not going to let it ruin the evening. Don't say anything, Katie, I tell myself. I want to shout ARSEHOLES! and struggle to restrain myself. The only reassuring thing is that I don't think Bells has noticed. Has she?

'Excuse me?' I hear Mark saying as he stands up. The auditorium has darkened as the film crackles on to the screen. It's deathly quiet except for the sound of crisp and sweet packets being opened and ice-cream wrappers being peeled off. The couple turn around. 'I'm sorry to stop you in your tracks but is there something wrong with your seats?' I can feel everyone listening. 'Because if there is, maybe you should report it?'

They look at one another sheepishly. 'I think we should be in the row behind,' the man weakly gives as an excuse.

'You should be ashamed of yourselves,' Mark says quietly, but firmly, and sits down again. The film begins.

He takes off his glasses, wipes them clean on the sleeve of his jumper and then puts them on again. He looks tired, something is clearly worrying him. I wish he would tell me. He must be aware that I'm looking at him because he turns to me. 'What? What is it?'

'Thank you.' I touch his hand and we link our fingers.

'What for?'

'For telling them off,' I whisper.

'Shh,' we hear from the row behind.

We both turn back to the screen, withdrawing our hands quickly.

I love Mark for speaking out. The only thing is that Bells is now painfully quiet. I hand her the popcorn, but she doesn't take any. I think she understands far more than I give her credit for.

I think she always has.

38

Bells sits on my bed as she watches me get dressed. I'm wearing a pale blue jumper tied at one side with a ribbon, jeans and pointed shoes with a small heel.

I brush my hair in front of the mirror and catch Bells in the reflection. She's rummaging through my make-up bag, picking out lipsticks, powder and generally making a mess. 'What's this?' she asks, holding up an eyelash curler. 'You and Mark gonna get married?'

'Me marry Mark? I don't think so,' I laugh as I tie my hair back and then let it loose again. 'It's an eyelash curler, by the way.'

'Why you not going marry Mark?'

She's now trying to put on some of my nail varnish. 'Er, he hasn't asked me,' I reply, still watching her carefully as she attempts to paint her nails with my silver nail polish.

'Not same as you, am I?'

She has never asked me this question directly, although

I know she has asked Mum. I don't know what to say. Oh, please, someone tell me what is the right thing to say. I can't lie and pretend she is to please her. Bells will see right through that anyway. I turn round and see a great circle of silver on the white linen. 'Bells, oh no!' I rush over to examine the stain.

She throws the bottle across the room and it hits the wall, polish oozing out and on to the carpet.

'Bells! What's wrong? Why are you so angry?' I retrieve the bottle and put the top back on tightly.

'Can't do like Katie,' she shouts, punching one hand with the other, silver smudging across her palms. 'Not same,' she says firmly. 'Not normal, am I?'

I sit down next to her. 'What's brought all of this on?' I ask gently.

'Not normal,' she emphasizes again, cross that I don't understand what she's saying. 'People stare, not nice.'

'Bells, you're normal to me, to Dad, Mum, to all the people who love you.'

Bells doesn't look convinced. She's heard that one before. 'Not like Katie.'

'Why do you want to be like me? I'm not half the person you are.'

'You beautiful.'

'That's not what makes a person,' I say adamantly. 'Don't you ever think that.'

'Not beautiful like Katie.'

'Well, I'm not a good cook like you. I can make chips and steak, and that's about it. And a boiled egg. I'm like Dad.'

She still looks upset.

'Look at the way you ran the house when Mum was so ill. I don't think you realize how much you can do, Bells.'

She stops hitting her hands together and laughs weakly. 'Am good cook, aren't I?'

'You are. This stuff doesn't matter, it really doesn't,' I say, holding the nail polish in front of her. 'It's all pretty superficial. You are you, don't ever change. Wave, smile, say hello to people like you always do.' I am thinking of the time when Bells was in my shop and I was ordering her not to say hello to customers. 'Or if they're being plain rude, you stare back, don't let them get away with it. You can rise above all that, Bells. That's why people love and admire you. Look at Mark, or Eddie at the deli, or Robert and Ted, Mr Vickers, or the *entire* football team for that matter. I've never seen such a fan club.'

A small smile lights up Bells's face.

'I feel like we're really getting to know each other now,' I stumble on, 'and I love being with you. You're a top person, Bells.'

'You pretty,' she says again, looking at my clothes. Bells is wearing a patchwork skirt, with a black evening top from the shop, and around her wrist is a black leather bracelet with silver studs. She's also wearing her three small stud earrings in the left ear. 'Won't ever look like you, will I?'

'I haven't got your beautiful-coloured hair.'

'Mum's hair,' she says.

'Yes, Mum's. Do you still want to put some of this nail varnish on?' I ask, holding up the pot.

She gives me her hand and I carefully apply the silver over her short bitten nails. 'Look, I've made a mess too.' I smile, wiping away the excess nail varnish with a tissue. 'You are you, Bells, Katie is Katie, Mark is Mark. If we were all the same, life would be pretty dull, don't you think?'

'Yes, Katie, that's right. Thank you, Katie.'

'Can I get you another drink?' I ask Eve, who has brought Hector along too. He is looking plumper than usual and is wearing a royal blue tank top.

'Katie, what a great party!' She's already tipsy.

'What a lovely home,' Hector adds, looking around the room.

Emma, Bells and I decorated the Christmas tree with silver and gold balls, silver, red and gold ribbon, and chocolate Santas wrapped in foil. Emma put fairy lights in the kitchen and bunches of holly in the windows with fake robins nestled in the leaves. We made canapés all day. Sausages, cheese puffs, mini-mince pies. If I have to wrap one more shrivelled prune in bacon I shall go mad.

'Eve, I wanted to thank you so much for keeping the

shop going these last few months. I couldn't have done it without you.'

'It is no matter. I was happy to. You know, Mr Vickers helped me too. He likes to count the day's takings.' She smiles widely. *'Mon Dieu!'* she exclaims, hitting my arm. 'I tell you, Mr Vickers, he is amazing! He sorts out my love life. He tell me to go for it with Hector, that looks are not the most important thing in the world.'

Ouch! Poor Hector, but to my surprise he finds this rather funny.

'Excuse me, I am here,' is all he says.

Then they both laugh together, Hector gently nudging her against the hip, and it's the most touching thing I've seen.

'Oh my God! How did you get that bruise the size of a tennis ball?' I ask Eve. It's on her left arm, near the elbow.

Hector chuckles. 'I might not be number one in the looks department but there are other departments I'm rather good at,' he says proudly as he walks away from us. Eve looks at me mischievously. 'Hector and I, we have sex last night,' she whispers. 'Against the bath sink, on the kitchen table, on the . . . oh, what is the word?'

'The bed?'

'Non! Katie, you are so boring, so dull. We make love everywhere. By the fire, on the . . .'

'That's enough!' I laugh, putting my hands over my ears. 'Stop it. Actually, I'm wildly jealous. You seem really happy.'

331

'I am. Touching wood.' She leans across to touch the mantelpiece. 'You must be sad to leave your friends, no?'

'I don't want to live with newly-weds.' I smile. 'We were doing the table seating plan today and that was bad enough.' I tell Eve how we sat for hours writing down the guests' names on small coloured Post-it notes, and then tried to arrange them around imaginary tables. At one point Jonnie shouted and swore at Emma, telling her he didn't want any of her 'fucking psychology friends' sat near him. Emma and I were speechless. Jonnie rarely loses his temper. Emma then fired back, telling him it was unfair for anyone to have to sit next to his parents. I was with her on that one, but thought I'd better not utter a word.

The doorbell rings again. 'You must be Mark,' I hear Emma say. 'I've heard so much about you.'

Oh, Emma, I cringe. Why did you have to say that?

'I can't believe we haven't met before,' she blunders on. 'Hello,' she says to Jess.

Jess is wearing a sea-blue-coloured satin top over jeans. She barely has any make-up on but her skin is flawless. Then I catch sight of Mark, and before I know it I've bolted upstairs and run into my bedroom, swinging the door shut. I don't think he saw me. What was that all about, Katie? What's wrong with me? I realize I have never felt this way about anyone before. I don't know what to say or how to act in front of him any more. I don't recognize myself. Keep calm, Katie, I tell myself, only to feel my face getting redder and hotter. 'What's meant to be is meant to be,' I mutter. 'You don't really believe any of that rubbish, do you? Oh God, stop talking to yourself!' I take in a deep breath and count to five, before willing myself to go back downstairs.

Bells stands at the CD player with Mark, the Beatles playing in the background. She holds a can of ginger beer towards him, her silver nails sparkling. Mark looks as if he has tumbled out of the washing machine. His hair is ruffled and he's wearing dark jeans with a loose white shirt. He puts the can down and takes Bells's hand. 'Can't dance very well,' she's saying.

'Yes, you can,' Mark shouts above the music, turning her around.

'You can't take your eyes off him, can you?' Emma says, sneaking up on me.

'I was watching Bells.'

'He looks at you too, you know.'

I turn to her. 'Does he?'

'A lot, but you don't care, do you?'

'No, no.'

'Rubbish, Katie. This is me, Emma, your best friend. I know you inside out and back to front. You like him, I mean, *really like him*, don't you?'

'I can't do anything about it, though,' I sigh, still watching him.

Mark looks in my direction and smiles before turning back to Bells.

'It stinks, doesn't it?' I say to Emma. 'And there's nothing I can do.'

'What do you mean? Come on, you can do something.'

'He has a girlfriend.'

She nods. 'I know, but why don't you tell him? Give yourself a chance, at least. What have you got to lose?'

I watch him laughing with Bells. 'Everything,' I say.

'Katie?' Mark says quietly, taking my hand and leading me out of the room. We stand alone, facing one another.

'Yes?' The music dies out.

'There's something I want to tell you.'

'Tell me,' I whisper.

'I don't know where to start.' He looks at me, absorbing every feature of my face. His finger gently outlines the curve of my cheek.

'What is it?'

He takes his hand away but I long for him to touch me again.

'It's all over between Jess and me. I think it has been for a long time. I've wanted to say this since we first met but I haven't had the courage. I had to say something tonight; I can't keep it a secret any longer. I am hopelessly . . .' He stops. Please don't stop.

'Yes?'

'And utterly . . .'

'Where are you moving, Katie? Katie?'

'I'm sorry,' I say, shaking my head free of fantasy. Jess is standing in front of me. 'Chiswick. I've found a small flat close to the shop. The rent's not too bad and . . .'

'Talking of moving, isn't it wonderful news about Mark?'

'Sorry?'

'Mark? He's been offered a transfer to Edinburgh.'

'He's moving away?' I know Jess is watching me. I feel as if I am on stage, thrust into the limelight and I've forgotten my lines. 'No, I didn't know.'

Jess looks genuinely surprised. 'Well, he only found out yesterday. I'm sure he was going to tell you.' There is definitely a hint of pleasure in her voice. She stands back from me. 'I'm surprised he hasn't told you. I thought you saw him last night?'

'When's he going?' Emma intervenes, allowing me to try and compose myself. I hadn't even noticed her approaching us.

'January. This new school has great drama facilities and he'd be involved in the Edinburgh Festival. It's too good an opportunity to miss. I think it will be good for our relationship too,' she continues in this soft, calm voice, but she's still watching me closely. 'It's hard being separated, I think Mark and I need to spend more time together.'

'I heard my name being mentioned,' Mark says, joining us.

'Jess was telling me about your move to Edinburgh,' I tell him. 'Congratulations.'

Mark's smile rapidly disappears. 'Jess, it was my news to tell.'

'Sorry, I didn't realize it was a big secret,' she says, her eyes widening.

Mark looks furious. 'Jess, are you ready?'

She frowns. 'What? Right now?'

'Yep. We need to go.'

'Fine. I'll get my coat.'

'Why didn't you tell me?' I ask him, when Jess is out of earshot.

'I've only just made the decision,' he tries to explain. 'I was going to . . .'

'I wish you had,' I say quietly.

'Katie, I'm so sorry.'

I fake a smile. 'I'll miss you.'

'I'll miss you too.'

I'm sure he wants to say something more. 'Happy Christmas,' he mutters finally, leaning forward to kiss me on the cheek. I can hear Jess's footsteps behind me.

And then he's gone.

39

Bells and I are catching the train home together for Christmas. The day after the party I moved into my new flat with the help of Emma and Jonnie. It was strange leaving. It was like facing my first day at boarding school when we unpacked the boxes.

My mobile rings and Mark's name appears in the screen.

'Are you still in London?'

'No, Bells and I are on the train.'

'The choo-choo,' Bells announces.

'Katie, look, I'm sorry.'

'It doesn't matter.'

'No, it does. You're a good friend . . .'

There's that word I hate. Friend.

'Well done,' I speak over him. 'A book deal and now Edinburgh. What a year!'

'Katie, I really need to talk to you.'

'That Mark?' Bells asks. 'Hello, Mark.'

'Hi, Bells,' he says in a flustered tone. 'Katie, it's about the other night . . .'

Bells takes the phone from me. 'Happy birthday, Mark.'

'It's not my birthday, Bells, not yet, but thanks anyway. Can I have Katie back?'

'When are you leaving?' For an insane second I allow myself to imagine he's going to tell me he isn't going.

'Two weeks.' The line crackles as the train goes through a tunnel. Mark is saying something but I can't make it out.

I fight the urge not to cry. 'Mark, I'll see you in the New Year. And it's great news.' I swallow hard.

'Hello, Mark,' Bells repeats. 'Happy birthday.'

He doesn't say anything back to her this time. 'You're coming to my birthday party, Katie, aren't you?'

The line goes dead.

Christmas is good fun and I stay on for New Year. I have never seen the New Year in with my parents and Bells – well, not since I was about twelve – so this one feels important.

On New Year's Eve, Aunt Agnes joins us, bringing home-made crackers. Agnes is ten years older than my dad. She's dressed in a fake fur coat and scarlet beret with scarlet lipstick to match, and is wearing a solid silver heart pendant that looks as if it came from an expensive Bond Street jeweller. We discover Aunt Agnes has met someone through setting up a fundraising scheme in the community to raise money for a children's hospice. His name is Peter. Since Uncle Roger died two years ago she has lost at least two stone in weight. 'Aunt Agnes, you look amazing,' I tell her.

'Thank you, darling,' she says, eyelashes fluttering over her almond-shaped eyes.

'What's your secret?'

She smiles. 'I don't make homemade chips and Black Forest gâteau any more.'

We put on our paper hats, tell silly jokes and light indoor fireworks. Bells has a snake. It looks like a brown pill, but once lit turns into a black mamba. Mine is a cowboy smoking a cigarette which, when I light it, puffs out smoke. At the stroke of midnight we all drink to Mum's health. Her cheeks look flushed from the alcohol and she's getting emotional. Her hair is very short and soft, like fluff. She still covers it with her patterned silk scarves. Bells asks if she can look at the scar again; and Mum guides her hand across the back of her head. Bells touches it gently.

Mum, Dad, Bells and I are watching *Who Wants To Be A Millionaire?*, the special New Year celebrity edition. It's my last night at home before I head back to London.

'I can't believe this cretin is phoning a friend. It's "D", you fool!' Dad says when the phone rings.

'Maybe he's phoning you, Dad,' I suggest.

'Darling, can you get that?' Mum asks him, her eyes glued to the screen.

Seconds later he comes back into the room. 'It's Mark.' Dad hands me the phone and settles back in his seat.

I shove it back in his direction. 'I'm not here,' I mouth at him.

'Mark, can she call you back?' Dad puts the phone down. 'I don't like lying, Katie. Make sure you call him.' His attention returns to the television.

'Why don't you want to talk to Mark?' Mum asks.

I pretend not to hear.

'Katie?' Mum presses. 'Has something happened?'

'He's moving,' I tell her.

'Unless your old father is missing anything, why is that so bad?' Dad doesn't look away from the television.

'He's going to Edinburgh.'

'Hmm,' Dad acknowledges. 'You'll miss him. He's a very nice young chap. What's he going to do in Edinburgh then?'

Parents never get it, I think to myself.

'Oh, darling, do shut up,' Mum says to Dad. 'You're getting the wrong end of the stick, as usual.' She turns to me. 'Look, I'm not blind. Something is going on here, more than Mark moving on,' she says. 'Why won't you talk to him?'

'I don't feel like it, OK? I want to watch this.'

Mum sighs impatiently. 'Come on, Katie.'

'Fine.' I give in. 'I do like him, but what's the point if he's going away?'

'Much worse things can happen. It's not the end of the world, is it? It doesn't mean you won't see him again,' she reasons.

'I know, but . . . I've got so used to him being around, that's all. I'll really miss him. He's my soulmate.'

Mum glances sideways at Dad, who sits in the large arm-chair wearing his leather slippers, squinting at the television.

We both smile. 'He was attractive when he was younger,' Mum whispers to me.

'He's asking the audience now, can you believe it?' Dad says, outraged. '*They* won't know!'

'This must sound so . . .' I can't think of a word to use after everything Mum has been through, '. . . silly to you.'

'No, darling. What's silly is if you don't tell him. When are you seeing him next?'

'He's having a party, tomorrow night. It's in Battersea. His parents are going and everything.'

'And you're going too, aren't you?'

I look unsure.

'You love him?' Bells asks. She's lying on her front on the floor, leaning on her elbows, watching the television. I hadn't been aware she was even listening because she had been so quiet.

'No,' I stammer, caught off-guard by her directness.

'Stupid Katie.'

'I'm not,' I bite back, thinking I have not been called stupid since I was little.

'Stupid, isn't she, Mum?'

'Stop calling me stupid,' I gasp. Then I remember how I told Bells over and over again how stupid she was when she cut out the labels from the T-shirts.

'Do you love Mark?' Mum asks.

'What? You love Mark?' Dad chips in now.

I bury my head in my hands.

'Oh, darling, do keep up. I think you're right, Bells,' Mum says. 'She's stupid if she doesn't tell him.'

They all look at me expectantly now.

'How do I tell him? He's going away. He has a *girlfriend*.'

Mum shrugs her shoulders. 'What have you got to lose?'

'My pride?' I suggest.

'Well, it is a risk, but you've got to ask yourself this question. Is Mark worth it?'

I think about this for a second. 'Yes. I've never met anyone like him.'

'Right, well, in that case, you have a large vodka, you go to the party, you walk over to him and be brave. You tell him exactly how you feel. If he's in love with his girlfriend, you accept it and move on, but at least you had the courage to tell him. You only regret the things you don't do, Katie.'

'That's right,' Dad says now.

'Maybe it wasn't meant to be,' I say in a final bid to spare myself from humiliation.

'That's the easy way out, only cowards say that,' Mum says with a sniff.

Mum and I stand at the top of the stairs. We're about to go to bed. 'Buy yourself a new dress for the party,' she says, touching my face. 'Don't wear black. Wear red,' she insists. 'It goes with your dark hair. And put your hair up.'

'Anything else?' I smile.

'No, that's it.'

We kiss on the cheek.

'Thank you,' I say, putting my arms around her. 'I love you.' It's the first time I have said that to her since I was a child.

'I love you too.' It's the first time she has told me since I was a child too. I feel a glow of warmth in her arms, something I realize has been lacking for years.